Almost against his will, Jake felt a slightly sickening shiver run down his spine. It occurred to him that something had been in here with an appetite, and for the first time, he had a mental image of what might have happened to the original crew of the vessel.

He leaned over to examine the cage from which two bars had been wrenched out, in the light of his lamp which he had set against the wall just inside the door. He put his hands on two of the bars and felt them turn in his grasp. He took his hands away and stared. The bars appeared solid, but they had been twisted loose in their sockets. He twisted one again and it came neatly out in his hand, being loose at the top and broken off at the bottom. He put it back— and suddenly, without warning, there was a smashing sound; and he was plunged into total darkness.

GORDON R. DICKSON

THE MAN THE WORLDS REJECTED

A TOM DOHERTY ASSOCIATES BOOK

ACKNOWLEDGMENTS

"The Man the Worlds Rejected," *Planet Stories*, July, 1953; copyright © 1953 by Love Romances Publishing Company, Inc.

"Jackal's Meal," Analog, June, 1969; copyright © 1969 by Condé Nast Publications, Inc.

"Minotaur," IF, March, 1961; copyright © 1961 by Digest Productions Corporation.

"Turnabout," IF, January, 1955; copyright © 1954 by Quinn Publishing Co.

"Strictly Confidential," *Fantastic Universe*, Dec., 1958; copyright © 1956 by King-Size Publications, Inc.

"In Iron Years," *Magazine of Fantasy and Science Fiction*, Oct., 1974; copyright © 1974 by Mercury Press, Inc.

"The Monster and the Maiden," *Stellar Short Novels*, 1976; copyright © 1976 by Random House, Inc.

"A Matter of Perspective," *Analog*, Dec., 1971; copyright © 1971 by Condé Nast Publications, Inc.

THE MAN THE WORLDS REJECTED

First printing: August 1986

A TOR Book

Published by Tom Doherty Associates
49 West 24 Street
New York, N.Y. 10010

Cover art by Alan Gutierrez

ISBN: 0-812-53572-3
CAN. ED.: 0-812-53573-1

Printed in the United States

0 9 8 7 6 5 4 3 2 1

CONTENTS

The Man
the Worlds
Rejected

I

Thick fingers of a giant's hand moved softly, caressing the ancient binding of the dark volume under the iridescent rainbow of the ceiling lights in the private library.

"So you want it back?" said Doreleyo.

Pioneer and crime boss of the City of Jark on Tenia, latter-day human with his near seven feet of height and three hundred pounds of heavy bone and muscle, he raised his leonine head from contemplation of the book. A golden tunic of living cloth, the voorlyct pseudo-life form that the Pioneer worlds had domesticated, clung about his massive shoulders. A Tenian love-bird perched on his gargantuan fist, gazing upward at her master with obsessed eyes, pouring out a song of adoration for him.

The young man who stood opposite the giant on the far side of the desk with two seven foot guards a pace behind was slim and a bare six feet in height. His tunic, breeches and boots were of the archaic wool and leather, drab in comparison with Doreleyo. But for all that, there was a sureness about him. The boss looked without kindness at him as he answered.

"Yes," said Jack Thorpe. "It belongs to Earth."

There was a small whisper of movement behind Jack, reminder of the two other Pioneers, musclemen for the city boss, who stood waiting just inside the room.

"To Earth!" echoed Doreleyo's heavy voice derisively. "Look, Earthman, the good is gone from that planet of yours. It's been gone for a thousand years. Only the dregs of the race are left there; little slugs like yourself, rotting in the ruins."

It was the common argument of the younger planets. A worn record, so deeply engraved in the minds of those who echoed it that protest was useless. But protest was also instinctive.

"That's not true," said Jack.

"No?" grinned Doreleyo. Behind his back Jack could almost feel the answering grins of the two henchmen—bait the Earthman.

"We have had it hard," said Jack. "It has been a bare, hand to mouth existence since Earth was deposed as business and government head for the other planets five hundred years ago. We were left with an exhausted planet; too many cities and a population untrained in the skills of fending for itself. But we have come back."

"How?" grinned Doreleyo as the love-bird fluttered on his fist.

"Through training," said Jack. "We have made the most of what little we had. Each Earthman or Earthwoman is trained from birth to do several jobs and do them well. At night we tore down the old cities. In the daytime we planted crops where the buildings had stood. We have lived and we've kept our art, our science and our literature alive. And we didn't ask for help."

"You're a runt," said Doreleyo, looking at Jack. "Bred from dregs, you're dregs." He paused. "And now you come whining to me to get your Shakespeare back."

"The first Folio," said Jack, steadily, with a touch of reverence, looking at the dark book on the polished surface of the table. "One of the few treasures that rich off-planet collectors have left us."

"I'm no collector," said Doreleyo.

"It was sent to you by mistake," said Jack. "We are a poor people, but a collection was taken up to send me all the way to Tenia to get the folio back."

"You touch me," replied Doreleyo.

"I'm glad," Jack returned calmly.

"In fact—" the big man stretched himself upright in his chair. "I am disposed to be charitable. As I say I am no collector."

Jack smiled. It was a smile of relief that lit up his tanned face.

"Earth will be deeply grateful to you," he said. The crime boss dismissed Earth's gratitude with a wave of his hand.

"Not at all," he continued. "You may have the book."

"Thank you."

"And I will even be lenient in the matter of the price," said Doreleyo.

The smile froze on Jack's face.

"The price?"

"You didn't expect to get it back for nothing, did you?" replied the crime boss. "The price—five million interstellar units."

Jack stared at him unbelievingly. The love-bird trilled a melody of sheer beauty.

"Well?" demanded Doreleyo. "What do you say?" Jack looked at him.

"I am trying," said Jack, coldly, "to decide whether you are a fool or—"

"What's that?" The bull roar of the Pioneer's angry voice thundered through the library.

"Only a fool would seriously entertain the notion," said

Jack, "that Earth could afford to pay five million, or even five thousand interstellar units for the return of the Folio, precious as it is to us. I was empowered—" he hesitated.

Doreleyo checked his anger suddenly. A touch of cupidity narrowed his eyes.

"Go on," he said harshly, "you were empowered—"

"In the event," Jack said, "that you returned the Folio to us in good condition, I was empowered to convey to you Earth's most sincere thanks: and to give you—this."

He reached inside his cloak to the pocket of his tunic and brought out a small square box.

Doreleyo snatched it up. Under the pressure of his heavy fingers it snapped open and a small medal tinkled on the table. Five small rubies made the points of a star around a cluster of tiny white diamonds and a short, green ribbon depended from it.

"The diamond star," said Jack reverently. "Earth's highest honor."

"You—" The crime boss choked. With a sudden gust of rage he picked up the medal and flung it at Jack. The sharp point of one of the gems slashed Jack's cheek, letting a tiny trickle of blood well out on the surface. The medal dropped back to the table in front of the Earthman.

As he got to his feet the enormous hands of the two musclemen encircled Jack.

Doreleyo's face was livid.

"An Earth decoration!" he said, thickly. "Do you think I could wear *that* with pride?" He jerked his head at the two men holding Jack. "Throw him out! Him and his toy star for a book worth a fortune!"

Jack was dragged toward the entrance. At the door, however, the sound of Doreleyo's voice checked the musclemen.

"Wait a minute," said the boss of the City of Jark. "See what he's got on him."

A large hand reached inside Jack's cloak to his tunic pocket and came away holding the contents.

"Bring them here," said Doreleyo. While one man continued to hold Jack, the other took the small handful of valuables to the desk where Doreleyo spread them out. A return ticket to Earth and a thin sheaf of unit notes. Doreleyo raked them into a pile and grinned vengefully across them at Jack.

"I'll accept the money as the price of an option on the repurchase of the folio," he said. "As for the ticket—this world was good enough for my ancestors when they landed here broke, driven out by your wealthy Earth business and government men. It should be good enough for you. Take him away, boys."

Jack felt himself tumbled out on to the hard pavement. He rolled over and sat up, dizzy and half stunned.

The diamond star flashed in the light of Tenia's hot, blue sun and tinkled on the pavement beside him.

He picked up the star and staggered to his feet. Wrapping the star carefully in his handkerchief he turned away and stepped on the traveling walkaway powered by Tenia's great solar accumulators—the common carrier of surface traffic in the City of Jark.

"Honor me, Friend—" the Pioneer greeting, in the soft, musical tones of a woman's voice made him spin around.

"You're the Earthman, aren't you?" the girl went on.

Jack stared at her in surprise. She must have come up behind him silently on the resilient surface, walking, or perhaps even running to better the speed of the walkaway. But it was neither this, nor the fact that she was undeniably beautiful with black hair, a slim, patrician face, and level green eyes, that startled him so. What caused the sense of shock was the fact that he found himself looking down, not up, into her eyes. This woman, whose dress and accent left no doubt that she was a Pioneer, was a good six inches shorter than he—no taller than an ordinary Earth woman.

"That's right," he answered, "I'm Jack Thorpe. You—"

"Neya Varden," she introduced herself. "Look—" her voice was urgent, "I want to talk to you."

"Go ahead," he said.

She hesitated. A touch of indecision and embarrassment became obvious in her manner.

"Not here," she answered. "I mean—well, not in public." He looked puzzled.

"I'm sorry—" she really was embarrassed now. It showed in the nervous twisting of her hands. "It's just that I have my job to think of; and—well, you are an Earthman."

For a moment he continued to stare at her. Then comprehension slowly dawned. Almost, he looked at the slim softness of her in disgust.

"Am I that much of a leper?" he asked bitterly. "Just because I come from the home world?"

"Not to me," she said swiftly. "Look, my cube isn't far from here. Let's go there, and I'll tell you what I want to see you about."

Jack looked at her curiously.

"All right," he answered, "I will."

Neya Varden's cube—the one room, all-purpose living quarters which honeycombed the interiors of the great apartment buildings of the poorer classes in Pioneer cities—was barely large enough to let them sit comfortably together at the table that let down from the wall. Neya Varden produced a couple of small bottles of Krysla, the native wine, which with their tops removed, became instead rather large glasses of the mildly alcoholic beverage. Jack touched his to his lips out of politeness and set it down again.

"You aren't drinking," said Neya, nervously.

"I'm sorry," there was a note of regret in Jack's voice.

"It's not drugged!" she snapped sharply.

"I'm sure it's not," said Jack. "But on Earth we're trained from the cradle on to keep ourselves always in the most efficient working order. There's not much alcohol in this, but—" he hesitated—"after a lifetime of that you get hyper-sensitive. Where this merely relaxes you and induces a slight euphoria, I can feel the slight blunting of my senses and the dulling of my perceptions. Instead of making me feel better, it makes me feel worse. Even a little fuzziness irritates me.''

"I see," she answered, looking down at the table.

"I'm sorry," said Jack. "What was it you wanted to talk to me about?"

She lifted her head. Beneath her purple tunic, her breasts rose and fell almost defiantly.

"How'd you like to hire me?" she asked.

Jack allowed some of the surprise he felt to show in his face.

"What?"

"Startles you, doesn't it?" she laughed a little harshly, "A Pioneer girl offering to lower herself by hiring out to an Earthman."

"As a matter of fact, no," said Jack. "What surprises me is the fact that you should think I need help of any kind."

"People can always use servants," she said, innocently, "can't they? And I could be useful—" she went on with a rush. "I can do office or household work. I've been working in one of the night clubs here because the money's better, but I can get good references. And—" she sat back with a smile, playing her trump card—"I'll pay my own way back to Earth."

"My dear Miss Varden," said Jack helplessly, with a touch of embarrassment. "Nobody has any servants on Earth."

She stared at him.

"I don't believe you. Who does all the dirty work?"

"If there's dirty work to be done," answered Jack, "I guess everyone does his own." He looked at her sympathetically. "Earth is still a poor world, even five hundred years after the Separation." He paused. "You don't understand, do you?"

She shook her head, her eyes bright with suspicion.

"I think you're just trying to put me off."

He tried to explain.

"When the empire got too big for Earth to control," he said, "and the younger planets pulled away, the first few generations nearly reverted all the way to savagery. You see the Earth population had been just about ninety per cent executives, with no practical knowledge outside of the rarefied work they did as Government or industrial heads of far-flung firms. Earth nearly collapsed. And when we did start to pull ourselves together, we realized that a drastic change would have to be made."

A slight smile touched the corners of his lips as these last words came out. This following part of the story was one that all Earth people of his generation looked on with fondness and a touch of pride.

"Half measures wouldn't work," Jack went on. "Drastic steps had to be taken. We left the adults to muddle along the best they could. But we turned to the children with the future of the home world in mind; and we began to set up a system of training that would give them the greatest chance of survival."

He paused, looking at her a little sideways, to see if she understood.

"Humans as a race," he said, "had never exploited their own minds and bodies, really. Not properly, not fully. Here and there there had been an individual who fell in love with the possibilities inherent in himself; and made his own effort at self-training. But it had never been put on an organized basis as we started to put it then."

She stared at him—puzzled, a little uncertain and disbelieving. But he was caught up in his story and had nearly forgotten her.

II

"There were many things to do," he went on. "It took a number of generations to do them. First we needed good aptitude tests—tests that could begin to function from the time the child began to walk and talk. Then we had to arrange to squeeze our meager standard of living still tighter to allow the individual full time and opportunity for his training and his schooling while he was growing up. And we had to set up a system that made it certain that we did not hammer the growing mind and body into a mold, but instead let it develop in its own natural direction and aided it to fulfill all the potentialities of that development. In the maximum development of the individual we pinned our hopes of the future of the world."

He looked back at her.

"And it worked," he concluded.

"I didn't ever hear that," she said, somewhat defensively. He sighed.

"You don't, of course," he answered. "They teach us the truth back home. The Pioneers, as all you people call yourselves on the younger planets, did have just cause to hate Earth for a time when my world was nothing but one planet-wide glorified board of directors. They haven't, any longer. But the historical attitude persists," he grimaced slightly. "There's a guilt complex partly responsible for that, too, on the part of your Pioneers."

"Us?" said Neya, resentfully. "Why?"

"We are still the source of your traditions," Jack said. "Earth is still the home world, the birthplace of the race. The younger planets are like a son who, having thrown off parental control and gone on to rise to a more fortunate state, now feels his conscience nagging him, and to justify his past and present actions, keeps reminding himself of old grievances."

She bit her lip and looked away from him. Then she looked back.

"What's all this got to do with my being hired by you?" she demanded.

"I was just trying to explain why that's impossible," he said. "I can't hire anyone—" he chuckled ruefully, "particularly now."

"Why not—*now?*" she pounced on the word.

Briefly, he told her of his reason for coming; and of his interview with Doreleyo. For a moment she sat, stunned. Then her face lit up.

"You're broke!" she cried triumphantly.

He nodded, puzzled.

"Well then, there's no problem," she went on, happily. "You don't have your ticket to get back on, do you? And Earth hasn't any consulate here."

"No," agreed Jack, wondering what she was driving at.

"I've saved enough money for my passage to Earth," she said. "But I didn't dare go by myself. I'd land there without a unit to my name and not knowing where to turn. Now I'll tell you what. I'll lend you enough to put in a deep-space call back to Earth for money to come home on. You pay me back when you get it. We can both leave on the next ship two weeks from now." As if to clinch her argument she added, "There won't be another one for over a year."

He shook his head.

"Why not?" she cried, exasperated.

"I can't send for more money," he said. "They don't have it to spare, back there. We have almost no trade with other worlds, and interstellar units are precious. Besides—I haven't gotten what I came for."

"The book?" she said, incredulously. "But Doreleyo said he wouldn't give it to you."

"I'm sorry," said Jack. "But I can't go back without it." She stared at him, her green eyes wide with amazement.

"You're insane!"

"I don't think so," said Jack. He checked himself suddenly. "Just why do you want to go to Earth so badly, anyway?"

"Do you have to ask that?" she answered bitterly. "Look at me!"

He looked at her, at the black hair, the smouldering eyes, the firm and pleasant mouth. He shook his head.

"I don't understand," he said. She looked incredulous, then—

"Perhaps you don't," she replied slowly. A touch of scorn came into her voice. "Of course you don't. An Earthman like you wouldn't. But it's plain enough to me. No man on a Pioneer world would look twice at me. I'm not good. A throw-back. A sport. A runt. Like you."

There was a moment's embarrassed silence between them following her declaration.

"I see," said Jack, gently, at last.

He got to his feet.

"I'm sorry I can't help you," he said, an honest note of regret in his voice, moving toward the door.

"Wait—" she was up on her feet and coming around the table to face him again and halt him. "You can't be serious about trying to get the book from Doreleyo, now."

"I must," he answered. "It means too much to Earth."

"He'll kill you," she cried. "Don't you know that? Here in the city of Jark, the Boss controls everything. All the businessmen, the criminal gangs, even the police are his. The city officials are his men. No one will help you. Do you hear me? No one! Earthman, you're insane!"

"Thanks for the warning," he said. "I was going to talk to the police and the city council."

"Then you've changed your mind?" She sighed a little.

"No," he said, quietly.

She stood back to let him pass. He inclined his head politely to her and opened the door. As he was stepping out she caught his arm.

"Come back here," she said. He yielded to the pressure of her fingers. She drew him slowly back into the apartment, shut the door and stood for a long moment looking at him.

"I don't understand you," she said at last, wonderingly. "Are all Earthmen like you?"

"We are what we are," said Jack.

"But why? Why?" she said. "Don't you believe me when I tell you how things are here?"

"I believe you," answered Jack.

"Then what is it in this for you—to make you try the impossible and risk your life this way?"

"In it for me?" Jack echoed, bewildered. He smiled a little sadly. "There's nothing in it for me. It's just a belief—my own belief—that the Folio belongs to Earth and should go back there."

She released him.

"You are a very strange man," she said. "Or else you are insane."

Jack bowed to her in the Pioneer fashion and turned to go.

"Wait," she said. "What are you going to do now? You say your money is gone. Where will you stay? How will you eat?"

"I don't know," he replied honestly. She drew a deep breath.

"Then stay here," she said. "At least for a few weeks. At least until you get this mad notion out of your head."

"Here?" he echoed.

"I can support both of us," she said. "I do rather well waitressing odd nights in one of the bars. I'm—" her tone became bitter—"something of a novelty."

"And you want me to stay," repeated Jack, gently. He looked at her. There was a hopeless sadness in her eyes— the look of an outcast.

"I've been lonely all my life," she said, frankly, answering his look. "Yes, Jack Thorpe, strange man from Earth. I want you to stay."

—Later that night she woke him, clutching at him fiercely in the darkness.

"But when you go back to Earth, you take me with you!" she hissed. "Promise!"

"I promise," Jack answered.

The next two days Jack spent at the City Library. The second night Neya worked, and late the following morning when she woke up, Jack was already dressed and waiting with questions for her.

"Tell me," he said abruptly, as she propped herself up on one elbow in the bed and pushed the heavy hair back from her sleepy eyes, "who'd be liable to object if I suddenly started making money here in Jark?"

She blinked at him uncomprehendingly.

"Object?" she echoed. "Nobody'd object. Why should they?"

"This city," he said patiently, "is very tightly organized. Surely—"

"Oh, I know what you mean," she yawned. "You'd just have to pay. Your boss, your union—"

"I was thinking of working for myself in a professional, advisory capacity," said Jack. "I was thinking of offering a sort of advisory service to local businessmen."

Her eyes came wide open. Her warm lips parted in amazement.

"Could you do something like that?" she asked, incredulously. "Would it pay?"

"It should pay very well," he replied, a trifle stiffly.

"Why, Jack!" she said, sitting up suddenly, her eyes alight. "That's marvelous. You go check with our district gang leader right away. His name's Ki Maneo—" she hopped out of bed and ran to the writing table. "Here, I'll give you the district headquarters address." She smiled at him almost shyly and picked up a stylus.

"District Leader?" echoed Jack. "Ki Maneo."

"Oh, I forgot you didn't know," she answered, busily

writing. "There's four district leaders in the city, one for each section. They head all the musclemen of the gangs for that section. You've got to let them know ahead of time what you're going to do and then pay them a percentage of what you make or they'll queer your job." She picked up the sheet of white plastic on which she had pressed the name and address of the District Leader and brought it over to him. "Don't forget, now." A note of concern warmed her voice.

A little smile touched the corners of his lips.

"That's the last thing I'll do," he promised her.

"All right, Earthman," said the businessman. "I'll listen. But it better be worth my while."

The Pioneer who spoke was a tough, sallow-faced giant. His cold eyes went across the desk to meet Jack, seated in front of him. A miniature artificial sun burned glaringly in the air above them.

"It's simple," Jack answered. "Most of the fabrication on these young worlds of yours is done by machinery. There's only a few shops like yours who do custom work requiring skilled workers. On Earth nearly all our production is the result of physical labor. We have evolved production techniques which you might find useful, Kel Lennan."

"I take it that you're an expert in these techniques." Kel's fingers ran over a row of buttons on his desk.

"Among other things," said Jack. "Yes."

"All right. Go on."

"Here's my proposition. I will show you how to increase the productivity of your workers for ten per cent of any profits over a ten year period, or a flat two thousand interstellar units payable a week from now provided production has increased by at least twenty-five percent."

Kel laughed and reached for the buttons.

"You're crazy," he said. "Go on, peddle your nonsense to somebody else."

"All right," said Jack. He rose and left. He was leaving the outer office when a secretary came running after him to call him back. He returned.

"What's the matter with you?" grumbled Kel Lennan. "Don't you know anything about business? You don't have to rush off. I was just building up to saying your terms are too steep."

"Sorry," said Jack, turning again, "if they're too steep, you shouldn't have called me back."

"Come back here!" roared the Pioneer. "Sit down. Let's talk this out like sensible men."

Three-quarters of an hour later, Kel had agreed to the two thousand flat rate. Mopping his brow and looking disgusted he pressed one of the buttons. One apparently solid wall of the office dissolved, revealing the shop.

Jack looked it over. It was a small plant engaged in turning out custom scanners. The scanners themselves came in a kit from a larger factory and were assembled by apprentices at one long table. At another long table the case builders did the finishing work. There were several types of scanners and it was the apprentice's job to pick the type that the master workman needed to fit the custom job he was building. When the kit was assembled, the apprentice would carry it over to his particular master and that man would begin work on turning its outward appearance into whatever the customer wanted. There were some pretty weird wants, evidently. Jack saw scanners being disguised as everything from stuffed animals to large windows. It was a simple organization, and, to Jack's Earth-trained eye, a horribly inefficient one.

"Well?" demanded the outworld businessman. "See any way to cut corners?"

Jack considered half a dozen and picked the quickest.

"There's one," he said slowly, "that I think would just about double production."

Kel Lennan stared at him.

III

In the following days, Jack talked to other factory owners. At the end of the following week he was back in the office of Kel Lennan, this time with Neya. The businessman met him with a beaming face.

"Marvelous," he said, "marvelous." And he led them to the factory room.

The physical appearance of the plant had been changed. Instead of two long tables at opposite sides of the room, the space was occupied by a double tier of desks, an upper desk alternating with a lower, all along the line. Directly beside and below each master craftsman sat his apprentice, so that once a kit was completed, it merely needed to be passed up.

"Wonderful," said Lennan. "Production is way up." He led them back to his office. "Though to be honest with you, I can't understand why saving the apprentices a few steps should make such a difference."

"It doesn't," answered Jack, calmly, as they entered the Pioneer's office. "You saved something there, but not much. What makes the real difference is the fact that now the masters and apprentices are separated from their fellows. Before, with each worker at his own class table, there was a natural temptation to talk and dawdle. Now, with this separation, everybody is isolated and has nothing to do but get on with his work. The physical change merely maneuvers them into keeping their nose to the grindstone."

Kel stared at him and then burst into a roar of laughter.

"I'll be shot!" he roared, his big voice making the walls echo. "I will be shot! So that's the trick." He went around the desk in his office and sat down, pulling out a voucher book. He picked up a stylus.

"It's a good thing I'm an honest man," he said. "Otherwise I'd be tempted to cheat you out of your two thou-

sand, now that I know how you made it. But—'' he started
to write. Jack reached out and caught his hand.

"Not that way." he said.

"What?" the big businessman looked up with a sudden
frown.

"I've got an account at the City Bank," said Jack.
"Call them on the viseo and sign a facsimile tab for a
transfer of funds from your account to mine."

"What's the matter?" rumbled Kel angrily. "Isn't my
check good enough for you?"

"Your check is perfectly good," said Jack. "It's just
that I have a dislike of carrying it out into the street." His
eyes met those of Kel and locked. "It shouldn't make any
difference to you. As you say, you're an honest man."

Neya stared at Jack. It was on the tip of her tongue to
protest. This was no way for an Earthman to treat even a
minor businessman.

"Well?" said Jack.

Kel snorted, but complied.

Once out on the street again Neya turned toward Jack
and opened her mouth with the intention of giving him a
lesson in Pioneer manners, but he spoke first, cutting her
short.

"Go home," he said.

"What—?" she cried.

"Or, on second thought," he went on. "Don't go home.
Go someplace else. Anyplace where you're unknown; and
stay there until I get in touch with you."

"But why?"

"I can't explain now."

"It looks to me," she said, her eyes narrowing, "as if,
now that you've got some money in your hands, you want
to get rid of me."

For answer, he reached into his pocket and brought out
the tab of his account at the city bank. It was a joint
account, in her name as well as his. Her face burned.

"Now will you go!" he said impatiently.

"Yes—" she stammered. "I—" She turned and made off through the crowd. He stood and watched until her slender figure disappeared among the looming seven foot forms, then turned and hailed a ground cab.

He had just come out of the place where he was making his fourth collection on a job such as he had done for Kel when two large Pioneers closed in upon him. They herded into a waiting ground cab. They sped into the traffic tunnels below the city level.

Jack asked no questions. He did not even protest when, during the later part of the ride, they blindfolded him with impersonal neatness and dispatch. These were not the ordinary kind of bodyguard, but accredited thugs of the gangs themselves, men completely outside and above the law who made no secret of their profession, but flaunted its badges—the scalp-lock on the shaved skull, the warp pistol worn openly on the hip, the duelling scars and the knife rings on each man's index finger that had made them. Killers, nothing more. Words would be wasted on them.

After awhile the car stopped, Jack was made to walk a short distance, and the blindfold was removed. Jack found himself facing four large, scalp-locked Pioneers seated behind a long table. Beyond them, in a corner, stood Neya. Tears filled her eyes as she looked at him from between the two thugs that held her.

"Well, Earthman," said the largest of the seated men, "do you know where you are?"

"I have a fairly good idea," replied Jack. His voice was as steady as ever. The man leaned forward. "Central City Headquarters for the Gangs of Jark," Jack went on. "You, I imagine, will be Ki Maneo, and these others, leaders of the other four city sections."

The man who had spoken looked at him steadily for a long minute.

"Since you know that," he said, "you won't deny you knew that you're supposed to contact a Leader before

working in his district, or that you've been working in all
sections without notifying any of us?''

"I won't," said Jack. "I did it deliberately."

"Why?"

"I wanted to get you all together," replied Jack.

It was a simple answer but it produced a surprising
reaction. The glances of all four men flickered uneasily
towards each other. The voice of Ki Maneo was harsh,
when he spoke again.

"Why?" The grim reiteration held its own threat.

"As you know," said Jack blandly, "I came here to get
back the Folio of 1623. Doreleyo has offered to sell it back
to me for a price. Consequently, I am raising money; and I
have a weapon in which you gentlemen might be interested."

"What weapon?" broke in one of the other Leaders, a
man whose heavy features were already sagging into fat.
"The young worlds are five hundred years ahead of your
planet scientifically, Earthman."

"That is no longer true," said Jack. "In the past century we have made fantastic strides, due to several important basic discoveries. It is we who are five hundred years
ahead. Do you think I would have deliberately invited you
to have me brought here otherwise?"

"I think," said another one of the Leaders, "that you're
doing some fast talking to save your neck. You know
damn well we'd never have let you get away with this
advisory service if you'd come to us first. There's no jobs
for Earthmen in Jark. You tried to make a killing and get
off planet without letting us know. Now you're talking
fast."

Jack chuckled. Neya, watching, stared at him in disbelief. It was inhuman to be that cool in the face of the
situation.

"Luckily I've got proof," Jack was saying.

"Proof?" It was the first speaker again.

"A model of the weapon," said Jack. "I knew you'd

pick me up, so I've been carrying it with me." He reached for his wallet pocket.

"Hold it!" At a sharp command from the man who had been doing most of the talking, one of the two who had picked Jack up came forward. He rifled Jack's pocket and came up with a small cube surmounted by a disk, which he carried to the table and set down. The four men looked at it blankly.

"It's crude," said Jack, "because it's homemade. One of your factories could turn out a better product." He half rose from his chair. "If you'll let me—"

Heavy hands of the guard at his back forced him down again.

"Never mind that!" snapped the spokesman of the group. He reached out and picked the object up curiously. As he did, the disk began to revolve slowly, unfolding as it went until it had spread to a good eight inches in diameter. Hastily, at the first sign of movement, the Leader had set it down again. Now he and the others watched the spinning disk closely. It was colored with an odd pattern of black lines on the white plastic that was the disk proper, lines which twisted and melted together with the rotation of the disk, that caught and held the eye with a strange fascination.

"You pressed the warm-up button there," Jack was saying. "The disk is the real secret of the weapon. Observe the disk closely, notice the pattern made by the lines. In addition to other functions, the pattern is very relaxing. Most relaxing. It makes you feel sleepy. Watching it, you feel quite sleepy. In fact, you are going to sleep. You are falling into a deep sleep. You are falling deeper into a deep, deep sleep. You are deeply asleep. Join your hands together in front of you."

Like automatons, the four Leaders and Neya clasped their hands in front of them. Turning around, Jack saw that the two men who had brought him in had also obeyed.

"You cannot pull your hands apart," said Jack. "Try."

The faces of the various people in the room contorted as they made the effort to separate their hands. But the fingers remained locked.

"You will do whatever I tell you," said Jack. "You are falling deeper asleep. You are falling very deeply into deep, deep sleep. You are fast asleep."

The room slumbered. Jack let out a long breath, then got up and walked over to Neya.

"Everybody else will go on sleeping," he said. "They will sleep deeper into deep, deep sleep. But Neya Varden will wake up, now!"

Neya stirred, blinked, and opened her eyes. She looked up at him.

"What happened?" she whispered.

"I hypnotized all of you," said Jack.

"Hypnotized?"

"An old technique," answered Jack. "Your people have forgotten now that psychology and medicine have become so effective. Stand over in the corner now and don't look at the disk. I've got to give these people some instructions."

She obeyed. He walked back to stand at one side with the six hypnotized men in view.

"You are deeply asleep," he said. "And you are falling still more deeply asleep. You will forget anything I have said to you and remember only what I tell you to remember. You will remember only that when you had me brought here I revealed to you that the science of Earth far outstrips the science of any of the other planets; and that I am a master of that science. You will realize that any attempt to harm me may result in Earth, with its advanced science, destroying you all. You will believe whatever I tell you; and you will leave orders with your underlings that any message or visit from me is to be called to your attention at once. And finally, whenever I tell you in the future to go to sleep, or snap my fingers like this—" he snapped his fingers by way of illustration—"you will go to sleep at once. Now you will remember all this when you wake up, but forget anything I said before you went to sleep. And you will not know you have been to sleep. Now—'' He slapped the table sharply with his hand.

—"WAKE UP!"

The men moved, opened their eyes and looked up blankly.

"Well, gentlemen," said Jack, sharply. "Now that I have shown you what I really am, I'm sure I can trust you to keep my secret." His voice took on a hard edge. "It would not be a good idea if the knowledge got out."

His eyes probed down the table, and, one by one, they muttered assent.

"If I need you, then, I'll call on you. Good-bye, gentlemen. Come on, Neya."

Obediently, she followed him. They went past the guards and out the door of the room, shutting it behind them. And they found themselves in a long corridor, stretching off to both sides of them.

"This way," Jack directed, turning to his left and starting off briskly. She hurried after him.

"Do you know where you're going?" she whispered sharply. He looked to one side and down at her.

"Of course," he said.

"But you were blindfolded when they brought you in," she persisted, still in a whisper.

"Oh, that," said Jack, and chuckled. He said no more until, after descending several levels of stairs and traversing several corridors, they came abruptly out into a traffic tunnel through a small door that from the outside looked as if it opened on a tunnel service storeroom. Jack flagged down a cab.

"It's just a matter of training," he explained, when they were safely on their way. "It was easy to get lost in the wildernesses of the great cities, when Earth people started tearing them down, so they taught us too how to find our way back from anywhere. It's a matter of a highly developed directional sense, plus a practised time sense, and a good memory. That's all."

He smiled down at her.

IV

They were seated together at lunch on the terrace of Jark's best hotel. Below them, the Pioneer city lay spread out from horizon to horizon, a limitless cluster of low, well-spaced buildings. The hotel they were in was no more than a dozen stories and it was far and away the tallest building in Jark.

He turned back to Neya, who was sitting across the table from him and toying with her meal.

"You aren't eating," he said.

She had been mincing up her meat with the little, sharp-edged silver tongs that were the standard Pioneer eating utensils. Now she laid them down with almost an air of relief and looked squarely at him.

"No, I'm not."

"Something bothering you?"

"You might as well know it now. As fast as you were putting money into that joint account, I was taking it out." She reached into her purse pocket and came out with two stamped strips of plastic. "I bought these."

He looked at them. They were a pair of one way tickets to Earth.

"That's how they picked me up and brought me to the City Headquarters," she said, half-defiantly. "They were waiting outside the space terminal when I came out."

"Well—" Jack shrugged. "It's a good use for the units."

She continued to look at him, a little baffled.

"It isn't going to work," she said, after a short pause. "You know that, don't you?"

"What isn't?"

"Getting that book back," she said fiercely. "Don't you—can't you see that you're playing with fire?"

He looked at her in surprise.

"I thought you were interested in helping me?" he said.

"I didn't think you'd be trying the sort of thing you're doing," she cried. "I thought you'd see sense after a few days and give up."

"You actually don't believe I have a chance, do you?" he asked sadly, watching her closely.

"I know you don't!"

"Didn't that last little scene give you any confidence in me?"

"That!" she said, desperately. "A trick. And what good did it do you, except to take the pressure off our necks for the moment? We're safe now, yes. If we stay quiet and don't attract any attention we can take off without any more trouble, probably. But you're still thinking about that book."

"Of course," he said soberly. "I think I told you I wouldn't leave without it."

She forced her voice down to a whisper so that its passion would not carry. But the tension in her voice came to him.

"But why?" she whispered bitterly between her teeth. *"Why?"*

"You mean why risk my life for a book?"

"Yes."

"It's my job," he said.

"Oh," she leaned back in her chair, her voice flat and empty. "A job. Is that it?"

"You don't understand," he said.

"I think I do."

"You don't!" His tone left no doubt of the matter. There was a hard note in it she had never heard before. "Listen. Earth is a poor planet, but she doesn't have to be."

"I know," she said coldly. "You told me. You're rebuilding her. She has a great future."

"That's not what I mean," he answered. "Earth never had to be poor. Even right from the moment when her

power was stripped away she could have been well off.
Well off on charity.''

She looked at him with uncertain suspicion. Tensely, he
leaned across the table toward her.

"Do you remember what I told you about the Pioneer
guilt complex where Earth was concerned?'' he said, lowering his voice. ''Right from the start of her downfall there
were people on the younger planets who wanted to help
her—secretly. On all the inhabited worlds they added up to
several millions who revered the mother planet. That ancestral tie is not something all people can ignore. We
could have had help—private help—right from the start.
We can have it now.''

She looked at him as if she no longer had any doubt of
his complete insanity, and the insanity of the world from
which he came.

"Why don't you take it then?''

His mouth was a grim line with something of harsh
pride in it. In an odd mixture of emotions she put her hand
over his.

"We are a people too,'' he said.

His fury gripped her, at the same time as her mind
stumbled in its lack of comprehension. She could only
stare at him, fascinated. With a sudden angry gesture he
threw her hand off.

"If we were wrong,'' he said, leaning across the table,
"if we were wrong to try to rule the race, how much more
wrong we'd be if, having failed, having lost everything but
our guts and brains, we let ourselves be turned into pets of
that same race. Runts, you Pioneers call us. Dregs, leav-
ings of the adventuresome spirit of the people. You're
wrong. The thing that took men up from the dust in the
first place rebuilds him again and again. We were wrong
in thinking we were masters; but by heaven above and the
eternal stars we're equals and we'll stand as equals until
the last one of us goes down forever.''

His hand had closed about a silver vase in the center of

the small table. Under the whiplash of his emotion, it tightened; and before Neya's astonished eyes, the slim fingers, so fragile-looking to her Pioneer-born eyes, were crushing the soft metal inward. His words drove through her.

"That book belongs to Earth," he said. "And I am Earth. And I will get it back, alone if necessary, without help and without favors." He stood up abruptly. Through all the violence of his utterances, he had held his voice to so low a pitch that the neighboring tables had not been disturbed. Now, with his sudden movement, some few people nearby looked up at him. He looked at her with the bitter look of a man who feels himself betrayed. He leaned across the table and flicked the two Earth tickets toward her.

"I've got no need of these," he said. "Use them yourself or turn them in, whichever you prefer. But think it over before you run to Earth. It's no dumping ground or hiding place for weaklings!"

And with that he swung about abruptly on his heel and strode off.

"Jack!" she cried after him, desperately, not caring what the rest of the crowd would think, seeing a Pioneer girl pleading with an Earthman. But Jack was already gone.

Neya was deeply hurt. When Jack did not return to her cube she threw herself back into the old routine of her life, the heavy daytime sleeping, the night work and the jibes of the other, normal-sized waitresses—for by now it was common gossip that Neya had fallen for an Earthman, who had *cut gravs* with her, in the old space lingo that still lingered here and there in Pioneer slang. Six, eight, ten months went by. The hurt inside her faded to a dull ache and when a year was nearly up, she had herself almost convinced that she had put him out of her mind for good.

Then something happened to show her how wrong this supposition was.

Jack had continued with his advisory services. Occasionally she heard him mentioned as a rising young businessman. Then one day, a scrap of conversation between two gray-skinned centaurians she was serving made her heart stand suddenly still.

"—Jack Thorpe," the humanoid entrepreneur who spoke stumbled in pronouncing the archaic cognomen, so that the words came out something like 'Shack Torb'—but they were clear enough to arrest Neya in the process of moving away from the table, "he's due any day now."

It was all she heard. One of the two centaurians, looking up at that moment, happened to catch her eye and she was forced to move away. But it was enough to set her on the trail.

In the City of Jark, like many Pioneer cities where all the social elements were tightly bound up together, almost any kind of information could be bought if you knew where to hunt a seller. Neya put herself on the track. The end of her quest was a little room in the alien section of Jark where she sat alone and listened to a recording played by she knew not who and piped in from she knew not where. Several voices in social conversation together came to her ear and one of them was the voice of Doreleyo. The bit she heard was brief enough.

"—the fable about the goose who laid the golden eggs."

There was the sound of male laughter, a pause, then a different voice.

"All right, I'm dumb. I don't understand it."

Doreleyo's laughter, alone this time.

"A man had a goose who laid golden eggs. He got greedy and chopped the bird open to get more than his egg a day. He killed the bird and that was all the golden eggs he ever got. Thorpe's laying up eggs for me. That bank account."

"That's why you've been leaving him alone?"

"I—" there was a sudden break where the recording had been censored. Sellers of information gave only what they had been paid for. Doreleyo's voice cut in again suddenly "—Only to a point. He's got nearly a million and that's enough. I'll make it look like he paid that for the book and then took off for Earth."

"And then—"

The recording stopped abruptly, cutting off the unknown speaker. Neya stood up, laid her money on a small table in the room and went out.

V

The city directory located Jack for her. He was occupying a suite in one of the better hotels. The check-board showed that he was in. She went up in the tube. Purely as an experiment, she bribed a bellboy to give her a pass key. She got it immediately, which meant that Jack had not even attempted the customary practice of a protective bribe. The omission exasperated her for it was so typical of his blithe innocence in this city of wolves. She dismissed the boy and let herself in.

She found herself facing a white wall of light, although the floor-to-ceiling windows that made up one wall of the room were brilliant with daylight. She closed the door behind her and, reaching out a hand, cut the study switch.

The light vanished, revealing Jack seated at a desk piled high with plastic figure sheets and holding a stylus in his hand. He looked up at her.

"Hello, Neya," he said.

She stood and looked at him. The change in his appearance shocked her.

Eleven months appeared to have thinned and aged him. The once-boyish touch to his features had disappeared. A brown stubble shadowed the lower half of his face; and below it the line of his jawbone was thin and sharp. Fatigue had hollowed his eyes and deepened his voice. He was so altered, so different from the man she had been expecting to see, that a strange pang shot through her and the carefully rehearsed scene of her warning that was to bring him at last to his senses fell apart like a tinsel toy before the solid facts of reality.

"You're tired—" the words rushed from her mouth instinctively.

"Tired I am," he answered with a smile of triumph that lit up his gaunted face. "But I'm through, Neya. I finished last night. I've just been checking."

She came up to him and leaned over the table, putting her hand on his shoulder for support and feeling momentarily the tense hardness of the muscles beneath his tunic. She stared at the sheets of plastic, acrawl with incomprehensible symbols.

"What's this?" she asked. "What have you got?"

He reached out, shook one sheet free of the pile and set it before her. She stared at it, baffled.

"I can't understand it."

"I'll explain it to you," he uncoiled and was on his feet in one smooth motion. "Come on and have lunch with me. We'll celebrate."

"But you need sleep."

"Later," he answered feverishly. "Come and have lunch." He turned away from her; and, striding across the room to a closet which opened at his touch, he took out a dress cape of voorlyct which flickered through the whole spectrum of colors as he twirled it about his shoulders. "We'll go to the Chijaha."

"The Chijaha!" She caught her breath. It was a tourist trap, the most expensive eating place in the City of Jark. Shock brought back the memory of her purpose.

"I came to tell you something—" she began.

"After lunch," he cut her short. "We can talk then."

He hurried her out, placing the sheet of plastic he had shown her in his cape pocket.

The Chijaha derived its name from the planet of a strange, barbaric people. It was a large, circular, blue-lighted establishment where the staff and entertainers dressed in odd, opulent costumes and weird, unfamiliar music played in the background, softly. But the food was excellent. Neya, somewhat timid in such lavish surroundings, stuck conservatively to the more common dishes, creo-soup, butter fried neyderlings and protein aspic gumbo, watching Jack meanwhile in some awe as he ordered strange things with exotic names such as bluepointoysters, crabmeatsalad, and T-bone-steak. The climax of his lunch was a sweet concoction known as applepie, so rare and so obviously a gourmet's dish that the Chijaha's Alderbaran chef himself brought it in; and, regardless of the fact that Jack was an Earthman, insisted on serving the portion with his own hands.

When the stir caused by this unusual action had died down and Jack and Neya were left to their hot drink, Jack finally allowed their talk to drop to a serious level. The triumph was still in his eyes but he offered the floor to Neya first.

"You had something to tell me—" he prompted.

Neya pushed her hot drink away and leaned forward.

"Doreleyo"—she spoke urgently, instinctively lowering her voice to a secretive level—"I've been checking up. He's been leaving you alone to make money in the hope that he'll sell you back the book. But now he's decided to crack down on you. I think he's afraid you'll get too much money—become too prominent. He'll get the money from you some way, probably by pretending to sell the book for what you've got. Then he'll have you killed. Jack—" her voice was suddenly tight with emotion—"you've got to believe this. You've got to give up this crazy idea and go hide somewhere until we can get you on the Earth ship. It's due again.''

"So soon?" he asked, a touch of interest flaring suddenly in his eyes.

"Early tomorrow morning," she said. "Don't you ever read the shipping news? They've been rescheduling all the flights. Jack—''

His laugh checked her.

"Why, that's perfect!" he said happily. "That ties right in with my own plans.''

"Your plans?" she repeated, stunned.

"Of course, my plans," he leaned forward to her in his turn, pulling the sheet of plastic from his pocket. "You didn't think I had any real hope of saving up the money for the book? The market for the kind of services I've been offering is just about worked out; and the financiers here in Jark have no intention of letting me get into the investment end of things. Besides, all that I've made belongs to Earth. We're desperately in need of interstellar credits at home. No—" he shook his head—"what I needed was time; and I've had time. The solution's here," and he shoved the sheet of plastic toward her.

"What secret?" she demanded suspiciously.

"The secret," he answered triumphantly, "of how to destroy the power of Doreleyo completely here in Jark. To make him as helpless as I was when he first threw me out into the street." He tapped the sheet with his finger. "The blueprint for a revolution.''

She stared at him.

"I see," she said at last, her voice oddly withdrawn.

"Here," he said, eagerly. "Let me explain it to you. Every society is rendered stable by careful balancing of its different social elements. Here in Jark, because of rigidity of the setup, we have relatively few powerful groups. I've spent this last year learning about them, their relative positions of power in city management. The present state of things can be resolved into the terms of symbolic logic—''

He talked on, stabbing odd figures on the plastic sheet to illustrate as he went, his voice low but tense, his eyes bright. Neya let his words wash over her, paying them no attention. She was busy thinking.

It had struck her that two things were true and had been true for a long time, although for some strange reason they had not penetrated to the conscious level of her mind. For some reason it was this moment here, in this unreal setting of the fantastic restaurant with Jack droning incomprehensible things, that they had chosen to make themselves inescapably obvious to her. One was that Jack was infinitely precious to her. And the second was that he was, tragically, but beyond any shadow of a doubt, insane.

She hid these thoughts behind a half-smile and an interested look on her face as she pretended to follow his explanations. At the first opportunity, she excused herself, saying—''I'll be right back—'' and went off toward the ladies' lounge.

She headed for the nearest exit and made her way out into the street.

A force-lift leading down to the traffic tunnels was only a few steps away. She took it, floating down into the shadowed blackness of the tunnels. She stopped for a moment in a public booth to put in a viseo call; then flagged a cab and gave the driver the number of Doreleyo's headquarters.

VI

It was deceptively easy for her to gain audience with the crime boss. But only someone unused to the big Pioneer cities would have been surprised by it. To Neya, it was simply one more grim proof that Doreleyo had the situation firmly in hand. Indeed, the boss himself made a point of confirming this opinion as she entered and took the chair his huge hand waved her to.

"Did you enjoy your dinner?" he asked.

"It was pleasant," she answered. He nodded his heavy head gravely. His love-bird preened itself on his fist.

"Our Earthman is quite a gourmet," he said. Abruptly, his manner shifted and his tone became businesslike. "You wanted to see me?"

"Jack Thorpe is psychotic," she answered without preamble. "Did you know that?"

He half smiled at her, stroking the love-bird.

"No," he replied. He paused, as if to let her continue, then, when she said nothing, went on himself. "What of it? What's that to me?"

"Don't you understand?" The words rushed from her lips. "He's not responsible. He wasn't responsible when he landed here. He was right about Earth wanting the book back; but he was lying about the fact that they couldn't and wouldn't pay to get it." Desperation tightened her voice. "Everything he's been doing here has been his own idea. He's insane. I've just been talking to him. He's been working on some fantastic project which he thinks will let him take over the city and force you to give him the book."

"Well—" his voice prodded her, inflexibly, "I repeat— what of it? How does it concern me?"

"Don't you see? Earth will still pay four million credits for the book if you get a sane Terran representative to talk to you. But they won't send anyone else unless it's proved to them that Thorpe is incompetent. Send him back with your demands. You can have him put on the ship forcibly."

Doreleyo stroked his chin. The black voorlyct of his tunic flashed.

"And what about you?"

"I want to get him back safe," she answered. "I won't try to fool you. I'll go on the ship with him and see that your offer reaches the proper people there. And I can take charge of him on the ship. I have some control over him. He—" she lied—"he thinks he's in love with me."

Doreleyo sat in silence, his eyes tilted down toward the desk top in front of him.

"I'd need some guaranty—" he said, finally.

She fumbled in her purse and came up with a bank tab that she tossed on the desk top.

"He set this account up in my name as well as his," she said. "He's never changed it. I called just now to make sure. I can make out a tab turning the whole account over to you and the bank will honor it."

Doreleyo looked her steadily in the face, his expression unreadable.

"Go ahead," he said.

She took a credit strip and filled it out, then pushed it across the desk to him. He picked it up and frowned at it.

"I've dated it ahead—after the ship leaves," she said, her heart thumping wildly in mingled fear and elation. "That way, right up to the moment we leave, I can stop payment."

A smile crept slowly over his large face.

"You're quite clever, Neya Varden," he said, gently, putting the slip away. "I like clever people. I'm one myself."

"I know it," she answered, watching him closely and wondering.

"I imagine you do," Doreleyo said. "You'll be interested in hearing that I went to the trouble to check up on Earth after your friend's first visit."

Fear began to grow inside her.

"—One of the things I found out," he went on, "was that Earth was actually as poor as our young Earthman said. In fact, when I spaced off my offer to Earth headquarters—which I did immediately after Thorpe had refused it—they replied that such a payment was not only against their customs, but impossible—" he smiled down into her stricken face—"so I don't imagine we'll have to put you to the trouble of that Earth trip after all, Neya Varden. Instead, you can be my guest for a couple of days until the deadline on this check is passed."

He raised his head and looked behind her toward some unseen presence.

"All right," he said. "You can take her away, now."

Neya rose numbly to find her arm grasped by one of Doreleyo's thugs. Furious, she tried to twist herself free, fighting and clawing unsuccessfully.

"Don't take it so hard," said the Crime Boss amiably. "Consider, Neya Varden, the Earthman may still work his plan successfully and rescue you."

His laughter rang in her ears as the thug carried her away.

They had doped her with *senesal*. Now they were trying to revive her and her body was sick and dead, pickled in sleep. It did not want to revive.

"No—no—" she moaned.

But the battering against her drugged state went on. She was being shaken. She was being forced to walk, stumblingly, while a pair of big hands held her. And, worst of all, some new chemical had been forced upon her which was inexorably pushing back the oblivion.

She opened bleary eyes, caught one brief glimpse of the room in which Doreleyo had interviewed her.

Doreleyo was alone with her, looming over the couch on which she lay, his eyes glaring hate.

"You!" said Doreleyo thickly. All the rage the man was capable of was in that one word. The love bird came thrilling to comfort him, but he knocked it away with a sudden sweep of one hand.

She stared up at him blankly. He reached down with his two great hands and shook her. The room blurred about her once again. The breath was knocked out of her as he flung her back down on the couch.

"Or maybe it wasn't you," muttered Doreleyo, staring down at her. "You haven't the brains; you haven't the guts to come in here deliberately and mislead me. It's *his* doing. You were a tool."

Abruptly, he knelt down by the side of the couch and laid his hands heavily upon her. His eyes caught hers and held them.

"You were the Earthman's tool, did you know that?" he asked. "He used you. He used you deliberately. Do you hear me?"

She shook her head weakly. Her voice came out thin and unnatural when she tried to speak.

"What are you talking about?" she said weakly. "I don't believe you."

"He used you. He used you," repeated Doreleyo. "Just like he fooled me. But there's a chance yet. For me and you. For both of us. Help me with this and I'll give you the whole city. You can write your own tab. You can have anything. You can even have me if you want. I'll marry you legally and make a settlement. You'll be rich in your own right. Just remember what he told you."

"I don't know what you're talking about."

"It was a trick," said the Crime Boss. His eyes were staring. "Even the book, probably. There's some reason there besides the book. Nobody would do all that for a book, would they?"

His hands closed on her shoulders, the fingers crushing them. She gave a little cry of pain and they relaxed.

"Do what?" she said. "How can I tell you anything when you won't tell me?"

"Don't you know what I'm talking about?" He thrust his face close to hers. "Don't you really know what's happened?"

"No!" she cried.

He took a deep breath.

"I'm stripped," he said. "I'm alone, waiting to get my throat cut, like an animal in the slaughterhouse. My boys here in the house have run off and left me. I can't raise the gangs by phone. I can't raise the cops. I can't get answers or help from anybody. And there is fighting in the streets—listen!"

Swiftly he was on his feet. He crossed the room and touched a hidden stud. A section of the wall faded and glowed into a screen.

The walkway outside Doreleyo's house took shape bright under the lights and the distant glow of the night sky. It was deserted but off in the distance, hidden by other buildings, came sporadic flashes, the sound of guns and shouting voices.

For a long moment she still did not understand. Doreleyo loomed tall against the street and buildings on the screen, like some titanic legendary figure. Then comprehension came with a rush.

"The revolution," she said. "What Thorpe was talking about."

"Yes, the revolution," said Doreleyo in low tones, talking as if to himself. "Jack Thorpe has done something— something—I wish I knew what. Why is it they won't come near me? Why do they fight?" He turned abruptly, crossed the room and came back to her. "He told you what he was going to do. He knew. You know. Tell me, and once I know what I'm fighting I can change it all back. I promise you that."

A strange gladness was welling up inside Neya. She looked up at the Boss in triumph.

"I can't tell you," she answered. "Even if I knew I couldn't tell you because I didn't understand."

"Don't lie to me, woman—" Doreleyo's voice rumbled in the empty room like thunder.

"I'm not lying," Neya sat up on the couch. "Jack talked but I didn't understand."

"But he told you!" cried Doreleyo. "If you heard it,

I'll get it from you. I'll probe it out of you. Then—''
laughing suddenly, he picked her up like a rag doll and
carried her across the room to a chair beside his desk. She
felt herself flung into it, and, as she gasped for breath from
the impact, Doreleyo dipped behind the desk and came out
with something that looked like an oversized grease gun
ending in a tip from which two small needles projected.

Neya had never seen one of these instruments but she
had heard of them. They were quite simple and drastically
effective. If the needles were inserted into a person's
skull at the right point an electrical charge effectively
destroyed that section of the brain that stored the moral
sense and the sense of personal identity. There were other
effects, equally bad or worse. She felt herself pinned down
by Doreleyo's broad hand, and the needle points on the tip
of the probe came closer.

As they touched her scalp Neya screamed. There was
the distant sound of footsteps running along the corridor
outside the room. Then everything exploded.

VII

The blackness cleared from before her eyes and she
struggled upright to face a strange tableau. Doreleyo stood
upright, half turned away from her, the probe, one needle
badly bent, lying on the floor at his feet. And in the
doorway, facing them both, the long barrel of a warp
pistol glistening in his fist, was Jack.

"Well, Earthman," said Doreleyo. "I'm very glad to
see you."

And indeed, he sounded as if he was. All the tension,
all the wildness that Neya had seen in him since he had

revived her, was gone. Neya, automatically wiping away the thin trickle of blood that had seeped down from the single needle puncture in her scalp, looked at the big Pioneer and understood. At last he was face to face with concrete reality, a situation he understood. A man with a gun was something the Crime Boss had had experience with; something he knew how to handle.

"Stay away from him, Jack!" she cried in instinctive warning.

"You hurt, Neya?" Jack asked, without taking his eyes from the other man.

"No—"

"Then come over here."

Neya pushed herself to her feet, and, shakily circling the Pioneer out of arm's reach, walked across the room to a couch near Jack, where she once more allowed her shaking body to collapse into a seated position.

"Now," said Jack to Doreleyo. "The Folio."

"It's in my desk drawer," responded Doreleyo, half turning toward that article of furniture and reaching out his hand.

"Stand still!" ordered Jack. He came forward and around the opposite side of the desk, keeping his gun trained steadily on the giant. At a touch of his finger on the drawer button the drawer slid out. Jack removed the book and put it under his arm.

"Tell me one thing," said Doreleyo, as Jack shut the drawer again. "What did you do?"

"Nothing unusual," Jack smiled. "Nothing that wasn't possible back in the ancient days when all men were Earthmen."

"Tell me," said Doreleyo. His voice was calm and interested. "I'd like to know."

"I used old skills," said Jack. "Skills you Pioneers have forgotten or discarded, but which were an instinctive part of the highly concentrated training all we of Earth must take nowadays. My weapons were invisible to your society, much as a savage might smuggle a blowgun and poison dart safely past an electric eye set to detect the metal of latter-day weapons.''

"Tell me," repeated Doreleyo.

"All right," said Jack. "I sold factory efficiency techniques out of ancient industrialized Earth to your custom builders. I attracted the attention of your seconds in commands and hypnotized them into adding myself to the list of things they feared. I made money and studied your city, people, classes, and society. In less than a year I determined that the essential elements of your society were that five principal powers worked together to produce a stable situation. Briefly, if the City of Jark was to continue running smoothly, and you were to stay in power, the following seemed to be necessary: that the police back up the power of the Boss, the gangs of the underworld cooperate with the police if the small businessmen do too; the small businessmen are cooperative with the unions, provided, that is, that if the financiers help the small businessmen, the unions do so too; the gangs cooperate with the police if the police remain loyal to the Boss; and the small businessmen help the unions if the financier group help the small businessmen.''

Doreleyo's eyes were baffled and furious. The love-bird fluttered unheeding on his shoulder, singing to him.

"I discovered something more," Jack went on softly. "I checked back some years into the City's history and I discovered that this tangle of power was mainly your doing. You had risen to power here in Jark as others have done in other Pioneer cities by playing one group against each other. It is a good scheme but it has one weakness, invariably, and that is that it depends on the kingpin for stability. I set myself to find the single point upon which the kingpin rested."

He smiled.

"One more of the old skills that has been largely forgotten is something called symbolic logic," he said. "Nowadays the situations that benefitted from its use have largely disappeared and only a few pedants on your Pioneer worlds bother to know it. Machines do, in some ways, too much for you. With us on Earth it is different. With symbolic logic, Doreleyo, your carefully built up maze of power resolves to this equation—'' and, reaching out to the desk with his free hand, Jack picked up a stylus and pressed upon a sheet of plastic a row of symbols. He twirled the sheet around and showed it to Doreleyo.

"From which—" he continued, "by a simple transformation we get this—"

Twirling the sheet back, he once more set down a set of symbols and showed them to the Boss.

"I won't go into details," he said. "It's enough for you to know that from this it's apparent that P or G are the only elements truly essential to stability, the rest being irrelevant when logically analyzed. P stands for the support which the police give the Boss, which is the thing I was trying to destroy, by creating an unstable situation. So I hit at G, which stands for the cooperation of the gangs with the police. If the police begin to fear that the gangs will not cooperate with them, then they are not likely to lend any support to the titular chief of the gangs."

Doreleyo's face looked like a stone image. He spoke between his teeth.

"I had the cops in my pocket," he said.

"You did," said Jack, "as long as they were sure that you controlled the gangs. Make them uncertain who is really in control and they will refuse to stand by anybody until they know for sure. With the hypnotic entree I had into the minds of your District Leaders it wasn't hard to inflame their hates against each other to violence when the time was ripe."

He stopped speaking. Through the silence of the room drifted the distant mob sounds from the screen.

"LOOK OUT, JACK!" screamed Neya.

During the time that Jack had been talking, Doreleyo,

with a silence and delicacy of movement incredible in a man his bulk, had gradually been drawing closer to the speaker. Now, as Jack finished, he launched his three hundred pounds at the Earthman.

If it had not been for the Folio, Jack might have eluded him. But Jack hesitated for just a second, pushing the Folio across the desk to safety. In that moment Doreleyo's hand closed about the warp gun and its thin plastic barrel snapped like a straw under the pressure of the thick fingers. For a split second it looked as if Jack also would be overwhelmed, but he flipped backward across the desk and landed on his feet.

"Jack—" Neya moaned.

Jack was breathing somewhat hard, but his face was calm, even interested, as he faced the Boss. He spoke to the girl without turning his head.

"It's all right," he said. He made a sudden quick movement towards the Folio but Doreleyo's hand was there before him. The giant Pioneer swept it off the table to the floor. His eyes were red with hate.

"Now, Earthman!" he rumbled.

Neya ran to the door of the room and flung it open.

"This way, Jack!" she cried. "RUN!"

"He has the book," said Jack tensely. And, slowly, incredibly, he began to move around the table toward Doreleyo. Doreleyo moved to meet him.

With a sudden movement, the Pioneer charged. What happened then was simplicity itself, but to both Doreleyo and the watching Neya it seemed magical. As the Boss' outstretched hand reached Jack, he seized it in both of his own, and, turning swiftly, levered the larger man into the air and over on his back. As Doreleyo slammed to the floor, Jack rose into the air, turning like a cat and came down on the Pioneer with all his weight, driving his knee into the man's solar plexus. The air thudded out of Doreleyo's lungs, and he flopped back, limp.

Jack scooped up the Folio. Then he turned to Neya, smiling a little at the shock on her face.

"Judo," he told her. "More tricks—as Doreleyo would say. Now that I've got the book we can leave." She stared at him.

"So it was the book, after all," she said.

"I tried to tell you that," he answered gently. She shook her head bewilderedly.

"I should have guessed—" she began. Her face contorted suddenly and she screamed, "Jack—BEHIND YOU!"

Jack tossed the book to her and started to whirl, only to feel a heavy body crash into him from behind and forearms like logs come thudding across his chest, imprisoning him, crushing his arms to his sides. Doreleyo's hot breath hissed in his ear.

"Now!" grunted the giant.

His arms tightened. Jack lifted his heel and brought it down hard on Doreleyo's instep. The big man grunted and his arms relaxed. As his left arm came free Jack slipped beneath it and struck backward with the edge of his hand at the base of the giant's spine. The thud of the blow covered the sharp crack as the spine broke. Doreleyo's legs gave way beneath him.

But in going down he managed to fasten his hands about Jack's neck. He dragged the lighter man down with him, throwing the weight of his body across Jack's legs and lower trunk. Like a huge bulldog, ignoring the dead weight of the paralyzed lower half of his body, Doreleyo gripped Jack's throat in his two huge hands and hung on, death staring in his eyes.

Jack's body and one arm were pinned to the floor. He fastened the fingers of his free hand at a sensitive point on Doreleyo's upper arm and squeezed. But the Pioneer was oblivious to anything except his determination to kill. His face writhed with the pain from the nerve pinch, but he held on.

Jack's sight was glazing; and he could feel his strength

going from him. The man holding him had crossed the borderline that divides the sane from the insane. With a fleeting impulse of regret and disgust, Jack raised the edge of his free hand and struck one quick blow on the thick neck.

Doreleyo's neck broke. He slumped limply, his hands relaxing from Jack's throat. Lungs gulping greedily for air, Jack struggled free and pulled himself to his feet. He crossed over to where the Folio lay and picked it up. He turned to Neya.

"Let's go," he said.

They went. The love-bird hung crying on beating wings above the dead body of Doreleyo. For a long minute it hung there. Then, with a tiny scream of agony, it flung itself head on at one of the flickering walls, smashed there, and dropped to the floor, a pitiful lump of scarlet feathers.

Jack led Neya at a run to the traffic tunnels. A rented car was waiting there, low and sleek under the overhead lights. But a huge thug, warp pistol holstered at his side and with the blades of his ring knives full-extended on bloody fists, was trying to force the locked controls.

Jack seemed to fly through the air at him. Their fighting bodies locked and toppled over the low hood of the car to fall from sight beyond. There was a long, drawn-out worrying noise and Jack rose to his feet alone, holding the warp pistol.

"Quickly," he snapped, vaulting into the car and holding a door in the cockpit open for her. "There's green blood on him. The aliens will be loose."

Neya's eyes widened. Pioneer born and bred, she knew only too well what happened in a city where the rioting spread to the foreign quarter. She jumped into the car. Jack snapped the transparent, warp-proof top down and the car shot forward.

Three times they detoured to avoid struggling groups. Twice Jack had to take to the air, a suicidal maneuver

under the low ceiling of the tunnels, when there was no
other way of avoiding battle. And once he shot his way
through a group of barrel-chested Sagittarians, killing
cleanly and without mercy, for the squat humanoids were
mad with the taste of blood and could be passed no other
way. Then they burst forth onto the surface at the edge of
the city; and Neya gasped at what she saw.

"The spaceport!" she cried, recognizing their destination.

The city behind them was red with flames. Jack flicked
back the top and pushed her from the car.

"We're in time," he cried, above a mounting, thunderous rumble that came from within the spaceport gates,
where a titanic shape loomed upright against the smoky
night sky. "The ship for Earth is still warming up. Come
on!"

He seized her wrist and dragged her after him. Numbly,
she allowed herself to be pulled through the gate where a
platoon of Interstellar Guards stood at ready with a warp
cannon pointing its ominous snout along the way to the
blazing city. Only the two tickets in Jack's hand got them
through.

Then they were inside the gates. Neya allowed herself to
be hurried along for a dozen paces toward the great spaceship. Then she dug in her heels and stopped.

Jack whirled on her.

"What's wrong?" he shouted over the thunderous noise
of the reactors warming up. "Come on, we've just time to
make it."

"I'm not going," said Neya. Her face was white. He
gripped her fiercely by the arms.

"Why not?" he shouted.

Tears were rolling down her cheeks. She shook her
head.

"It's all right," she said. "I made you promise to take
me. You don't have to. You go ahead."

"What are you talking about?" raved Jack. Above both

of their heads, the great floating spaceport clock ticked off
the seconds toward launching time.

"I made you promise—"

"What of it!" Jack shouted. "What's that got to do
with it? I want you to come, you little fool." He stared at
her in the lucid light of the burning city.

"I love you!" he cried.

Neya's eyes went wide with shock. She swayed toward
him and for a moment he caught her. Then she was
fighting like a demoncat, pulling herself free. Astonished,
he let her go.

"No!" her voice was determined. "That doesn't help.
That makes it worse. I wouldn't fit in back there. I haven't
been trained. I'd be helpless. No use to you, Jack! Go
on—quickly. Go alone!"

He grabbed her in exasperation.

"You can be trained!" he bellowed above the mounting
sound. "In six months—a year—you'll be just as good as
I am."

She smiled sadly, her white face resigned.

"You think I haven't realized?" she cried. "You're no
ordinary Earthman. They don't send ordinary men half
way across the galaxy to do the job you did. You aren't
just any man back there. I know I could never come up to
you, no matter what I did. And you know it too. Tell me
the truth. Tell me what you really are back there on that
world where everybody seems to be a superman!"

For a long second he stood staring at her, a look of
incredulity spreading over his face. Then, with a sudden
whoop of joy, he swept her up off her feet and started at a
run for the gangplank of the ship.

"Put me down!" she screamed, kicking, but he paid no
attention. In spite of the fact that she weighed over two-
thirds his own weight, he ran lightly and easily as if she
was no burden at all. Pressed tight against him, Neya felt
his chest shake slightly as if he was silently laughing.

He reached the gangplank and was up it in three bounds.

For a second the port loomed, then they were inside and the great plug of metal swung shut behind them. And the floor pressed up against their feet as the ship began to lift.

"What's this?" demanded a spruce young deck officer sharply. He stood, very stiff and erect in his white and gold uniform, looking at them as if he doubted their sanity.

"Nothing," said Jack, setting Neya down. "It's all right. We've got tickets." And he produced them.

"Cabin four thirty-six to the right," said the officer, glancing at them. "All right." He swung abruptly on his heel and was off down the corridor, snapping out commands to a couple of crewmen who were reeling in the gangplank.

Jack and Neya moved off down the corridor to the right until they came to a door where 436 glowed whitely against the imitation paneling. Jack pressed a ticket against the scanner and the door swung open. He took Neya by the hand and drew her through into a small stateroom, cleverly furnished to give an illusion of size and great comfort. Green carpeting was beneath their feet and soft lights glowed overhead. The silence after the thunder was almost shocking.

They faced each other.

"You won't get away with this," said Neya. "I'll talk to the Captain." He ignored the threat.

"So you thought I was something unusual," he said. The smile that had been on his face ever since her demand outside to know who he really was was broadening.

"I suppose you'll try to tell me you aren't," she replied, coldly.

"Not only that—" he said. He was openly grinning at her now in pure delight. "I'm not only very ordinary. I'm worse than that. I'm very blundering and inept. So you want to know who I am?"

Neya's face was hard and unfriendly. Jack took both her hands in his.

"Young lady," he spoke the words with great emphasis, jerking his thumb toward his chest, but without letting go of her hand, "I—*I*—am the incredibly stupid and woolyheaded librarian who made the original mistake and sent the Folio to Doreleyo in the first place!"

For a second she just stared at him, and then her face began to crumple. Jack let go of her arms and pulled her to him. She sobbed on his shoulder.

"I'm no good," she said in a choked voice, after a moment, moving her lips against the soft cloth of his tunic. "I'll never be any good no matter how much they train me. When you find that out, you won't like me. So I'll just go away and not bother you any more."

"The hell you will!" said Jack, grimly, tightening his arms around her.

Jackal's Meal

If there should follow a thousand swords to
  carry my bones away—
Belike the price of a jackal's meal were more
  than a thief could pay . . .
      "The Ballad of East and West,"
      by Rudyard Kipling

In the third hour after the docking of the great, personal spaceship of the Morah Jhan—on the planetoid outpost of the 469th Corps which was then stationed just outside the Jhan's spatial frontier—a naked figure in a ragged gray cloak burst from a crate of supplies being unloaded off the huge alien ship. The figure ran around uttering strange cries for a little while, eluding the Morah who had been doing the unloading, until it was captured at last by the human Military Police guarding the smaller, courier vessel alongside, which had brought Ambassador Alan Dormu here from Earth to talk with the Jhan.

The Jhan himself, and Dormu—along with Marshal Sayers Whin and most of the other ranking officers, Morah and human alike—had already gone inside, to the Headquarters area of the outpost, where an athletic show was being

49

put on for the Jhan's entertainment. But the young captain in charge of the Military Police, on his own initiative, refused the strong demands of the Morah that the fugitive be returned to them. For it, or he, showed signs of being—or of once having been—a man, under his rags and dirt and some surgicallike changes that had been made in him.

One thing was certain. He was deathly afraid of his Morah pursuers; and it was not until he was shut in a room out of sight of them that he quieted down. However, nothing could bring him to say anything humanly understandable. He merely stared at the faces of all those who came close to him, and felt their clothing as someone might fondle the most precious fabric made—and whimpered a little when the questions became too insistent, trying to hide his face in his arms but not succeeding because of the surgery that had been done to him.

The Morah went back to their own ship to contact their chain of command, leading ultimately up to the Jhan; and the young Military Police captain lost no time in getting the fugitive to his Headquarters' Section and the problem into the hands of his own commanders. From whom, by way of natural military process, it rose through the ranks until it came to the attention of Marshal Sayers Whin.

"Hell's Bells—" exploded Whin, on hearing it. But then he checked himself and lowered his voice. He had been drawn aside by Harold Belman, the one-star general of the Corps who was his aide; and only a thin door separated him from the box where Dormu and the Jhan sat, still watching the athletic show. "Where is the . . . Where is he?"

"Down in my office, sir."

"This has got to be quite a mess!" said Whin. He thought rapidly. He was a tall, lean man from the Alaskan back country and his temper was usually short-lived. "Look, the show in there'll be over in a minute. Go in. My apologies to the Jhan. I've gone ahead to see everything's properly fixed for the meeting at lunch. Got that?"

"Yes, Marshal."

"Stick with the Jhan. Fill in for me."

"What if Dormu—"

"Tell him nothing. Even if he asks, play dumb. I've got to have time to sort this thing out, Harry! You understand?"

"Yes, sir," said his aide.

Whin went out a side door of the small anteroom, catching himself just in time from slamming it behind him. But once out in the corridor, he strode along at a pace that was almost a run.

He had to take a lift tube down eighteen levels to his aide's office. When he stepped in there, he found the fugitive surrounded by the officer of the day and some officers of the Military Police, including General Mack Stigh, Military Police Unit Commandant. Stigh was the ranking officer in the room; and it was to him Whin turned.

"What about it, Mack?"

"Sir, apparently he escaped from the Jhan's ship—"

"Not that. I know that. Did you find out who he is? What he is?" Whin glanced at the fugitive who was chewing hungrily on something grayish-brown that Whin recognized as a Morah product. One of the eatables supplied for the lunch meeting with the Jhan that would be starting any moment now. Whin grimaced.

"We tried him on our own food," said Stigh. "He wouldn't eat it. They may have played games with his digestive system, too. No, sir, we haven't found out anything. There've been a few undercover people sent into Morah territory in the past twenty years. He could be one of them. We've got a records search going on. Of course, chances are his record wouldn't be in our files, anyway."

"Stinking Morah," muttered a voice from among the officers standing around. Whin looked up quickly, and a new silence fell.

"Records search. All right," Whin said, turning back to Stigh, "that's good. What did the Morah say when what's-his-name—that officer on duty down at the docks—wouldn't give him up?''

"Captain—?'' Stigh turned and picked out a young officer with his eyes. The young officer stepped forward.

"Captain Gene McKussic, Marshal,'' he introduced himself.

"You were the one on the docks?'' Whin asked.

"Yes, sir.''

"What did the Morah say?''

"Just—that he wasn't human, sir,'' said McKussic. "That he was one of their own experimental pets, made out of one of their own people—just to look human.''

"What else?''

"That's all, Marshal.''

"And you didn't believe them?''

"Look at him, sir—'' McKussic pointed at the fugitive, who by this time had finished his food and was watching them with bright but timid eyes. "He hasn't got a hair on him, except where a man'd have it. Look at his face. And the shape of his head's human. Look at his fingernails, even—''

"Yes—'' said Whin slowly, gazing at the fugitive. Then he raised his eyes and looked around at the other officers. "But none of you thought to get a doctor in here to check?''

"Sir,'' said Stigh, "we thought we should contact you, first—''

"All right. But get a doctor *now!* Get two of them!'' said Whin. One of the other officers turned to a desk nearby and spoke into an intercom. "You know what we're up against, don't you—all of you?'' Whin's eyes stabbed around the room. "This is just the thing to blow Ambassador Dormu's talk with the Morah Jhan sky high. Now, all of you, except General Stigh, get out of here. Go back to your quarters and stay on tap until you're given other orders. And keep your mouths shut.''

"Marshal,'' it was the young Military Police captain,

McKussic, "we aren't going to give him back to the Morah, no matter what, are we, sir . . ."

He trailed off. Whin merely looked at him.

"Get to your quarters, Captain!" said Stigh, roughly.

The room cleared. When they were left alone with the fugitive, Stigh's gaze went slowly to Whin.

"So," said Whin, "you're wondering that too, are you, Mack?"

"No, sir," said Stigh. "But word of this is probably spreading through the men like wildfire, by this time. There'll be no stopping it. And if it comes to the point of our turning back to the Morah a man who's been treated the way this man has—"

"They're soldiers!" said Whin, harshly. "They'll obey orders." He pointed at the fugitive. "That's a soldier."

"Not necessarily, Marshal," said Stigh. "He could have been one of the civilian agents—"

"For my purposes, he's a soldier!" snarled Whin. He took a couple of angry paces up and down the room in each direction, but always wheeling back to confront the fugitive. "Where are those doctors? I've got to get back to the Jhan and Dormu!"

"About Ambassador Dormu," Stigh said. "If he hears something about this and asks us—"

"Tell him nothing!" said Whin. "It's my responsibility! I'm not sure he's got the guts—never mind. The longer it is before the little squirt knows—"

The sound of the office door opening brought both men around.

"The little squirt already knows," said a dry voice from the doorway. Ambassador Alan Dormu came into the room. He was a slight, bent man, of less than average height. His fading blond hair was combed carefully forward over a balding forehead; and his face had deep, narrow lines that testified to even more years than hair and forehead.

"Who told you?" Whin gave him a mechanical grin.

"We diplomats always respect the privacy of our sources," said Dormu. "What difference does it make—as long as I found out? Because you're wrong, you know, Marshal. I'm the one who's responsible. I'm the one who'll have to answer the Jhan when he asks about this at lunch."

"Mack," said Whin, continuing to grin and with his eyes still fixed on Dormu, "see you later."

"Yes, Marshal."

Stigh went toward the door of the office. But before he reached it, it opened and two officers came in; a major and a lieutenant colonel, both wearing the caduceus. Stigh stopped and turned back.

"Here're the doctors, sir."

"Fine. Come here, come here, gentlemen," said Whin. "Take a look at this."

The two medical officers came up to the fugitive sitting in the chair. They maintained poker faces. One reached for a wrist of the fugitive and felt for a pulse. The other went around back and ran his fingers lightly over the upper back with its misshapen and misplaced shoulder sockets.

"Well?" demanded Whin, after a restless minute. "What about it? Is he a man, all right?"

The two medical officers looked up. Oddly, it was the junior in rank, the major, who answered.

"We'll have to make tests—a good number of tests, sir," he said.

"You've no idea—now?" Whin demanded.

"Now," spoke up the lieutenant colonel, "he could be either Morah or human. The Morah are very, very, good at this sort of thing. The way those arms— We'll need samples of his blood, skin, bone marrow—"

"All right. All right," said Whin. "Take the time you need. But not one second more. We're all on the spot here, gentlemen. Mack—" he turned to Stigh, "I've changed my mind. You stick with the doctors and stand by to keep me informed."

He turned back to Dormu.

"We'd better be getting back upstairs, Mr. Ambassador," he said.

"Yes," answered Dormu, quietly.

They went out, paced down the corridor and entered the lift tube in silence.

"You know, of course, how this complicates things, Marshal," said Dormu, finally, as they began to rise up the tube together. Whin started like a man woken out of deep thought.

"What? You don't have to ask me that," he said. His voice took on an edge. "I suppose you'd expect my men to just stand around and watch, when something like that came running out of a Morah ship?"

"*I* might have," said Dormu. "In their shoes."

"Don't doubt it." Whin gave a single, small grunt of a laugh, without humor.

"I don't think you follow me," said Dormu. "I didn't bring up the subject to assign blame. I was just leading into the fact the damage done is going to have to be repaired, at any cost; and I'm counting on your immediate— note the word, Marshal—*immediate* cooperation, if and when I call for it."

The lift had carried them to the upper floor that was their destination. They got off together. Whin gave another humorless little grunt of laughter.

"You're thinking of handing him back, then?" Whin said.

"Wouldn't you?" asked Dormu.

"Not if he's human. No," said Whin. They walked on down a corridor and into a small room with another door. From beyond that other door came the faint smell of something like incense—it was, in fact, a neutral odor, tolerable to human and Morah alike and designed to hide the differing odors of one race from another. Also, from beyond the door, came the sound of three musical notes, steadily repeated; two notes exactly the same, and then a third, a half-note higher.

Tonk, tonk, TINK! . . .

"It's establishing a solid position for confrontation with the Jhan that's important right now," said Dormu, as they approached the other door. "He's got us over a barrel on the subject of this talk anyway, even without that business downstairs coming up. So it's the confrontation that counts. Nothing else."

They opened the door and went in.

Within was a rectangular, windowless room. Two tables had been set up. One for Dormu and Whin; and one for the Jhan, placed at right angles to the other table but not quite touching it. Both tables had been furnished and served with food; and the Jhan was already seated at his. To his right and left, each at about five feet of distance from him, flamed two purely symbolic torches in floor standards. Behind him stood three ordinary Morah—two servers, and a musician whose surgically-created, enormous forefinger tapped steadily at the bars of something like a small metal xylophone, hanging vertically on his chest.

The forefinger tapped in time to the three notes Whin and Dormu had heard in the room outside but without really touching the xylophone bars. The three notes actually sounded from a speaker overhead, broadcast throughout the station wherever the Jhan might be, along with the neutral perfume. They were a courtesy of the human hosts.

"Good to see you again, gentlemen," said the Jhan, through the mechanical interpreter at his throat. "I was about to start without you."

He sat, like the other Morah in the room, unclothed to the waist, below which he wore, though hidden now by the table, a simple kilt, or skirt, of dark red, feltlike cloth. The visible skin of his body, arms and face was a reddish brown in color, but there was only a limited amount of it to be seen. His upper chest, back, arms, neck and head—

excluding his face—was covered by a mat of closely-trimmed, thick, gray hair, so noticeable in contrast to his hairless areas that it looked more like a garment—a cowled half-jacket—than any natural growth upon him.

The face that looked out of the cowl-part was humanoid, but with wide jawbones, rounded chin and eyes set far apart over a flat nose. So that, although no one feature suggested it, his face as a whole had a faintly feline look.

"Our apologies," said Dormu, leading the way forward. "The marshal just received an urgent message for me from Earth, in a new code. And only I had the key to it."

"No need to apologize," said the Jhan. "We've had our musician here to entertain us while we waited."

Dormu and Whin sat down at the opposite ends of their table, facing each other and at right angles to the Jhan. The Jhan had already begun to eat. Whin stared deliberately at the foods on the Jhan's table, to make it plain that he was not avoiding looking at them, and then turned back to his own plate. He picked up a roll and buttered it.

"Your young men are remarkable in their agility," the Jhan said to Dormu. "We hope you will convey them our praise—"

They talked of the athletic show; and the meal progressed. As it was drawing to a close, the Jhan came around to the topic that had brought him to this meeting with Dormu.

". . . It's unfortunate we have to meet under such necessities," he said.

"My own thought," replied Dormu. "You must come to Earth some time on a simple vacation."

"We would like to come to Earth—in peace," said the Jhan.

"We would hope not to welcome you any other way," said Dormu.

"No doubt," said the Jhan. "That is why it puzzles me,

that when you humans can have peace for the asking—by simply refraining from creating problems—you continue to cause incidents, to trouble us and threaten our sovereignty over our own territory of space.''

Dormu frowned.

"Incidents?" he echoed. "I don't recall any incidents. Perhaps the Jhan has been misinformed?"

"We are not misinformed," said the Jhan. "I refer to your human settlements on the fourth and fifth worlds of the star you refer to as 27J93; but which we call by a name of our own. Rightfully so because it is in our territory."

Tonk, tonk, TINK . . . went the three notes of the Morah music.

"It seems to me—if my memory is correct," murmured Dormu, "that the Treaty Survey made by our two races jointly, twelve years ago, left Sun 27J93 in unclaimed territory outside both our spatial areas."

"Quite right," said the Jhan. "But the Survey was later amended to include this and several other solar systems in our territory."

"Not by us, I'm afraid," said Dormu. "I'm sorry, but my people can't consider themselves automatically bound by whatever unilateral action you choose to take without consulting us."

"The action was not unilateral," said the Jhan, calmly. "We have since consulted with our brother Emperors—the Morah Selig, the Morah Ben, the Morah Yarra and the Morah Ness. All have concurred in recognizing the solar systems in question as being in our territory."

"But surely the Morah Jhan understands," said Dormu, "that an agreement only between the various political segments of one race can't be considered binding upon a people of another race entirely?"

"We of the Morah," said the Jhan, "reject your attitude that race is the basis for division between Empires. Territory is the only basis upon which Empires may be differentiated. Distinction between the races refers only to differences in shape or color; and as you know we do not regard any particular shape or color as sacredly, among ourselves, as you do; since we make many individuals over into what shape it pleases us, for our own use, or amusement."

He tilted his head toward the musician with the enormous, steadily jerking forefinger.

"Nonetheless," said Dormu, "the Morah Jhan will not deny his kinship with the Morah of the other Morah Empires."

"Of course not. But what of it?" said the Jhan calmly. "In our eyes your empire and those of our brothers are in all ways similar. In essence you are only another group possessing a territory that is not ours. We make no difference between you and the empires of the other Morah."

"But if it came to an armed dispute between you and us," said Dormu, "would your brother Emperors remain neutral?"

"We hardly expect so," said the Morah Jhan, idly, pushing aside the last container of food that remained on the table before him. A server took it away. "But that would only be because, since right would be on our side, naturally they would rally to assist us."

"I see," said Dormu.

Tonk, tonk, TINK . . . went the sound of the Morah music.

"But why must we talk about such large and problematical issues?" said the Jhan. "Why not listen, instead, to the very simple and generous disposition we suggest for this matter of your settlements under 27J93? You will probably find our solution so agreeable that no more need be said on the subject."

"I'd be happy to hear it," said Dormu.

The Jhan leaned back in his seat at the table.

"In spite of the fact that our territory has been intruded upon," he said, "we ask only that you remove your people from their settlements and promise to avoid that area in future, recognizing these and the other solar systems I mentioned earlier as being in our territory. We will not even ask for ordinary reparations beyond the purely technical matter of your agreement to recognize what we Morah have already recognized, that the division of peoples is by territory, and not by race.''

He paused. Dormu opened his mouth to speak.

''Of course,'' added the Jhan, ''there is one additional, trivial concession we insist on. A token reparation—so that no precedent of not asking for reparations be set. That token concession is that you allow us corridors of transit across your spatial territory, through which our ships may pass without inspection between our empire and the empires of our brother Morah.''

Dormu's mouth closed. The Jhan sat waiting. After a moment, Dormu spoke.

''I can only say,'' said Dormu, ''that I am stunned and overwhelmed at these demands of the Morah Jhan. I was sent to this meeting only to explain to him that our settlements under Sun number 27J93 were entirely peaceful ones, constituting no human threat to his empire. I have no authority to treat with the conditions and terms just mentioned. I will have to contact my superiors back on Earth for instructions—and that will take several hours.''

''Indeed?'' said the Morah Jhan. ''I'm surprised to hear you were sent all the way here to meet me with no more instructions than that. That represents such a limited authority that I almost begin to doubt the good will of you and your people in agreeing to this meeting.''

''On our good will, of course,'' said Dormu, ''the Morah Jhan can always depend.''

''Can I?'' The wide-spaced eyes narrowed suddenly in the catlike face. ''Things seem to conspire to make me doubt it. Just before you gentlemen joined me I was informed of a most curious fact by my officers. It seems some of your Military Police have kidnapped one of my Morah and are holding him prisoner.''

"Oh?" said Dormu. His face registered polite astonishment. "I don't see how anything like that could have happened." He turned to Whin. "Marshal, did you hear about anything like that taking place?"

Whin grinned his mechanical grin at the Morah Jhan.

"I heard somebody had been picked up down at the docks," he said. "But I understood he was human. One of our people who'd been missing for some time—a deserter, maybe. A purely routine matter. It's being checked out, now."

"I would suggest that the marshal look more closely into the matter," said the Jhan. His eyes were still slitted. "I promise him he will find the individual is a Morah; and of course, I expect the prisoner's immediate return."

"The Morah Jhan can rest assured," said Whin, "any Morah held by my troops will be returned to him, immediately."

"I will expect that return then," said the Jhan, "by the time Ambassador Dormu has received his instructions from Earth and we meet to talk again."

He rose, abruptly; and without any further word, turned and left the room. The servers and the musician followed him.

Dormu got as abruptly to his own feet and led the way back out of the room in the direction from which he and Whin had come.

"Where are you going?" demanded Whin. "We go left for the lifts to the Message Center."

"We're going back to look at our kidnapped prisoner," said Dormu. "I don't need the Message Center."

Whin looked sideways at him.

"So . . . you *were* sent out here with authority to talk on those terms of his, after all, then?" Whin asked.

"We expected them," said Dormu briefly.

"What are you going to do about them?"

"Give in," said Dormu. "On all but the business of

giving them corridors through our space. That's a first step to breaking us up into territorial segments."

"Just like that—" said Whin. "You'll give in?"

Dormu looked at him, briefly.

"You'd fight, I suppose?"

"If necessary," said Whin. They got into the lift tube and slipped downward together.

"And you'd lose," said Dormu.

"Against the Morah Jhan?" demanded Whin. "I know within ten ships what his strength is."

"No. Against all the Morah," answered Dormu. "This situation's been carefully set up. Do you think the Jhan would ordinarily be that much concerned about a couple of small settlements of our people, away off beyond his natural frontiers? The Morah—all the Morah—have started to worry about our getting too big for them to handle. They've set up a coalition of all their so-called Empires to contain us before that happens. If we fight the Jhan, we'll find ourselves fighting them all."

The skin of Whin's face grew tight.

"Giving in to a race like the Morah won't help," he said.

"It may gain us time," said Dormu. "We're a single, integrated society. They aren't. In five years, ten years, we can double our fighting strength. Meanwhile their co-alition members may even start fighting among themselves. That's why I was sent here to do what I'm doing—give up enough ground so that they'll have no excuse for starting trouble at this time; but not enough ground so that they'll feel safe in trying to push further."

"Why won't they—if they know they can win?"

"Jhan has to count the cost to him personally, if he starts the war," said Dormu, briefly. They got off the lift tube. "Which way's the Medical Section?"

"There"—Whin pointed. They started walking. "What makes you so sure he won't think the cost is worth it?"

"Because," said Dormu, "he has to stop and figure

what would happen if, being the one to start the war, he ended up more weakened by it than his brother-emperors were. The others would turn on him like wolves, given the chance; just like he'd turn on any of them. And he knows it."

Whin grunted his little, humorless laugh.

They found the fugitive lying on his back on an examination table in one of the diagnostic rooms of the Medical Section. He was plainly unconscious.

"Well?" Whin demanded bluntly of the medical lieutenant colonel. "Man, or Morah?"

The lieutenant colonel was washing his hands. He hesitated, then rinsed his fingers and took up a towel.

"Out with it!" snapped Whin.

"Marshal," the lieutenant colonel hesitated again, "to be truthful . . . we may never know."

"Never know?" demanded Dormu. General Stigh came into the room, his mouth open as if about to say something to Whin. He checked at the sight of Dormu and the sound of the ambassador's voice.

"There's human RNA involved," said the lieutenant colonel. "But we know that the Morah have access to human bodies from time to time, soon enough after the moment of death so that the RNA might be preserved. But bone and flesh samples indicate Morah, rather than human origin. He could be human and his RNA be the one thing about him the Morah didn't monkey with. Or he could be Morah, treated with human RNA to back up the surgical changes that make him resemble a human. I don't think we can tell, with the facilities we've got here; and in any case—"

"In any case," said Dormu, slowly, "it may not really matter to the Jhan."

Whin raised his eyebrows questioningly; but just then he caught sight of Stigh.

"Mack?" he said. "What is it?"

Stigh produced a folder.

"I think we've found out who he is," the Military Police general said. "Look here—a civilian agent of the Intelligence Service was sent secretly into the spatial territory of the Morah Jhan eight years ago. Name—Paul Edmonds. Description—superficially the same size and build as this man here." He nodded at the still figure on the examining table. "We can check the retinal patterns and fingerprints."

"It won't do you any good," said the lieutenant colonel. "Both fingers and retinas conform to the Morah pattern."

"May I see that?" asked Dormu. Stigh passed over the folder. The little ambassador took it. "Eight years ago, I was the State Department's Liaison Officer with the Intelligence Service."

He ran his eyes over the information on the sheets in the folder.

"There's something I didn't finish telling you," said the lieutenant colonel, appealing to Whin now that Dormu's attention was occupied. "I started to say I didn't think we could tell whether he's man or Morah; but in any case— the question's probably academic. He's dying."

"Dying?" said Dormu sharply, looking up from the folder. "What do you mean?"

Without looking, he passed the folder back to Stigh.

"I mean . . . he's dying," said the lieutenant colonel, a little stubbornly. "It's amazing that any organism, human or Morah, was able to survive, in the first place, after being cut up and altered that much. His running around down on the docks was evidently just too much for him. He's bleeding to death internally from a hundred different pinpoint lesions."

"Hm-m-m," said Whin. He looked sharply at Dormu. "Do you think the Jhan would be just as satisfied if he got a body back, instead of a live man?"

"Would you?" retorted Dormu.

"Hm-m-m . . . no. I guess I wouldn't," said Whin. He turned to look grimly at the unconscious figure on the table; and spoke almost to himself. "If he *is* Paul Edmonds—"

"Sir," said Stigh, appealingly.

Whin looked at the general. Stigh hesitated.

"If I could speak to the marshal privately for a moment—" he said.

"Never mind," said Whin. The line of his mouth was tight and straight. "I think I know what you've got to tell me. Let the ambassador hear it, too."

"Yes, sir." But Stigh still looked uncomfortable. He glanced at Dormu, glanced away again, fixed his gaze on Whin. "Sir, word about this man has gotten out all over the Outpost. There's a lot of feeling among the officers and men alike—a lot of feeling against handing him back . . ."

He trailed off.

"You mean to say," said Dormu sharply, "that they won't obey if ordered to return this individual?"

"They'll obey," said Whin, softly. Without turning his head, he spoke to the lieutenant colonel. "Wait outside for us, will you, Doctor?"

The lieutenant colonel went out, and the door closed behind him. Whin turned and looked down at the fugitive on the table. In unconsciousness the face was relaxed, neither human nor Morah, but just a face, out of many possible faces. Whin looked up again and saw Dormu's eyes still on him.

"You don't understand, Mr. Ambassador," Whin said, in the same soft voice. "These men are veterans. You heard the doctor talking about the fact that the Morah have had access to human RNA. This outpost has had little, unreported, border clashes with them every so often. The personnel here have seen the bodies of the men we've recovered. They know what it means to fall into Morah hands. To deliberately deliver anyone back into those hands is something pretty hard for them to take. But they're soldiers. They won't refuse an order.''

He stopped talking. For a moment there was silence in the room.

''I see,'' said Dormu. He went across to the door and opened it. The medical lieutenant colonel was outside, and he turned to face Dormu in the opened door. ''Doctor, you said this individual was dying.''

''Yes,'' answered the lieutenant colonel.

''How long?''

''A cople of hours—'' the lieutenant colonel shrugged helplessly. ''A couple of minutes. I've no way of telling, nothing to go on, by way of comparable experience.''

''All right.'' Dormu turned back to Whin. ''Marshal, I'd like to get back to the Jhan as soon as the minimum amount of time's past that could account for a message to Earth and back.''

An hour and a half later, Whin and Dormu once more entered the room where they had lunched with the Jhan. The tables were removed now; and the servers were gone. The musician was still there; and, joining him now, were two grotesqueries of altered Morah, with tiny, spidery bodies and great, grinning heads. These scuttled and climbed on the heavy, thronelike chair in which the Jhan sat, grinning around it and their Emperor at the two humans.

''You're prompt,'' said the Jhan to Dormu. ''That's promising.''

''I believe you'll find it so,'' said Dormu. ''I've been authorized to agree completely to your conditions—with the minor exceptions of the matter of recognizing that the division of peoples is by territory and not by race, and the matter of spatial corridors for you through our territory. The first would require a referendum of the total voting population of our people, which would take several years;

and the second is beyond the present authority of my superiors to grant. But both matters will be studied.''

"This is not satisfactory.''

"I'm sorry," said Dormu. "Everything in your proposal that it's possible for us to agree to at this time has been agreed to. The Morah Jhan must give us credit for doing the best we can on short notice to accommodate him.''

"Give you credit?" The Jhan's voice thinned; and the two bigheaded monsters playing about his feet froze like startled animals, staring at him. "Where is my kidnapped Morah?"

"I'm sorry," said Dormu, carefully, "that matter has been investigated. As we suspected, the individual you mention turns out not to be a Morah, but a human. We've located his records. A Paul Edmonds.''

"What sort of lie is this?" said the Jhan. "He is a Morah. No human. You may let yourself be deluded by the fact he looks like yourselves, but don't try to think you can delude us with looks. As I told you, it's our privilege to play with the shapes of individuals, casting them into the mold we want, to amuse ourselves; and the mold we played with in this case was like your own. So be more careful in your answers. I would not want to decide you deliberately kidnapped this Morah, as an affront to provoke me.''

"The Morah Jhan," said Dormu, colorlessly, "must know how unlikely such an action on our part would be—as unlikely as the possibility that the Morah might have arranged to turn this individual loose in order to embarrass us in the midst of these talks.''

The Jhan's eyes slitted down until their openings showed hardly wider than two heavy pencil lines.

"*You* do not accuse *me*, human!" said the Jhan. "*I* accuse *you!* Affront my dignity; and less than an hour after I lift ship from this planetoid of yours, I can have a fleet here that will reduce it to one large cinder!''

He paused. Dormu said nothing. After a long moment, the slitted eyes relaxed, opening a little.

"But I will be kind," said the Jhan. "Perhaps there is some excuse for your behavior. You have been misled, perhaps—by this business of records, the testimony of those amateur butchers you humans call physicians and surgeons. Let me set your mind at rest. I, the Morah Jhan, assure you that this prisoner of yours is a Morah, one of my own Morah; and no human. Naturally, you will return him now, immediately, in as good shape as when he was taken from us.".

"That, in any case, is not possible," said Dormu.

"How?" said the Jhan.

"The man," said Dormu, "is dying."

The Jhan sat without motion or sound for as long as a man might comfortably hold his breath. Then, he spoke.

"The *Morah*," he said. "I will not warn you again."

"My apologies to the Morah Jhan," said Dormu, tonelessly. "I respect his assurances, but I am required to believe our own records and experienced men. The *man,* I say, is dying."

The Jhan rose suddenly to his feet. The two small Morah scuttled away behind him toward the door.

"I will go to the quarters you've provided me, now," said the Jhan, "and make my retinue ready to leave. In one of your hours, I will reboard my ship. You have until that moment to return my Morah to me."

He turned, went around his chair and out of the room. The door shut behind him.

Dormu turned and headed out the door at their side of the room. Whin followed him. As they opened the door, they saw Stigh waiting there. Whin opened his mouth to speak, but Dormu beat him to it.

"Dead?" Dormu asked.

"He died just a few minutes ago—almost as soon as you'd both gone in to talk to the Jhan," said Stigh.

Whin slowly closed his mouth. Stigh stood without saying anything further. They both waited, watching Dormu, who did not seem to be aware of their gaze. At Stigh's answer, his face had become tight, his eyes abstract.

"Well," said Whin, after a long moment and Dormu still stood abstracted, "it's a body now."

His eyes were sharp on Dormu. The little man jerked his head up suddenly and turned to face the marshal.

"Yes," said Dormu, a little strangely. "He'll have to be buried, won't he? You won't object to a burial with full military honors?"

"Hell, no!" said Whin. "He earned it. When?"

"Right away." Dormu puffed out a little sigh like a weary man whose long day is yet far from over. "Before the Jhan leaves. And not quietly. Broadcast it through the Outpost."

Whin swore gently under his breath, with a sort of grim happiness.

"See to it!" he said to Stigh. After Stigh had gone, he added softly to Dormu. "Forgive me. You're a good man once the chips are down, Mr. Ambassador."

"You think so?" said Dormu, wryly. He turned abruptly toward the lift tubes. "We'd better get down to the docking area. The Jhan said an hour—but he may not wait that long."

The Jhan did not wait. He cut his hour short, like someone eager to accomplish his leaving before events should dissuade him. He was at the docking area twenty minutes later; and only the fact that it was Morah protocol that his entourage must board before him caused him to be still on the dock when the first notes of the Attention Call sounded through the Outpost.

The Jhan stopped, with one foot on the gangway to his vessel. He turned about and saw the dockside Military Police all now at attention, facing the nearest command screen three meters wide by two high, which had just come to life on the side of the main docking warehouse.

The Jhan's own eyes went to the image on the screen—to the open grave, the armed soldiers, the chaplain and the bugler.

The chaplain was already reading the last paragraph of the burial service. The religious content of the human words could have no meaning to the Jhan; but his eyes went comprehendingly, directly to Dormu, standing with Whin on the other side of the gangway. The Jhan took a step that brought him within a couple of feet of the little man.

"I see," the Jhan said. "He is dead."

"He died while we were last speaking," answered Dormu, without inflection. "We are giving him an honorable funeral."

"I see—" began the Jhan, again. He was interrupted by the sound of fired volleys as the burial service ended and the blank-faced coffin began to be let down into the pulverized rock of the Outpost. A command sounded from the screen. The soldiers who had just fired went to present arms—along with every soldier in sight in the docking area—as the bugler raised his instrument and taps began to sound.

"Yes." The Jhan looked around at the saluting Military Police, then back at Dormu. "You are a fool," he said, softly. "I had no conception that a human like yourself could be so much a fool. You handled my demands well—but what value is a dead body, to anyone? If you had returned it, I would have taken no action—this time, at least, after your concessions on the settlements. But you not only threw away all you'd gained, you flaunted defiance in my face by burying the body before I could leave this Outpost. I've no choice now—after an affront like that. I must act."

"No," said Dormu.

"No?" The Jhan stared at him.

"You have no affront to react against," said Dormu. "You erred only through a misunderstanding."

"Misunderstanding?" said the Jhan. "*I* misunderstood? I not only did not misunderstand, I made the greatest effort to see that you did not misunderstand. I cannot let you take a Morah from me, just because he looks like a human. And he *was* a Morah. You did not need your records, or your physicians, to tell you that. My word was enough. But you let your emotions, the counsel of these lesser people, sway you—to your disaster, now. Do you think I didn't know how all these soldiers of yours were feeling? But *I* am the Morah Jhan. Did you think I would lie over anything so insignificant as one stray pet?"

"No," said Dormu.

"Now—" said the Jhan. "Now, you face the fact. But it is too late. You have affronted me. I told you it is our privilege and pleasure to play with the shapes of beings, making them into what we desire. I told you the shape did not mean he was human. I told you he was Morah. You kept him and buried him anyway, thinking he was human— thinking he was that lost spy of yours." He stared down at Dormu. "I told you he was a Morah."

"I believed you," said Dormu.

The Jhan's eyes stared. They widened, flickered, then narrowed down until they were nothing but slits once more.

"You believed me? You *knew* he was a Morah?"

"I knew," said Dormu. "I was Liaison Officer with the Intelligence Service at the time Edmonds was sent out— and later when his body was recovered. We have no missing agent here."

His voice did not change tone. His face did not change expression. He looked steadily up into the face of the Jhan.

"I explained to the Morah Jhan, just now," said Dormu, almost pedantically, "that through misapprehension, he had erred. We are a reasonable people who love peace. To soothe the feelings of the Morah Jhan we will abandon our settlements, and make as many other adjustments to his demands as are reasonably possible. But the Jhan must not confuse one thing with another.''

"What thing?" demanded the Jhan. "With what thing?"

"Some things we do not permit," said Dormu. Suddenly, astonishingly, to the watching Whin, the little man seemed to grow. His back straightened, his head lifted, his eyes looked almost on a level up into the slit-eyes of the Jhan. His voice sounded hard, suddenly, and loud. "The Morah belong to the Morah Jhan; and you told us it's your privilege to play with their shapes. Play with them then—in all but a single way. Use any shape but one. You played with that shape, and forfeited your right to what we just buried. Remember it, Morah Jhan! *The shape of Man belongs to Men, alone!*"

He stood, facing directly into the slitted gaze of Jhan, as the bugle sounded the last notes of taps and the screen went blank. About the docks, the Military Police lowered their weapons from the present-arms position.

For a long second, the Jhan stared back. Then he spoke.

"I'll be back!" he said; and, turning, the red kilt whipping about his legs, he strode up the gangplank into his ship.

"But he won't," muttered Dormu, with grim satisfaction, gazing at the gangplank, beginning to be sucked up into the ship now, preparatory to departure.

"Won't?" almost stammered Whin, beside him. "What do you mean . . . *won't?*"

Dormu turned to the marshal.

"If he were really coming back with all weapons hot, there was no need to tell me." Dormu smiled a little, but still grimly. "He left with a threat because it was the only way he could save face."

"But you . . ." Whin was close to stammering again; only this time with anger. "You knew that . . . that creation . . . wasn't Edmonds from the start! If the men on this Outpost had known it was a stinking Morah, they'd have been ready to hand him back in a minute. You let us all put our lives on the line here—for something that only *looked* like a man!"

Dormu looked at him.

"Marshal," he said. "I told you it was the confrontation with the Jhan that counted. We've got that. Two hours ago, the Jhan and all the other Morah leaders thought they knew us. Now they—a people who think shape isn't important—suddenly find themselves facing a race who consider their shape sacred. This is a concept they are inherently unable to understand. If that's true of us, what else may not be true? Suddenly, they don't understand us at all. The Morah aren't fools. They'll go back and rethink their plans, now—all their plans."

Whin blinked at him, opened his mouth angrily to speak—closed it again, then opened it once more.

"But you risked . . ." he ran out of words and ended shaking his head, in angry bewilderment. "And you let me bury it—with honors!"

"Marshal," said Dormu, suddenly weary, "it's your job to win wars, after they're started. It's my job to win them before they start. Like you, I do my job in any way I can."

Minotaur

When Jake Lundberg finally broke his way through the inner door of the airlock into the *Prosper Prince*, he found himself in pitch darkness.

"That's not going to work," he said, and went back along the line of the small magnetic grapple that held the two ships together and into his own *Molly B.*

The *Molly B.*, a range scout, while large enough and comfortable enough by the ordinary standards of a Government trouble-shooter, was at the moment looking rather minnowlike and feeling rather cramped, at the end of the fragile little line that was all that was required to keep the two vessels together in the absence of gravity. For the *Prosper Prince* had been a full-scale survey ship, with its own labs and shops and a crew of nine.

"What could happen to nine trained men twelve light-years from the nearest star?" said Jake, who was used to talking out loud for the benefit of the little throat microphone that connected him with the recorder on the *Molly B.*, no matter how far he might wander from her. "You tell me."

Molly B. made no effort to tell him. She was agreeable but dumb, in the literal sense of that word.

"Now I'm getting self-powered lights which I'll carry over and string out along the corridor to the control room there as I go," Jake added, for the recorder, as he dug into a supply locker. "Don't get lonely now, Molly."

He went back out and along the line into the *Prosper Prince* once more, moving a little awkwardly, for if the lights he was carrying weighed nothing, in the absence of gravity, they made a pretty full armload.

Through the airlock into the *Prosper Prince* proper, Jake encountered a small amount of weight. About one-half G. Which meant that although the lights were not functioning, the ship he was in was not completely dead. The air, however, though his helmet counter showed it as good, smelled musty when he flipped the helmet back. Whatever else was operating, the circulating fans were off.

Loaded, with his lights on, Jake headed down the main corridor in what he knew must be the route to the control area forward. Every forty feet or so, or at each bend in the corridor, he stopped to set one of the lights in place against the corridor wall. The magnetic base of each light stuck firmly, and its lens, with a theoretical thousand years of power self-contained behind it, began to flood the corridor with light as soon as it made contact with the wall. The main corridor, Jake noted as he went along, was comparable to the air in the ship. It looked all right, but it gave evidence of having been unused for some time.

A hundred yards down the corridor and up an emergency ladder (the lift tube was, of course, not working) and along the corridor above for another twenty yards brought Jake to the door of the main control center of the ship. He stepped inside, fixed one of his lights to a handy wall and put down the rest of his load while he looked the situation over.

The control center—except for the faintly musty odor of the air and the slight film of dust—might have been abandoned just a moment or so before. All the equipment was in workable-looking shape. The one exception was the coffee and water taps in a little alcove off the plotting board. These had been battered into the wall from which they protruded, as if by a sledge-hammer.

"Now what do you think of that?" said Jake, and proceeded to detail the situation for the benefit of the recorder back on the *Molly B*. He could imagine one of the think-boys back at Earth Headquarters, six months from now, pausing as this part of the tape was played back, and scratching his head.

"Don't let it get you down, Pete," he said. Jake called all the think-boys Pete. Headquarters had sent him several stiff memos about it. He paid no attention. He had to risk his neck as an occasional part of his job. They didn't. If they didn't like the way he made his reports, they knew exactly what they could do about it.

Jake moved over to the log desk, passing the main screen as he did so. The screen was dead, its silvery surface reflecting a picture of the control room and himself. He paused to inspect the two V-shaped inroads of scalp into his hairline. Yes, they were definitely going back. There was no use blinking the fact. And that was no good. All right, perhaps, for some skinny intellectual type to have a high forehead, but a broad, square-jawed character like himself—he just looked half-shorn. He'd probably better see about repilation, next trip home to Earth.

"—or else a good hair tonic," he said out loud. "Make a note of that, Pete."

The logbook was also turned off. But when he flipped the switch, it lit up in proper shape. He ran the tape back to the last entry.

June 34, 2462: Still on twelfth jump between Runyon's World and Ceta. Biochemist Walter Latham, slight case of hives. Taking infra-red treatments. Acid condition of soil in grass plantation tank of air-freshener room corrected. The coffee continues to have a burned taste. No evidence of spoilage, but suggest Quartermaster look into this on return to Earth. Today was the nineteenth anniversary of the launching of this ship, and the event was duly celebrated by the crew and staff at a dinner at which an original poem written in honor of the occasion by Engineer's Assistant Rory Katchuk was recited and, by unanimous vote of the whole crew, ordered to be written into the ship's log. It is as follows:

> *Oh, Prosper Prince*
> *You made me wince,*
> *Right from the start,*
> *And ever since.*

Some more of the corridor lights have been smashed about the ship. If this is one of the elaborate practical jokes that sometimes crops up on long voyages, it is in bad taste, and the man responsible, when found, will be severely dealt with. This applies also to whoever is responsible for the sobbing noise.

Jake raised bushy eyebrows upward into the growingly naked scalp he had just been examining. He read off the entry in the log for Pete's benefit.

"Sobbing noise?" he echoed. "Now, that's a new one. Let's look a little farther back."

He spun the tape back at random and stopped it. He read off the entry before him out loud.

"*April 29, 2462: Due to lift from Runyon's World tomorrow. All reports complete and planet looks good. The Prosper Prince may well congratulate herself on having discovered and tested a prime colonizable world. Breathable atmosphere, benign temperature range, flora and fauna. Largest native life-form encountered, the creatures we have named Goopers. These are very similar to the Earthly baboon in appearance, but have marked internal differences, and large, apparently atrophied glands for which no purpose can be discerned, on the underside of their forearms. It is difficult to figure why these creatures do not overrun the planet, since they are entirely herbivorous and seem to have no natural enemies. Perhaps their racial fear of entering the forests or any shadowy or enclosed place acts as a process of natural selection. (See Jeffers-Bradley report #297, log inclusion Jan. 3, 2462.)"*

Jake spun the log back to January the third of that year and discovered the report inclusion.

"We found the forest to consist of vegetation similar to our hardwood forests—oaklike trees with many small branches and twigs, but no leaves. The twigs, however, are so numerous and thick that sunlight is cut to a minimum; there is almost no ground-cover or small vegetation between the trees but a sort of moss, and no animal life to be seen, except an occasional firefly kind of insect. Phosphorescence noticeable in darker spots coating tree trunks and even the ground, due to a fungoid life-form which excretes a zinc-sulphate phosphor."

Jake spun the log ahead to April 29th and finished reading the entry there.

"A possible clue may lie in the fact that these creatures avoid the streaks of zinc-sulphate phosphors which make their appearance mysteriously at night even in the open meadows. At any rate, this is a puzzle for later investigation, if the planet is opened for colonization."

Jake shut off the log, thoughtfully.

"Well, Pete," he said, "what do you think of that? They lifted for home on April 30th. By July they were posted overdue. I was sent out to look for them July 10th and it's only taken me 40 days to find them. They're right where they should be if they'd just quit jumping on the 12th jump. No sign of trouble—except those coffee and water taps over there. But no sign of anybody aboard either. You don't suppose they just all decided to walk right out of the airlock?"

There was no answer to that question, of course, so Jake

shook his head, gathered up his armload of lights and went on exploring and distributing illumination about the *Prosper Prince*.

He found the ship in good shape, but empty. The control section was empty, the officer's quarters were empty, the recreation areas were empty, and the men's quarters were empty.

Going down one level, he found himself in the section reserved for the labs and shops—and it was here that he reached the end of his supply of lights. Taking the last one and hand-activating it, he proceeded, carrying it like a searchlamp before him, and began to work back aft toward the greenery, where the grass plantation tank that renewed the oxygen supply in the ship had its existence, with the water reservoir, and the drive units.

When he stepped through the door into the greenery, at first sight it looked as a greenery should. It was a large, almost empty-seeming room with the equivalent of two city lots planted in a very tall grass which looked totally undisturbed. But at one end, where the ventilating system was, the fan housing had been completely wrecked and the fan inside it smashed.

"Aha!" said Jake to his mike. "Somebody decided to dispose of the ventilating system, Pete. Suppose we just take a closer look at that." He moved forward toward the fan housing.

But before he could reach it, noise exploded upon his eardrums. It was distant but thunderous noise, coming from the front end of the ship, a racket like a gang of medieval smiths working on armor.

Jake spun about and burst out of the room. He ran back up the corridor. As he neared the noise, it echoed and reechoed through the metal walls about him.

He scrambled up the ladder to the mid-level of the ship and just as he reached the top, the noise stopped. He stopped, too. In the new and sudden silence, he could hear his own heart pounding.

He stood listening: then he went forward again. He moved down the mid-level corridor, the one he had first entered on coming into the ship. But he saw nothing amiss until he rounded the curve to the point where the airlock pierced the inner and outer skins of the vessel. The massive latch handle, which dogged shut the inner door to the lock, had been battered completely off.

For a long moment, Jake said nothing. Then he cleared his throat, but not noisily.

"Are you still there, Pete?" he half-whispered. There was no answer, of course, but the sound of his own voice shocked a little common sense back into him.

He looked up and down the corridor. The lights still burned, undisturbed.

"Pete," he said fervently, "there's something aboard here and it doesn't love me."

He looked again at the door. Damaged as it was, there was no hope of his opening it—not, at least, without tools. For a second he felt a completely irrational flash of rage. There was the *Molly B.* out there, a few feet from him, with the very tools he needed to break through to get to her. And for lack of the tools, he could not do so.

He suddenly reminded himself there should be tools aboard this ship as well. It was only a matter of finding them. He turned about and headed once more toward the control room. In there, there should be a master chart of the vessel and a list of the supplies and equipment she would have been carrying.

Back in the control room, Jake found his normal good spirits recovering. After all, he considered, it was only a matter of taking the time to locate tools on board this ship. Then he could break open the door and slap a tow-line from the *Molly B.* onto this ship and haul her to Earth, where whatever was aboard could be captured by properly armed and protected men. He even whistled a bit as he thought of it.

His whistling ended abruptly a few moments later. He had located the design chart, the equipment list and the arms locker. The arms locker, however, was locked. And Jake had discovered that the combination to it was missing from the papers in his hand.

"Oh-oh," said Jake. "I don't like this, Pete. I don't like it at all."

He reached for the locker door nonetheless—and abruptly he felt a crawling sensation on the back of his neck. He whirled about. But the control room was empty. The entrance to it was empty. And as far as he could see, down the corridor beyond it, that too was empty.

"Nerves," he told himself and Pete, out loud. "Nerves."

Suddenly, the light halfway down the corridor and out of sight of the doorway, from where Jake was then standing, went out. And there was a tinkling smash in the darkness.

Jake froze. And then the hair on the back of his neck began to rise. For, eerily, from the darkened corridor, there came to his ears the sound of a sobbing. A sobbing like that of a soul whose last hope had been stolen and lost forever.

Jake backed up against the drive control. His hand, groping instinctively behind him for some sort of weapon, closed about the short metal length of the captain's wireless microphone. He grabbed it up in one hand, an eight-inch club weighing maybe four pounds.

And the sobbing stopped. It stopped as short as if the sobber had had his breath choked off. Still bristling, Jake circled quietly about the room and approached the door, sidling along the wall. As he passed the wall of the control room he detached the lamp he had put against the wall there; and, hand-activating it to keep on burning, he carried it with him. When he reached the doorway, he swung suddenly into it and flashed its beam down the full long corridor.

The corridor was absolutely empty.

Jake stood there in baffled frustration. Then he turned and went back to the arms locker. He tried to batter it open, using the captain's microphone. He managed to bend the microphone, but he did not manage to open the door.

"Pete," he said softly putting the bent microphone down, "this is a heck of a situation. You heard that banging before, and you heard the sobbing this time. Tell me, Pete, what sort of something would want to make noises like that?"

He shook his head tensely and went back to the list. On it, he located the section that dealt with tools. The tools he would want, he discovered, were down in the tool shop on the lower level again, back by the greenery. Jake whistled tunelessly through his teeth as he read this little item of information.

"It *would* be out there!" he said. "Well, Pete, here we go down to the bottom level of the ship again. Down to the tool room to get ourselves a cutter torch and pry bar."

He took the lamp from the control room wall and placed it so it would catch part of the corridor as well as the control room. Then, picking up the light he had been carrying as a hand lamp, he headed back for the bottom level. He went off down the corridor, and when he reached the point where the other light had been, he stopped.

The light that had been there was lying on the floor of the corridor. It had been thoroughly smashed.

Jake puzzled over the remains, found no answer, and continued on to the ladder, careful to keep the light ahead of him. A little farther on, however, he moved into the area of another light, which was shining brightly, intact. He hooked his own light onto his belt. Then he went on until he came to the ladder leading both up and down, and climbed down it to the lower level once more.

He went along the lower level corridor to the greenery. He paused warily to glance in, but the room was empty. He continued on to where the corridor ended in a door. Opening this door, he stepped through into the tool shop of the ship. He was in a moderately sized square room, about twice the size of an ordinary earthside kitchen. A number of power tools stood around the wall and magnetic racks were fitted with hand tools.

He selected a portable torch flame cutter and a spring-operated pry bar. Then he came back out of the tool room into the lower level corridor. He started his walk back up the corridor toward the ladder. As he went he found himself wishing that he had been able to bring a second load of lights before he had been made a prisoner aboard this vessel. The lamp at his belt flung a brilliant glare before him. It was more than adequate to the subjects it illuminated. Nevertheless, darkness followed; and shadows jumped and slid along the walls as he walked. He had just reached the foot of the ladder when a sound reached his ears.

It was the sound of a light somewhere distant in the ship, smashing.

He stopped with his hands on the ladder. He found himself straining his ears to listen. But there was no other sound. He climbed up the ladder, went down the corridor a little way and came to the inner airlock door. He chose a spot along the corridor wall where the light would illuminate the door well, without shadows; and at this spot, some ten feet from him, he clamped the light to the wall and raised the torch to go to work on the door.

Once more, somewhere distant in the ship, a light smashed and tinkled.

Jake shut his jaw a little grimly and turned to the inner door of the airlock. The flame from the cutting torch in his hand splattered against the metal.

It was some moments before Jake realized that it was having little or no effect.

He stopped and checked, first the torch, then the door. The torch was in perfectly good shape. The door, however, carried in its lower right corner a little legend stamped into the metal. The legend consisted of a small "c" with a circle around it.

Jake straightened up, breathed deeply, and ran his thick fingers slowly through his close-cropped hair.

"Well, Pete," he said, his voice sounding odd in his own ears, "how do you like that? They *would* decide to make their airlock out of collapsed steel instead of something cuttable."

He glanced once more at the torch, hanging useless in his hand, and stuck the tool back into his belt. There was nothing that would get him through the collapsed steel of the airlock he faced now, he knew, but some of the special equipment he had on board the *Molly B*.

"O.K., Pete," he said softly. "Mohammed and the mountain, all over again. If I can't tow this ship home with the *Molly B*., maybe I can tow the *Molly B*. home with this ship."

He turned away and headed up the corridor toward the control room.

Some time later, with the door to the control room closed and welded shut with the torch at his belt against interruption, Jake was busy overhauling the controls. As far as he could see, they were in excellent shape. He had nothing to do now but simply start the vessel moving and keep it at it.

However, handling a ship this size was not simple at all. It was not so much the question of driving as it was of figuring where to. The process by which an interstellar ship moved in space was by making large "shifts." These shifts instantly caused the vessel to cease to be at one particular point in time and space and caused it to be at another point in space. There was literally no effort to it.

The calculations required to tell the person running the ship where he was and where he would be once he shifted, though, were very complicated indeed. In this instance, it was further complicated by the fact that Jake had to stop and figure out all over again where he was. That information was on board the *Molly B*. But, since the *Molly B*. was out of reach, Jake theoretically had to go back to Earth and retrace his steps all the way out to this point. Of course he had the great calculators of the ship here to do it with. But still, it was a time-consuming job.

It took two hours to get the ship in working condition. It took three more hours to find out where he was. Nearly six hours had gone by since Jake had entered the ship; and when he was finally done, he found himself tired, hungry and thirsty. But the shifts were programmed that would take the ship to Earth.

He started the *Prosper Prince* toward its first shift point, and then cautiously he cut open the door to the control room and looked out down the corridor. He saw utter darkness. No lamp, no light was showing anywhere. Through his teeth he whistled two short bars of a tune. Then he took down one of the two lamps that yet remained in the control room, the one he had carried in his belt; and taking this with him, holding it before him, he lit it and walked down the corridor.

He saw nothing as he went, although the sounds of his own footfalls were loud in his ear. Halfway down the length of the ship, past the officers quarters, he came to the ship's galley. Closing this door, he made welds at its four corners and set about preparing himself something to eat and drink.

It was not that he expected his welds would secure the door against whatever had had strength enough to smash the water and coffee taps in the control room, or dismember the blower equipment in the greenery; but he hoped its having to break through the door would give him time to adopt a posture of defense. And the cutting torch in his hand would be a weapon of sorts.

He made himself a pretty fair meal out of dehydrated stores, and a pot of coffee. After he had eaten, he sat at the galley table, with one eye on the welded-shut door, drinking the coffee. The ship's logbook hadn't lied; the coffee did have a burned taste. He mentioned this to Pete in passing.

Then his mind switched off onto speculation as to what it might be that roamed the ship and had evidently disposed of its original crew. He had a long talk with Pete about the matter, exploring several likely possibilities, but coming back to the pretty obvious conclusion that it must have been a life-form common to the Runyon's World that had somehow got on board.

"But how," Jake said, "something that large and dangerous could get on a ship like this without being seen or known about, I can't understand."

A sudden thought hit him. He cleaned up the remains of his meal, cut open the door and went back up to the control room. Sealing himself in there, he went to check the ship's records once more.

This time, in a different record section, he found a small list of livestock taken from the planet. This ranged from sub-microscopic life-forms, strain of the phosphorescent bacteria, and on up to one of the Goopers mentioned in the log and in the report he had read earlier. The record also told him where these were to be found—in the ship's organic laboratory on the top level. Jake put the record away thoughtfully.

He checked to see that the ship was properly approaching the point for its first shift through no-space, then took his torch and lamp, and unsealed the control room. He went down the corridor and up to the top level of the ship. A few doorways down the corridor of the top level, he discovered the entrance to the ship's organic laboratory.

The door was ajar. He stepped inside without touching it. The laboratory was a pretty large room, three-quarters of which were given over to chemical equipment and supplies, and one-quarter of which was equipped with cages and containers. Jake saw at a glance that all the cages and containers had been broken open, except the largest of them—a cage which might possibly have contained something the size of an adult chimpanzee.

Almost against his will, Jake felt a slightly sickening shiver run down his spine. It occurred to him that something had been in here with an appetite, and for the first time, he had a mental image of what might have happened to the original crew of the vessel.

He leaned over to examine the cage from which two bars had been wrenched out, in the light of his lamp which he had set against the wall just inside the door. He put his hands on two of the bars and felt them turn in his grasp. He took his hands away and stared. The bars appeared solid, but they had been twisted loose in their sockets. He twisted one again and it came neatly out in his hand, being loose at the top and broken off at the bottom. He put it back—and suddenly, without warning, there was a smashing sound; and he was plunged into total darkness.

Jake whirled, the torch which was in his hand coming up automatically. There was a sound of movement in the direction of the doorway. A strange and undefinable odor smote his nostrils. He sensed rather than saw a large body leaping at him and triggered the torch.

Its flame lashed out for a fractionary moment; then the torch was knocked from his hand. In that split second of light, he saw something hulking and vaguely manlike, but larger than any man had a right to be. Then he saw no more, because the torch was gone from his hand and automatically shut off. But a hideous howl rang through the room. There was a smashing noise from the direction of the doorway. Then the howl rose again, out in the corridor, and there was a sound of running. For a third time he heard the howl, distant half the ship's length from him, but hideous as ever. Then there was silence.

Down on hands and knees, with frantically searching fingers, Jake pawed about for the torch. He found it and pressed its trigger. By the lurid gleam of its flame he saw the light he had put against the wall lying smashed on the floor.

Jake drew in a shaky breath.

"Well, Pete," he whispered with a dry throat. "Here we are in the dark with just a cutting torch. And whatever it is isn't feeling too happy right about this moment." He got to his feet in the darkness. "I'll try to make it back to the control room," he said, "using the torch here to light me."

Cautiously, keeping the torch triggered, Jake moved out into the corridor. The flame it threw was not an effective light. It illuminated poorly and glared in his eyes at the same time. Half-blinded, and half-smothered in darkness, Jake found the ladder and fumbled his way down it to the main level. Still holding the torch, he headed back to the control room.

At that moment the first of the shifts hit him. He was conscious of the peculiar fleeting moment of nausea that marked one of the great jumps in space. It was disturbing, coming when his nerves were wire-tense, but it was also reassuring. The ship, he knew, was headed home.

He had paused when the shift hit him. Now, as he started forward again, the torch in his hand sputtered and went out. For a second, he stood paralyzed in the dark. Then the torch flamed on once more.

Instantly, he realized what was happening. The torch was nearing the end of its charge and it was the only weapon he had—and the tool room from which it had come was clear across the ship away from him.

Hastily, he shut it off. Blackness rushed in around him. Utter blackness. He strained his eyes in both directions up

and down the main level corridor, but there was not the
faintest glimmer of light. It came to him then that all the
lights he had set up must have been found and smashed.
He was alone, in the dark, with whatever was prowling the
ship.

He reached out to touch the wall with his fingertips for
guidance. And as he did so, he became aware for the first
time of a faint glow. His eyes were adjusting to a level of
illumination just barely above the level of darkness. He
stood still, letting his vision continue to adjust.

Gradually there emerged the eeriness of long streaks of
phosphorescence glowing on the walls of the ship. By
their total shape, he was able to make out the directions
and the dimensions of the corridor in both directions. His
breath caught in his throat in relief.

"How do you like that?" he whispered. "Looks like
Runyon's World can be useful, too."

He began to feel his way down the corridor toward the
control room. He was, he estimated, about halfway there
when an indescribable uneasiness caused him to hesitate.
He halted. He stood stone still in the darkness, his eyes
staring ahead.

Then he saw what instinct had warned him of—one of
the streaks of phosphorescence down by the entrance to the
control room was slowly being occluded by something
large and black, thirty feet or so from him.

In sheer reflex his finger tightened on the trigger of the
torch. Blue flame spurted blindingly from the torch's muzzle. And although the distance was far too great for the
flame to have done any damage, the animal howl of hate
and terror and pain he had heard before rang out.

Jake whirled about and ran stumblingly back the way he
had come.

He paused, finally, and leaned against the wall to catch
his breath. Looking back along the corridor he saw the
streaks of phosphorescence clear and uneclipsed. The crea-

ture, whatever it was, must have fled in the opposite direction.

His mind racing, Jake reached out one finger and touched the streak of phosphorescence close behind him, realizing suddenly that as he had seen the monster obscuring the phosphorescence, so the monster had also seen him. A little of the shining stuff came away on his finger, which glowed ghostlike before him. A wild thought leaped and hammered in his brain.

He turned about once again with his back to the control room and began to work his way toward the clinic. He found the entrance to it and slipped inside. Easing the door closed behind him, he risked the fading power of the torch in one brief sputter of light. Immediately it was dark again, but as blackness washed in, his hand closed around the stem of the infrared lamp that had been used in treating the crewman with hives he had read about in the log. Lamp and torch in hand, he stepped back out into the corridor.

"The phosphorescence is something that works for *it*, Pete," he whispered. "Let's see how it likes this!"

He switched on the lamp and began moving down the corridor. At one spot along its length he shut it off and paused to look back. What he saw then made him smile in the darkness with satisfaction.

Ten days later, a survey ship and the *Molly B.* were taken in tow just outside Earth's orbit. Aboard was found a very large baboonlike creature, somewhat burned about the upper arms or forelimbs but quite alive, although huddled in the welded-shut greenery, from which the creature had to be drugged before it could be removed. And a very much alive and self-possessed Jake.

"The thing is, Pete," explained Jake cheerfully later to Albin Rhinehart, a fat, hard-faced man who was Director of the Investigatory Bureau, "the vegetarian Goopers the crew got acquainted with on the planet were simply a pre-form, from which emerged an occasional black sheep, possibly mutant variety, which took to carnivorous ways and acted as a natural control by preying on its own species. The mutants grew much larger and normally hid out in the forest areas. The forest areas that were lighted at night by this fungoid which produced a marked zinc-sulphate phosphorescence.''

"But—" began Albin.

"Let me tell it my way, Pete," went on Jake, perching on the corner of the desk and wiping his forehead. His fingers explored his hairline for an absent-minded second. "You don't happen to know any good repilators, do you? . . . No, I didn't think so. Well, to get on with it, these large, carnivorous, mutant Goopers preyed on the vegetarians. Evidently the crew of the ship took aboard one of the vegetarian variety, not knowing he was also a mutant preform. The change came about, or perhaps something during the trip triggered it, and the Gooper grew large and escaped. One night it started preying on the crew in the darkness." Pete's face became grim. "I found some of their bones, as well as some of the bones of the lesser laboratory animals. These mutant forms are evidently pretty intelligent."

"What makes you think that?" said Albin.

"Well," answered Jake, "judging from the reports of smashed lights and sobbing noises, this one had been out of his cage and back in again several times before he ran wild. Otherwise there would have been a report in the log to the effect that he had broken out. Remember those two bars that looked all right but were actually broken loose?"

"Then what did happen, do you think?" Albin asked.

"I think," said Jake, "that the Gooper, following his instincts as well as his intelligence, went out first to spread phosphorescent fungus around the ship, then returned to his cage. Or he may have done it in several trips. Then one night, or at some particular time when most of the men were separated or asleep, it smashed all the lights, then hunted them down and killed them one by one. I found where one man had tried to hide in the ventilating blower, down in the greenery, and I suspect another must have been getting himself a cup of coffee when he was attacked.''

"Biology reports the creature's eyes are particularly adapted to seeing under the conditions of this phosphorescence," commented Albin.

"It figures," said Jake. "It probably lived off the men it killed for a couple of weeks at least, and after that polished off the laboratory animals. But it was evidently pretty well starving by the time I came aboard, judging by all the loose skin about it."

"That fungoid phosphorescence is interesting," said Albin. "Evidently it fostered cultures in the forearm glands, which were active in the carnivorous beast, and which it distributed by rubbing the glands over surfaces it passed."

"A form of symbiosis, maybe," suggested Jake. He yawned and stretched.

"Well," said Albin, staring at him, "you seemed to have come out all right. How come the phosphorescence didn't help it get you?"

"That infra-red lamp I told you about, remember?" replied Jake, grinning.

Albin did not grin back. "I don't get it."

"Red light quenches phosphorescence. In the dark, the beast, for all its size, was more afraid of me than I was of it. It'd already had a taste of the cutting torch and it couldn't know I was about out of fuel. I herded it into the greenery and sealed it there." Jake cocked an eye at Albin. "But I'm surprised at you, not knowing that little fact about phosphorescence and red light, a man in your position. Maybe you ought to take a few night study courses, Pete."

"The name's not Pete," said Albin stiffly.

Turnabout

Paul Barstow was saying,

"And this is the gadget . . ."

His square bright face under its close-cropped blond hair was animated. He seemed on the verge of reaching up to hook a finger in the lapel buttonhole of Jack Hendrix's sportcoat to pull the taller man down into a position where he could shout into his ear.

"You aren't listening!" he protested now. "Buddy! Jack! Pay some attention. Or has that crumb teaching job got you to the point where money doesn't mean anything to you any more?"

Jack Hendrix's long, heavy-boned face almost blushed.

"I'm listening," he said.

He hadn't been, of course. This was merely one more piece of evidence to add to the mounting pile of proof that he was totally incapable of doing anything right. He had been mooning instead over Eva Guen, whom he had lost some months back. But they had passed her in the corridor on their way to this small, hidden workroom, and something in the way she had looked at him had set him spinning again. Peculiarly, there had been what Jack could have sworn was a hurt look in her eyes, in that brief moment that they looked at each other in passing. Why there should be a hurt look in *her* eyes, Jack could not understand. She was the one who had left him to come to work for Paul—and very sensibly, too, he told himself, self-righteously, but with the same old twinge of unhappiness.

Eva had been his graduate teaching assistant at the University where he taught physics. She was tall and quiet-faced, with startling wide blue eyes under soft blonde hair. Quite naturally, he had fallen in love with her. And it was then the trouble started.

For from the moment Jack was forced to admit to himself that he was in love, he had to take an unbiased look at his chances of doing something about it. And that look was crushing in its effect. For in the process of assembling Jack Hendrix, a somewhat devastating oversight had occurred. Whatever minor god had been in the supervisory position that day had carefully mixed strength with intelligence, added just a pinch of genius and a sort of ugly-handsome good looks, but had totally forgotten at the last moment to install a governor on Jack's imagination. The result was that Jack was a dreamer.

And the result of that was that he, with three degrees to his name, and a couple of honoraries of various sorts lying around, continued to vegetate in his teaching job, while Paul, in his typical hyper-thyroid fashion, was already managing his own commercial research labs. Not that the comparison was strictly fair. Paul had always been more promoter than physicist. And Eva had gone out of Jack's life to a better job with Paul's outfit.

Not that that had anything to do with his accepting Paul's offer of a job as consultant on a little problem he claimed to have on hand at the moment.

"I'm listening," said Jack.

"Praise Allah," said Paul. "No one knows about this but you and me. It's top secret. *My* top secret."

Women, of course, thought Jack, were naturally secretive. They looked at you with unfathomable blue eyes and waited for you to make the proper move. But how could you make the proper move if you didn't know what they were thinking? That was why he had never gotten around to telling Eva how he felt about her. And then one day she was gone. He didn't blame her, even if without warning it had exploded—

"—Exploded?" stammered Jack, guiltily. "Well, er—when did that happen?"

"Are you sure you've been listening?" said Paul, suspiciously. "I just told you. A couple of weeks back." He went on to explain the circumstances while Jack listened with one ear, the image of Eva flickering like a candle luring his moth-like powers of attention in the back of his mind.

He forced himself to concentrate.

"But what happened to the man you had working on it?" he asked. "And what is it, anyway? You still haven't told me that."

"You mean Reppleman?" said Paul, quickly. "He had a nervous breakdown at the time of the explosion. Got a complete block on the whole thing, and now, they've got him in a nursing home."

A flicker of genuine interest stirred for the first time in Jack.

"Oh?" he said. "how come?"

"Well, that's the thing," said Paul. "I'm going to trust you, Jack. I've got something here that's worth more money than there is in the world today; and I'm willing to give you a slice of it if you can work this thing out for me. But we've got to have secrecy.

"Right at this moment, you and I are the only ones who even know this room has been entered since the explosion. I rebuilt the generator myself from Reppleman's records. And nobody, but you and I, knows we're back here today. The rooms at the back of the building here are all storerooms except this one."

"Generator?" said Jack, for a second momentary instant distracted from the lorelei mental image of Eva.

"A generator," said Paul, slowly and impressively, "of an impenetrable, planar field of force. Come over here."

The image of Eva went out as abruptly as if someone had dropped a candle-snuffer over it. Jack blinked and followed Paul, as he led him up to the equipment in question.

The small room which housed it was right at the bleak northern end of the labs and terminated one narrow wing of the building. It was L-shaped, with the generator in question tucked away in the narrow recess of the foot of the L. The length of the long part of the L, at right angles to this, was strewn with odds and ends of tools and equipment piled on two long benches fastened to the wall. Along the end away from the recess was the door that gave entrance to the room; and just to the left of this as you entered, at the end of the long part of the L, was the room's only window, open at the moment to the summer breeze and the gravel expanse of the parking lot behind the labs.

His mind for once wholly concentrating on the subject at hand, Jack followed Paul into the narrow cubbyhole that was the recess and listened to the other man's explanation of what was before him. It was not true that Jack could not focus on a problem. It was merely that a thing to hold his attention must first arouse his interest. Once it had, he dealt with it with almost fantastic effectiveness.

"You see," Paul was explaining, "it's a very simple sort of circuit. It's easy enough to produce it. The question is to handle it, after you've produced it. The initial power to run it comes from this storage battery hookup. That's all we need."

"Then what's the catch?" asked Jack, his nose half-buried in the creation's innards.

"The trouble is that once it's turned on, there seems to be a sort of feedback effect. Well, no, that isn't quite right. What it seems to do once it's turned on is tap some other source of power that's too much for it. It overloads and you get the explosion.''

"But while it's on you have a plane of force?"

"That's right."

"How long?" demanded Jack, his long fingers poking in the wiring.

"You mean from establishment of the field to explosion?" replied Paul. "About half a minute, as far as I can figure from Reppleman's notes and what I could reconstruct about what happened the day it blew up on him."

"You haven't tried it since you rebuilt it?" asked Jack.

"Do I look crazy?" demanded Paul. He put his hand on Jack's arm. "Listen buddy, remember me? The boy with the crib notes up his sleeve at exams?"

Half-lost in the machine before him as he was, Jack felt a sudden little stir of warning. Paul was anything but stupid; and when he went into his dumb-bunny act, there was usually a joker somewhere in the deck. But before he could concentrate on the sudden small danger signal he ran across something that drove it out of his mind.

"What's this?" he demanded, pouncing on a part of the apparatus.

"Oh, that," said Paul. "Just a notion of my own. Obvious answer. A timer setup. You set it, say, to turn the field on for perhaps a ten-thousandth of a second, then turn it off again. I'll let you play with it."

Jack frowned.

"Where are the notes?" he asked. "I'd like to see just what—Reppleman, you said his name was?—had written down."

Paul grinned and shook his head.

"Not so fast. First I want an answer from you on whether you think you can tame this baby for me or not."

"But how can I tell without the background?" protested Jack.

"Won't cost you a cent to say no," replied Paul. "Don't

look at me like that, Jack. Sure, I know I'm handing you a pig in a poke. But this thing is too big to take chances with. Do you want it or don't you?''

Jack hesitated. He was strongly tempted to tell Paul to take a running nosedive into the nearest lake, and walk out. Then he remembered the long life of financial ineptitude that had climaxed itself with losing Eva; and his good resolutions to mend his scatterbrained ways.

''All right,'' he said. ''I'll have a shot at it, anyhow.''

''Good boy,'' said Paul. He patted Jack's arm, in a way which was somehow reminiscent of approving a large, shaggy dog. ''I'll be in my office. You know where that is. If you want anything, just hustle me up.''

He gave Jack's shoulder a final slap and strode out.

Left alone, Jack sat down on one of the long workbenches, filled his pipe and considered the problem. The situation was peculiar to say the least. Paul's odd insistence on secrecy; and Eva's strange look when she had passed him in the corridor. And this story about the man who had developed the generator. Typically, it did not occur to him to doubt the generator. Jack was one of those men who have entertained the impossible in their minds so often that there is little reality can do to surprise them.

So it blew up did it? Jack puffed on his pipe and stared at the generator. But—hold on a minute—if it blew up and when it blew up it sent a man named Reppleman to a rest home, could it have blown up more than once? And if it had blown up only once it must have been turned on only once, and if that was the case, how did Paul know that it had produced a plane of force? Of course he had probably known the theory Reppleman was working on. And what was his purpose in keeping that theory a secret from Jack?

In fact, if the dingus worked, how did it work? Jack returned to the mass of equipment and wiring and began to prowl through it. After a while he stopped and scowled. Nine-tenths of the junk in the setup was mere window-dressing. The only thing about it that could possibly have any effect or function was an oddly wound coil of ordinary silver wire upon a core of some strange-looking silvery metal. Jack tapped this latter with a fingernail and it rang with a faint, light-sounding chime.

By the time this point was reached his interest had been captured. On a hunch he disconnected everything but the coil on its peculiar core. He disconnected the timer Paul had attached to the apparatus, hesitated a second, then made contact by crossing the two lead-in wires.

Nothing happened.

He disconnected the wires and sat back to think.

After a moment, he reached out and felt the winding on the coil. It was metal-cool—air temperature. On second thought, he connected the timer and set it to allow a warm-up period of fifteen seconds. At the end of that time the timer should activate the coil for the period of a ten-thousandth of a second.

Nothing happened.

Jack chewed the stem of his pipe. Once more he disconnected and felt the winding. It was faintly warm—but barely so.

Now let me see, said Jack to himself. We run two sorts of power through this thing. One, low power and steady. To warm it up? That's what I assumed, but there's no indication of it. On the other hand this timer is definitely set to give a sudden short pulse of relatively high current. I tried the high current direct. No result. I tried a short period of low current. What's next?

After he had smoked another pipeful of tobacco, all that occurred to him was to lengthen the warmup period. Let's do it right, he said to himself. Let's give it a good five minutes.

He turned it on once more and set the timer for another ten-thousandths of a second jolt at the end of five minutes of low power. It occurred to him that the two upright metal poles, about two feet in length, between which the field was supposed to be generated, might be too close to the coil, and he moved them out to the full length of their wiring, so that they were now actually in the long part of the room. He glanced at the timer. Almost four minutes yet to go.

He wandered down the long part of the room and stood gazing out the window. There was his car, sitting beside the row of others on the gravel of the parking lot. And there, farther down the row was Eva's. They were the two oldest cars on the lot. You'd almost think we had the same taste in automobiles, thought Jack, a trifle wistfully. Neither of them is worth much—

Abruptly, without warning, his traitorous imagination slipped its restraints and began to build a picture of Eva coming out on to the lot, seeing his old car not very distant from hers, and being overwhelmed by a flood of memories. He pictured her coming out the back entrance of the building as he stood here watching. She would walk across the lot with her smooth, lithe stride, toward her own old grey, four-door sedan. But partway there, her steps would falter as she caught sight of his equally ancient blue business coupe. She would not, of course, say anything, but she would stand there; and he, seizing the moment, would step from this window down onto the gravel only a few feet below and approach her.

The sound of his footsteps crunching the loose rock would warn her of his coming; and she would turn to look at him. She would neither move nor speak, but stand waiting as he came up to her and then—

He was just opening his mouth to speak to her in imagination, when unexpectedly from behind Jack there came the sound of a soft, insidious click . . .

For a moment he thought nothing had happened. The parking lot lay unchanged before him in the sunlight with its row of cars and the sky blue above them dotted with distant clouds. And then he tried to turn around and found he could not, with the slight movement of his effort the scene before him dissolved into a grey field streaked here and there by lines of various colors.

He froze, suddenly, and the scene came back to normal. He reached out to grab hold of the edge of the window to steady himself; but with the first movement he was plunged into greyness and his hands caught nothing. Once more he steeled himself into immobility, and for a moment he hung on the edge of panic. What had happened?

Slowly, he forced his mind back into control of his body and its emotions. Steady, he told himself, steady. Think it through.

As calmness returned he became suddenly and icily aware of two things. The first was that everything within his field of vision appeared somehow artificially frozen into immobility. Just what gave him this impression he was not able to understand. Part of it was the air. A small breeze had been bathing him as he stood in front of the open window. Now, there was nothing. The atmosphere around him was like intangible glass.

The second thing was the discovery that he was no longer standing with his feet on the floor, but lying crosswise athwart the window, in mid-air, at about the former level of his waist.

For a moment he was astounded that he had not realized this immediately. And then reasons began to appear to him. The first of these was the sudden realization that gravity appeared to have altered respective to his position. He felt not at all as if he were lying on his side, but as if he had remained quite normally upright. And another discovery following immediately on the heels of this was the sudden perception that while his body seemed to have moved, his point of view had not. He still looked out at the parking lot from the angle of vision of a man with both feet normally planted on the floor.

All of these, of course, were things that held true only as long as he remained perfectly still. The moment he attempted to move all his senses failed him and he seemed to swim in a grey mist. The conclusion was a very obvious one. Somehow, the generator had worked to produce its plane of force. And somehow he was caught in it.

The explosion should come at any moment now.

For one hideous moment he suffered death in imagination. Then reason returned to point out that the half minute Paul had mentioned as the time limit had undoubtedly been passed already. Still, it was a little while before he could completely fight off the tension of his body, bracing itself in expectation of the rending force that could strike at him from behind.

In the end it was his imagination that saved him. For long habit had made it independent of the rest of him; and its first move, once the facts of the matter had been grasped and the immediate danger of explosion discounted, was to draw him a very clear and somewhat ridiculous mental picture of himself as he must appear to anyone who might enter the room, floating broadside as he was, in thin air. It reminded him suddenly that positions were no respecters of persons; and he remembered almost in the same instant of what the White Knight had had to say to Alice on the subject after resting head-downward in a ditch. And so, by way of the ludicrous, he scrambled back onto the firm ground of his everyday sanity.

He was caught in a force field. Very well. And what could he do about it? The obvious answer was to turn around, go back to the generator and turn it off. And the one flaw in this plan was that he couldn't apparently, for some reason, make the turn.

On the other hand, he was able to make some movements. He experimented, waving first an arm and then a leg, cautiously. Barring the fact that the slightest motion caused the room to appear a nightmare of streaks and lines in a grey field, there was nothing unusual about the effects of these motions. The room? He became suddenly aware

that he seemed to have rotated around a center-point somewhere in the region of his belt buckle. He was now no
longer looking out the window, but turned at a slight angle
toward the bench on what had been the wall at his right
hand. Filled with sudden hope, he closed his eyes firmly
and took what should have been a long stride forward and
up. When he opened them again he was staring back into
the room, down the long length of the L.

For a long moment he hung, carefully motionless, con-
sidering the implications of what he had just done. It
seemed apparent, he thought, that what he had actually
accomplished was to turn himself about the way a paper
figure would be turned on a turntable—the difference between this and ordinary methods being that as he was now
facing in the opposite direction, his head was now where
his feet had been and vice versa. Or, to orient more
exactly by existing landmarks, where the force field had
flipped him into position with his head toward the right
wall, his rotation had changed him so that now his head
was toward the opposite wall, the one originally on his
left.

Conclusion?

Jack winced. The field itself appeared to be a two-
dimensional phenomenon; and he, himself, caught up in it,
to be restricted to two-dimensional movement. For a second the thrill of panic came back, and he was forced to
fight for a moment before he could go back to looking at
the situation sensibly and calmly.

The field appeared to be on a level with his waist as it
had been when he had been standing normally upright.
That was, in effect, level with the tops of the upright rods
that had been supposed to generate the field between them.
Hah!—*between* them, thought Jack, bitterly—and a few
inches above the level of the benches. As he looked down
the length of the room he noticed that whatever had touched
the plane of the field at any point seemed to have been,
like himself, caught up in it. He noticed a hammer and a

soldering iron, both of which had been hanging from
hooks on the left wall, now floating stiffly at right angles
to it. Furthermore, there seemed to have been some sort of
polarity involved. In both cases the end which had been
upright was at the left and the down end out at the right—
that was, of course, from his present point of view—and
corresponded exactly with the fact that his own head had
gone to the right, and his feet to the left.

But that was enough observing. The thing to do now
was to get to the generator and turn it off before something
else happened. Jack closed his eyes and made three quick
steps, right foot first left foot following, toe to heel. When
he opened them again he was mildly surprised to discover
that he was still a little short of the end of the room, but a
couple more steps solved that problem. He rotated himself
through a ninety degree arc and stepped *up* into the narrow
alcove that housed the generator and the timer on a bench
at its far end.

He banged his head on the wall and blinked with the
shock of it. He opened his eyes and looked down at the
generator.

With a sudden, sickening sense of shock, he realized
that it was below him, and therefore outside of the plane of
the field. His desperation was strong enough to make him
reach for it, anyway, and to his surprise it seemed almost
to flow upward to reach his fingers and his fingertips
pushed against a short length of wire, which bent before
them.

As they did so, there was a sudden flare of red light
from the coil and he snatched his fingers away as he
noticed that that part of the generator was apparently red
hot, glowing into incandescence. The whole apparatus, in
fact, seemed to quiver on the point of exploding into
flame. Curiously, however, there was no sensation of heat
emanating from the coil; and what was apparently a wisp
of smoke, rising above the generator and out of the field,
seemed frozen in midair.

Cautiously Jack retreated slightly from the generator. Two things were immediately apparent. One, that the generator was evidently a part of the field, and reachable, even though it had not been in the original plane as he had. Two, that he had better be careful how he went about shutting it off. It struck him somewhat belatedly that Reppleman's explosion had probably occurred through mishandling the generator when it was in its present state.

No, the way to turn the generator off was the way it had been turned on—through the timer. He looked at the portion of the generator and bench that lay below him but did not see the timer. Then he remembered that this was the left side of the bench at the alcove's extremity and that the timer was at the right. Carefully he rotated to the right as far as the narrow width of the alcove would allow him and out of the corner of his eye, caught a glimpse of the timer on the bench far to the right. The position was an awkward one, but he was in no mood to consider comfort. It might be interesting for a while to be the two-dimensional inmate of a single plane, but the novelty wore off quickly. He pushed his head into the right hand corner of the alcove and started to reach back past his hip to the timer.

It was impossible.

For a moment he hung still, stunned. Then as the truth penetrated, he had to restrain an urge to burst into hysterical laughter. Of course, being two-dimensional he could not move the line of his hand past the line of his body, any more than a normal three-dimensional person in a three-dimensional world can lie on his side on a flat floor and duplicate such an action without moving either floor or body. As long as he remained an inhabitant of the force field, he would never be able to reach behind his back. Around his feet or around the top of his head, yes, but behind his back—never.

For a moment he yielded again to panic and scrabbled around to find a position from which he could reach the timer, but the alcove was too small to allow him his necessary two-dimensional turning radius. He stopped finally, and common sense came to his aid.

Of course, the thing to do was to back out where there was room and turn around, so that he could come in facing in the other direction.

He moved back out into the long part of the room, mentally berating himself for having lost his head. He closed his eyes and rotated. He was getting quite used to this business of blinding himself while moving and made a mental note that eventually he must get around to keeping his eyes open just to get a clearer picture of what happened, when he did move. Reversed, he stepped back *up* into the alcove.

He opened his eyes to find himself not in the alcove but against the wall of the long room opposite the alcove. For a moment he stared in puzzlement, then understanding came.

"Of course," he said. "I'm reversed. I'll have to step *down*."

He did so. Two steps down took him into the alcove. He opened his eyes to find himself finally facing the corner which housed the timer—*but his feet were the parts of him next to it, and his head and hands were away from it*.

This is ridiculous! he thought. One way it's behind my back and the other way it's down by my feet. He crouched down, trying to squeeze himself into the corner close enough so that he could reach the timer. But it was no use. The alcove was too narrow to allow him to put his feet in the opposite corner and lean far enough over so that his hands could manipulate the timer. The sort of person who can bend over and put both hands flat on the floor could have done it easily, but Jack, like most males of more or less sedentary occupation, was not in that kind of shape. He tried kneeling, squeezing himself as tightly into the right hand corner as he could. But here the earlier prohibition of his two-dimensional existence came again into effect and he was blocked by his own knees. Not only did he have to reach around them, but they blocked off his view of the timer.

In a cold sweat, he finally gave up and backed out into the relatively open space of the long part of the room. It was fantastic. There was the timer directly in front of him. A touch of the finger would shut it off, for he could see its pointer frozen on the mark where it had turned the generator on. And it was a part of the field like the generator wire he had touched, so presumably he could move it. Yet, because of the restrictions of two-dimensional space, it was out of his reach.

To Jack, a born and native three-dimensioner, it seemed grossly unfair; and for one of the few times in his life he blew up.

After having cursed out force-fields, force-field inventors, all known physical laws, the generator, Paul, and himself for being a damn fool and daydreaming when he should have been watching the timer, he found himself feeling somewhat better. From being excited, he suffered a reaction to calmness. Let's look at this sensibly, he told himself.

He reminded himself that he'd been acting like a wild animal caught in a trap, rather than a thinking man. The thing to do was to make an effort to understand what it was that had hold of him rather than just fighting it blindly. If he could not reach the timer, he could not reach the timer. What other possibilities were there?

One—somebody, say perhaps Paul, would eventually come in and perhaps he could turn the timer off. Jack shook his head. No, whoever stepped through the door of the room would probably be caught up in the field the way he had been. If indeed the field was limited only to the room and did not extend beyond its walls already. Jack brightened. If the field was bounded by the room, then all he had to do was get out of it—

Painfully he maneuvered himself around until he was facing the door. The doorknob was below the field, but he had hopes of hooking his fingers onto the door's loose edge and pulling it open. It was a hope that was doomed to disappointment. Jack discovered that in two dimensions you could push, with fingertips, but not grab. The door, presumably because it was hinged to the walls outside the scope of the field, was strictly immovable.

It appeared to be a rule that whatever was loose and touched by the field was picked up by it, but whatever was attached to anything else beyond the limits of the field was not. It did not strictly make sense, because where do you draw the line of attachment? His body was attached to his limbs and his limbs had been outside the field. A matter of relative mass?

Concluding this to be an unrewarding field for speculation, Jack returned to the matter of field size, and at that moment it suddenly dawned on him that all this time the window at the end of the room had been open. If he could get out through that and beyond the limits of the field—

The wish was father to the act. Hardly had the thought occurred to him before he was jockeying for position in line with the window. He got it—back in the same position in which he had first found himself when the field caught him up—and simply walked out, presenting the unusual spectacle of a man strolling through mid-air while lying on his right side. It was all so easy that for the first time he found cause to wonder about the fact that the walking motion enabled him to progress when he was apparently doing nothing more than flailing the empty air. He experimented a little and discovered that he had the sensation of pressing back against something whenever he moved. Apparently the field had some kind of substance of its own, or a type of tension that reacted like an elastic skin when pressed longitudinally.

As soon as he was free of the building he rotated abruptly and *walked* sideways alongside it. His hope was that the field would be cut off by any solid obstacle. He traveled for some little distance before he admitted to himself that this hope was vain. Cheerfully, the field continued to buoy him up and imprison him, even when he reached the street in front of the labs.

The street was unusually silent and deserted. For a moment he considered waiting until somebody came by to help. But his natural shyness and sensitivity to embarrassment overcame the idea, and he turned back to cruise once more along the side of the building, peering in the windows with the hope of locating Paul himself, or at least someone connected with the labs.

The windows on the back and the side he had been down were all closed and the door had taught him that there was no use dealing with any three-dimensional object unless it was, like him, caught up in the field. He crossed past his own open window and started down the far side of the building.

Here there were several open windows, but they all gave on empty offices. But toward the front he came to one through which he could glimpse figures, at the far end. Without hesitation, he closed his eyes and stepped through the opening.

When he opened his eyes inside the room, he was astonished to see a tableau that was more than even his overactive imagination had ever conceived. Before him were Paul and Eva. They stood facing each other in a small room that seemed to be a sort of combination office and laboratory. Paul was leaning forward and his hand was on the smock-sleeved arm of Eva, who was pulling away from him.

For a moment the implications of the scene did not penetrate. When they did, Jack went skidding through the air toward the two figures, too angry even to remember to close his eyes.

When the grey field winked away to reveal the room in its proper dimensions again, he found himself floating in mid-air beside and a little above them. This room was evidently lower than the one from which he had started; and he glared down at the top of Paul's stubbled head and cut loose.

It was a fine exhibition of sizzling language, punctuated by flashes of streaky greyness, when in his excitement he forgot himself and moved or jerked his head. But when at last he began to run down, he was somewhat astonished to discover that neither of the people below had moved or shown any reaction to his presence. They had not even looked up.

In fact, Paul was still clutching Eva's arm and Eva was still leaning backward. They had not moved at all.

An awful suspicion struck Jack with the impact of a solid fist to the pit of the stomach. He had assumed until now that the timer had somehow stuck at the position in which it activated the generator, that no explosion had taken place because he had been careful after that first crimson flare not to monkey with the working parts of the generator. It had not occurred to him that the field in restricting him to two dimensions might *really* have restricted him to two dimensions.

Frantically he rotated until he was able to spot a large electric wall clock above the door of the room. Its hands were frozen at twelve minutes after two, and the long sweep-second hand stood motionless a little beyond the figure 12. He rotated back to where he could view the two people below. On the thick wrist above the hand that held Eva's arm was a large gold wristwatch, and this also stood with its hands immovably at twelve minutes after two. Jack was caught, not merely in a single plane, but in a single instant of time.

Up until now he had not really despaired. Always in the back of his mind had been the notion that even if he failed completely, sooner or later someone would come to his rescue.

Now he realized that no rescue was possible.

*   *   *

Somehow he survived that realization. Possibly because he was the kind of man who does survive, the sort of person who by birth and training has been educated to disbelieve in failure. It was just not in him to accept the fact that he was hopelessly trapped. And particularly in support of this was the discovery he had just made about Paul and Eva.

He looked down at them with a sort of bleak clarity of understanding that he had never succeeded in obtaining before. He realized now that he had been—for all effective purposes—blind while Eva had been working with him at the University.

He had introduced Paul to Eva himself some six months back when the other man had dropped by to see him on one of his occasional forays into the academic area in search of likely hired help. Jack had not considered the introduction important. It had not occurred to him that Paul would find Eva the sort of woman he would want. In fact if anyone had asked him about such a combination, he would have thought it rather funny. The two, by his standards, were opposite as the poles—Eva, with her cool depths, and Paul with his violent surface huckstering. It had not aroused Jack's suspicion that Paul should visit frequently during the months that followed, and that his visits should stop with Eva leaving the U.

No, Jack had been blind to the possibility of anyone else wanting Eva but himself, obsessed by the battle with his inner shyness that twiddled its thumbs and hoped vainly for a fortuitous set of circumstances that would do his wooing for him. Paul might not have the inner strength that had just brought Jack through where poor Reppleman had foundered, but he had push, and guts enough in his own way. While Jack dreamed, he had carried off Eva; and now, at this late date Jack was finally waking up to the fact that where the mating instinct is concerned we are still close enough to our animal forebears to have to fight for our partners on occasion.

He swung around and made his way once more out of the room. He needed space to think.

Once more in the bright sunlight outside, in the eternal out-of-doors of twelve minutes after two on a warm June afternoon, he continued his survey of the situation he was in. But he returned to it with the cold, dispassionate viewpoint of the trained mind. He marshalled the facts he had learned about his situation and considered them. They amounted to the following:

He was involuntarily imprisoned in what appeared to be a plane of two dimensions only and of unknown extent.

He was kept prisoner by a device operating at this moment.

The natural restrictions of movement in two dimensions, plus a matter of his original position in the plane, prevented him from reaching the means by which he could shut off the device.

Problem: How to shut off the device?

He returned to the room housing the generator and examined it. He studied the objects that, like himself, had been caught up in the field. He could not grasp any of them, but he could push them around within the limits of the field. It would, he thought, probably be quite possible to push the hammer, say, into the core of the generator and short it out. Also, probably quite fatal, if Paul had been telling the truth about the explosion. Reppleman had probably done some such thing. But he was in a rest home now with, again according to Paul, a complete block on the whole business. Still, the hammer possibility might be considered as a last-ditch measure.

"I have only begun to fight," quoted Jack softly to himself.

He studied the two upright rods from the top ends of which the field was generated. A thought occurred to him and he measured the distance between them (about three feet as nearly as he could estimate by eye) and the length of the room to the window in front of which he had been standing. He remembered that it had taken him more steps than he had expected to reach the generator from the window. He checked this and discovered that the first step back from the window was about the length of his normal stride, but that the second was only slightly more than half that, and the third diminished in proportion.

He returned to the window, went through it to the outside, and checked his stride in the opposite direction. His first step out from the window in a direct line away from the rods of the generator was not quite double his normal stride. With the next it doubled again, and half a dozen steps saw him sweeping over the countryside with giant's steps.

On impulse he closed his eyes and continued outward. After a few more steps he stopped and opened his eyes to look. Earth lay like an enormous, white-flecked disc below him. Space was around him. For a second, instinctively, he tried to gasp for air, then realized with a start that he was not breathing, nor had he been breathing for some time. Such things, evidently, were unnecessary in two dimensions.

He looked back down at Earth then ahead into space. Reppleman had gone mad at the end and wrecked the generator. But Reppleman was Reppleman; and he was— Jack. Moreover he had a score to settle back in his normal world. And he had every intention of getting back to settle it.

How far, he thought, had Reppleman wandered, before he had come back to destroy the thing that held him? The thought was morbid and he shook it from him. Firmly he faced away from the world and strode outward. For a moment he twinkled like a dot among the stars. And then he was gone, stepping into enormous distances with ever-increasing stride.

Jack closed the door of the little workroom behind him and turned left in the corridor outside. He went down the corridor, counting doors. At best it would have to be a guess, but if his estimate was right the room he wanted should be—

This one.

He pushed open the door and stepped in, interrupting two people in the midst of an angry argument. For a moment they stood frozen, interrupted and staring at him, and then Eva literally flew into his arms, while Paul's astonishment faded to a bitter smile and he sat down on a corner of the desk beside him and crossed his arms.

"Oh, Jack!" choked Eva. "Jack!"

Jack folded her in his long arms almost automatically, with a feeling of bewilderment that gradually gave way to one of pleasure. He had never seen the calm, self-contained Eva moved like this before; and the corresponding role it demanded of him was rather attractive. He felt sort of contented and self-righteous; and at the same time as if he ought to do something dramatic, like, say, picking up Paul and breaking him in half, or some such thing.

At that, however, it was Paul who got in the first punch.

"She's worried about you," he said, dryly, jerking a thumb at Eva.

"You are?" demanded Jack, looking down at her.

"Oh Jack!" said Eva. "You mustn't do it. You don't know how dangerous it is!"

"What is?" asked Jack, becoming bewildered again.

"The field," put in Paul, as dryly as before.

"Oh that," said Jack. "Well—"

"You don't know what it's like," interrupted Eva. "I was here when they took Max Reppleman out after the explosion. Jack—"

"Never mind that," said Jack, strongly. "Paul said you were worried about me."

"Jack, please listen. That whole business is dangerous—"

"You wouldn't be worried about me unless you were—well, worried about me," said Jack stubbornly. His blood was up now. He had almost lost this girl once to Paul through hesitation and delay. "Eva—" He tightened his grasp on her—"I love you."

"Jack, will you lis—" Eva stopped suddenly. Color flooded her face. She stared up at him in shocked speechlessness.

"Eva," said Jack, quickly, taking advantage of this golden opportunity and talking fast. "Eva, I fell in love with you back at the University, only I was always looking for the right chance to tell you and I didn't get around to it because I was afraid of making some mistake and losing you. And when you left and went to work for Paul I gave up, but I've changed my mind. Eva, will you marry me right now, today?"

Eva tried to speak a couple of times but no sound came out.

"The whirlwind lover," said Paul somewhere in the background.

"Well?" demanded Jack.

"Jack, I—" trembled Eva.

"Never mind," said Jack, breaking in on her. "Because I won't take no for an answer. Do you hear me?" He paused for a second to be astonished at his own words. "You're going to marry me right away."

"Ye gods!" said Paul. He might have saved his breath. Neither one of the other two was paying attention to him.

Jack let her go, and looked at Paul.

"Paul—" he said.

"Yes *sir!*" responded Paul, getting up from the desk and popping exaggeratedly to attention.

Jack looked at him with the jaundiced eye of a conquering general for his defeated rival. Though temporarily vanquished, this man was still potentially dangerous. Proceed with plan B? asked the front part of his mind. Proceed with plan B, responded the back of his mind.

"Paul," he said. "I've got the answers for you on the field."

Paul's ironic pose slowly relaxed. A wary, calculating look came into his eye.

"What?" he said.

"I'll show you," Jack said. "Come on with me. You too, Eva."

And he turned on one heel and led the way out of the room.

"You see," said Jack, "you were wrong in your picture of what the generator does." They were all three standing in the little L-shaped room and Jack had just told them what had happened to him. "It doesn't produce a field at all. What it does is affect certain types of objects close to it so that they become restricted to a certain limited two-dimensional plane in a single moment of time. The generator itself tries to exist both in this and in normal space at the same time, with the result that it blows up—what you might call a paradox explosion—not after some seconds, but immediately. Of course, this doesn't affect what's been caught up in the single moment-and-plane, because for them that single instant is eternity."

"But it didn't blow up on you," said Paul.

"I turned it off before it had a chance to," replied Jack, a little grimly.

"Now wait," said Paul. "Wait. You just finished telling us you couldn't reach the timer switch because of your position which was essentially unchangeable in two-dimensional space. How did you turn it off? In fact, how did you ever get back?"

Jack smiled coolly.

"What happens to a plane in curved space?"

Paul frowned.

"I don't get it," he said.

"It curves, of course," answered Jack. "And where it's dependent upon something like the generator, it curves back eventually to it."

Paul's eyes narrowed.

"Well—" he hesitated. "What good did knowing that do you, though? You could walk clear around the circle and still not change your position so as to reach the timer switch."

"Ah yes," said Jack. "If it was just a simple circle. But it was a Moebius strip."

"Now wait—" cried Paul.

"You wait," said Jack. "How many points determine a plane?"

"Three."

Jack turned and walked down the length of the room to where the two upright rods still stood connected to the generator. He touched their tips.

"And how many points do we have here?"

Paul looked bewildered.

"Two," he said. "But—"

"Then where's the third point we need? As a matter of fact you're standing right at it."

Paul started in spite of himself and moved slightly aside.

"What do you mean?" he asked.

"The third point," said Jack, "is the focal point of the two lines of force emanating from the two rod tips. They converge right in the middle of the window at the far end of the room there."

"But I still don't see!" said Paul.

"You will," said Jack. He turned and stepped into the alcove. There was a moment's silence, then the sound of tearing paper and he stepped back out holding a long thin strip of newspaper. He walked back to Paul.

"Let's see your thumb and forefinger," he said. "Now look here. This one end of the strip for the length of about an inch we'll say is the part of the plane in this room that's determined by the three points, the two rod tips and the focal point of their lines of force. Hold that."

He transferred one end of the strip to Paul's fingers. Paul held it pinched between thumb and forefinger and watched.

"Now," went on Jack, demonstrating, "the plane goes out like this and around like this and back like this in a big loop and the end approaches the generator between your fingers again. It comes in here and the last inch of it goes back between your fingers, and there you are, reversed and ready to shut off your timer."

"Wait," said Paul, now holding the two ends pinched between his fingers together and the big loop of paper strip drooping in mid-air. "Why does the end come back in the same place? Why doesn't it just circle around behind and touch ends?"

"For two reasons," answered Jack. "The plane must end where it began. Right?"

"Yes."

"*But*," said Jack. "To remain the same plane it must have the same three points in common. And the plane takes its position from the focal point, not the two rod tips. The result is what you've got in your hand there, a loop with a little double tag end."

"But I don't—well, never mind," said Paul. "The important thing is that this is still a straight loop, with no twist in it at all. "You could never get reversed on this. This is no Moebius."

"Think again," said Jack. "With that tag end it is." He turned to Eva. "Come on, Eva. We'll leave Paul to figure this out while you and I go get our own affairs taken care of." He took her hand and opened the door.

"Hey!" cried Paul. "You can't—"

"Oh yes, I can," said Jack, turning in the open doorway. "I've answered all your questions. Just take an imaginary little two-dimensional figure and run him around that strip of newspaper. You'll see."

And he led Eva out the door, closing it behind them. Once in the corridor, however, he took her shoulders in his two big hands and backed her against the wall.

"Tell me," he said. "Just why did you quit me at the U. and come down here?"

Eva looked guilty.

"He—Paul said—"

"What did he say?"

"He said," hesitated Eva, "you'd always told him you never intended to marry anyone." A small note of defiance came into her voice. "What was I going to do? Every day I'd come to work and you'd be there, and you never said anything—" she broke off suddenly, eyeing him curiously. "Why did you ask me that now, Jack?"

"Because," said Jack. "For a minute I was tempted to save Paul a walk—a long, long walk."

She stared up at him.

"I don't understand."

He smiled and took her hand.

"Some day," he said tenderly, "some day when we are very old and married and well supplied with grandchildren, I'll tell you all about it. Okay?"

She was too much in love with him to protest—then.

"Okay," she smiled back.

They went down the corridor toward the door leading out to the parking lot behind the labs.

In the room Paul stood frowning at the strip of paper in his hand. It didn't seem possible, but it was. He had just finished walking, in imagination, a little two-dimensional man all the way around the strip; and, sure enough, he had ended up facing in the opposite direction. It was simple enough. But it wasn't a Moebius. Or was it? If the two ends were one end—

Outside on the parking lot he heard the roar of a motor; and he looked up to see a battered old blue business coupe make its turn on the gravel expanse and head out the driveway. As it passed it stopped; and Jack stuck his head out the car window to shout something to him. Paul stepped to the window.

"What?" he yelled.

Jack's words came indistinctly to him over the distance and the racket of the ancient motor.

"—I said—stay right where you are—"

"What?" roared Paul.

But Jack had pulled in his head and the car pulled ahead out the driveway and into the street. Paul watched it merge with the traffic and get lost in the distance.

What had Jack said? Stay right where you are? *Why* should he stay right where he was?

Suddenly he felt the unexpected cold squeeze of suspicion. It couldn't be that Jack would—

—Behind him and from the direction of the timer came the sound of a soft, insidious *click*.

Strictly Confidential

To: Interstellar Bureau of Criminal Apprehension
From: Jake Hall
        Hall Detective Service "BEHIND
        THE EIGHT BALL? CALL HALL!"

My connection with the Topla Pong caper began at approximately 3:15 P.M. of August 3rd, 1965. I was sitting at my desk, cleaning the dried blood from the front sight of my forty-five and having a couple of eye-openers from the office bottle. Both of the windows in the office were open.

The windows are at right angles to each other, since the dump is a corner office. As I finished the shot and poured myself another, a large green and purple butterfly came fluttering in one window, picked up the forty-five and flew out the other.

I don't mind admitting this made me sore. That was a sweet little gun and I had conceived a sentimental attachment for it, due to having many memories attached to it. I ripped open the right hand bottom drawer of my desk, grabbed my second best gun—a .38 police special—and got to my feet determined to track down the butterfly that had taken it. Unfortunately, I made the mistake of turning

121

my back to one of the windows as I rose. I caught a glimpse of green and purple out of the corner of my eye and the ceiling fell in.

"What the hell—" I thought, and passed out.

When I woke up, a short, hefty individual in a grey business suit was splashing water in my face.

"Lay off, buster," I said. "This is my best and only tie." And I struggled to my feet. He stopped splashing water and stood back. My head was killing me. I located the bottle and poured myself a triple shot. Then I took a second look at him.

"Who're you?" I said, picking up the thirty-eight, which was still on the desk top. I was sore enough to let him have it. I'm glad now I didn't. Some guys are sensitive and I know enough now to realize it would have hurt his feelings.

"IBCA Agent Dobuk," he answered me. "I am a Memnian from Pesh—formerly of the Plagiarism Section."

"Listen," I said. "The last time I copied anything was in the third grade. State your business, or blow."

"I am an agent of the Interstellar Bureau of Criminal Apprehension," he said sadly. "An emergency has caused me to be transferred to the Violent Crimes Section. That same emergency has brought me to your office. Although it is ordinarily against Interstellar Commission Rules to admit the existence of other races to backward natives, events have forced my hand. "

I turned away from him and picked up my hat from the desk.

"See me later," I said. "I got a date with a butterfly."

"Wait," he said; and closed his fist around a handful of my suitcoat. "Let me explain first."

I tried to walk away from him, but it was like being held in a steel vise. Experimentally, I chopped his wrist with the barrel of the thirty-eight and bent it—the barrel of the thirty-eight, that is.

"Okay, bud," I said. "You talked me into it. I'll listen."

He let me go. I went back to the desk, put the bent thirty-eight away and got out my thirty-two from the filing case.

I felt better with that in my shoulder holster. I sat down.

"Take a chair," I said.

"Thank you," he answered. "I'll have to adjust my weight first. What should a human my size weigh?"

"I'd guess you at about a hundred and eighty," I said. He fiddled with his belt and sat down. The chair took it all right. "Sorry," he added. "I didn't want to take chances."

"Well, what's the dope?" I asked. He looked at me.

"What I have to say," he said, lowering his voice impressively, "must never go beyond this room."

"I'll shut the windows," I said, starting to get up.

"Never mind," he said, "I trust you."

"In that case," I said, "my fees are thirty bucks a day and expenses. If you feel like paying a retainer—"

He tossed me a thousand dollar bill. I stuffed it carelessly in my hip pocket. "Go ahead," I said. He looked at me grimly.

"You have just been visited by an interstellar criminal," he told me, lowering his voice. "In fact by one of *the* interstellar criminals."

"You mean the butterfly?" I asked.

"That butterfly, as you call him," he nodded. "He is, in reality, none other than Topla Pong, a Sngrian from Jchok." I shrugged. He was paying for the time.

"You're paying for the time," I said. "If you say so, okay. To me he's still a butterfly."

"A most dangerous butterfly," replied Dobuk. "A butterfly of the worst order. Not more than two weeks ago, sidereal time, he engaged a battle cruiser of the second class in the Coal Sack Area and destroyed it utterly. He is one of the great criminal minds of our present galactic era and one of the few great crime organizers."

"Crime organizers?" I asked.

"Criminal executives," he told me. "They do not belong to any particular branch of the criminal world, but to all. In two weeks he is capable of organizing the population of this planet and so infecting it with criminal ideas that the Interstellar Fleet will have no choice but to sterilize the globe by wiping out all intelligent life upon it."

"I get you," I said. "He's dangerous."

"We must stop him," Dobuk nodded. "You and I together must do what the IBCA has been trying to do for centuries."

"Why us?" I asked.

"The situation is critical," he answered. "Topla Pong has cropped up here where there is no one trained to stop him."

"What about you?" I said. He shook his head.

"I have the basic training, of course," he said mournfully. "But I'm strictly a plagiarism expert. I have no experience in violence. Also I'm too heavy for this world."

"Come again?" I asked. He gestured toward his belt.

"I have a gravity nullifier," he explained. "I adjusted it to one hundred and eighty of your pounds. Without it I would weigh approximately two of your tons."

He looked to me like a guy on short leave from a straitjacket, but he handed out thousand dollar bills. I picked up my hat.

"Okay," I said. "Let's go."

We went down the stairs and out into the street to where my battered forty-eight Chev was parked. It looked like a heap but things had been done to the motor and it was capable of a hundred and twenty if pushed. Detective Lieutenant Joe Haggerty was standing beside it. He glowered at me as I came up.

"Still clipping fruit stands for free apples, Haggerty?" I greeted him. His glower became a snarl.

"Listen, shamus," he said. "The fact that you saved

the Governor's life last year isn't going to protect you forever. One of these days I'll find something to connect you with these hoods that are being found dead around town with a forty-five, a thirty-eight, a thirty-two, or some other size slug in them. And when I do—''

He left the threat hanging in the air. We got in the Chev and pulled off. Dobuk was looking at me in awe.

"How can you stand to have anyone dislike you that much?''

"I manage,'' I said. Dobuk shook his head in disbelief.

"You humans have such tough emotions,'' he said. "There was a note on that in the IBCA guidebook to this planet, but I could hardly believe it.''

"Live and learn, buster,'' I said. I pulled out into the traffic.

"Where are we going?'' asked Dobuk.

"To the Platinum Wheel,'' I told him.

"But shouldn't we start trying to trace—''

"Look, bud,'' I said. "You hire me, you do things my way. Arson, gut-shooting, little things like that, I'll maybe cover up for a client. But if I find you're the guilty party, I'll throw you to the badges. After all, I'm in business in this town.''

"What?'' he said. He sounded bewildered.

We pulled up in front of the Platinum Wheel, the plushest nightclub in the territory—run by the Syndicate, of course. We left the car and walked inside.

"Jake!'' screamed a gorgeous, long-legged, red-haired cigarette girl the minute she saw me. "What are you doing here? Don't you know the Syndicate is out for your blood?''

"It's worth a couple of quarts just to see you, baby,'' I said, clutching her. We kissed. It was like drowning in a sunset colored sea. She was a good kid. I kissed her every time I saw her.

When I finally let her go, she stepped back revealing a hard-looking character in a head-waiter's outfit.

"Who let you in, Hall?" he grated.

"The pest exterminators," I said. "They got the small lice, but they wanted some help with the rats."

"A wise guy, huh?" he sneered and let fly a left with all of his two hundred and twenty pounds behind it. I ducked; and there was a nasty, splintering sound just behind my neck.

He had hit Dobuk.

"Oh, I'm so sorry!" said Dobuk, bending over him.

"Forget it and come on," I said. We left the hard guy writhing on the emerald green carpet, clutching his mashed mitt; and walked back toward the office in the rear of the building.

"Are you sure we're going about this in the right way?" asked Dobuk.

"In this territory, when you talk about organized crime, you talk about the Syndicate," I said.

"I just thought—a careful investigation of probabilities—a calculation of—"

"Let me give you a piece of advice," I said.

"What?" he asked.

"Don't think," I said.

"But that's impossible," said Dobuk.

We had reached the door of the office. I opened it and led the way in without bothering to knock. Inside, Mikey McGwendon sat wearing a tux, his nails smoothly mani-cured, behind a large desk on the front edge of which perched a platinum blonde—a knockout. Also present was a large gorilla-like character and a small weasel-faced character. They were wearing Brooks Bros. suits; but they weren't fooling me any. After you've been in this business as long as I have you can spot the type a mile off.

Mikey gave me a mechanical smile as Dobuk and I advanced to his desk. I thought to myself he had taken us for a couple of his well-heeled sucker patrons. But I was wrong.

"Well, if it isn't Jake Hall, the wonder boy shamus," he greeted me. "What can I do for you?"

"That depends," I said. Reaching out, I snagged the platinum blonde off the desk and crushed her in my arms. Our lips met. It was like drowning in a sea of black flame. This was a no good kid. I had never kissed her before, but one touch of her lips told me that. Holding her off at arms length, I saw I was right. Her green eyes were as cold as ice on a go-light.

"Care to try that again, shamus?" she inquired, throatily.

I pushed her away while I still had my strength left. I turned back to Mikey. I could tell he hadn't liked my little byplay with his girl friend, but he hadn't got where he was in the rackets without learning some self-control—I'll give him that. He took his hand out of his desk drawer, closed the desk drawer and gave me that same mechanical smile.

"I don't think I know your friend," he said.

"Client, Mikey, client," I answered. "We got a little something to talk over with you. How about some privacy?"

Not a muscle in his face twitched. He flicked his hand at the door.

"Beat it," he growled.

The blonde pouted, but undulated out. The two characters hesitated. But they wouldn't have been Mikey's boys unless they'd learned some self-control. They took their hands out from under their left armpits and went out.

"Well, shamus?" said Mikey, turning to me as the door slammed.

"Well, it's like this," began Dobuk, behind me. "We're looking for—"

"Can it!" I growled. I perched on Mikey's desk myself and helped myself to a cigar from his humidor and a stiff slug from a decanter that stood handy on the desk top. "I thought you had this town organized, Mickey."

"Who says I haven't?" he retorted.

"Nobody said it yet," I told him. "What if I told you

there's rumors of a freelance character running around with a forty-five?''

"There's no free guns in this town, Hall. If there is, I'll have the boys take care of him. What's he look like?''

"About eight inches long," I said. "Two and a half ounces, green with purple patches and about two feet across the wings.''

He was writing the particulars down on a note pad.

"Eight inches long—" he repeated and stopped suddenly, looking up at me. "Who you trying to kid, Hall?''

I reached over, grabbed him by the lapels and hauled him to me. He clanked a little coming across the desk and I reached in to grab what I figured was a gun in his inside pocket. I never made it. Before I could close my hand, the lights went out.

I came to lying on a couch. Raising my head, I saw a large room with dark wooden rafters overhead. I was in somebody's hunting lodge. Looking down, I saw a fireplace and the platinum blonde in something filmy curled up on a polar-bear skin in front of it.

"Where am I?" I said.

"In my hunting lodge," she answered, throatily. "Don't you like me on a polar-bear skin, shamus?''

I reached for a bottle of bourbon on an end table nearby and poured myself a healthy slug. It made me feel a little better. My head was killing me.

"Save the routine for Mikey," I growled.

"But I can't stand Mikey," she answered. "I want to run away from him. Oh, he buys me presents and things— like this hunting lodge. But I can't stand him.'' Suddenly she was up in a swirl of something filmy and had flung herself into my arms. "Oh, Jake, Jake," she sobbed, "you don't know what it's like, living the kind of life I lead.''

Looking down at her platinum blonde head, I almost felt sorry for her. Poor kid, it was the old story, I thought.

Miss Podunk Corners of nineteen sixty-three, a knockout at sixteen, chased by all the local punks, but with stars in her eyes. A beauty contest win, Hollywood, a contract as a starlet at two hundred a week—and then nothing. Nothing to do, week after week, but sit around drawing her two hundred and killing time. Never a part. In desperation, marriage—to a wealthy, handsome, older man, who, however, turned out to have no time for anything but his aircraft plant. Six weeks of this, and disillusionment. Reno, divorce, a modest hunk of alimony. Then—one day she had woken up to look in the mirror and see herself— twenty, no longer a kid.

In desperation, she had begun to live for kicks, started running with a tougher and tougher crowd. Finally, she had ended up with Mikey. Oh, I'd no doubt, he had attracted her at first, with his crude, unsophisticated ways; and then it had begun to dawn on her that she was trapped.

It was the sort of thing I saw all the time in my business. But that was neither here nor there. I was here, and where was Dobuk?

"Where's the guy that was with me?" I demanded.

She choked back her sobs.

"He's out back," she said. We got up and went out. In a shed at the rear of the building we found a stack of hickory logs piled up like so much cordwood. On top was Dobuk, out cold.

I shook him out of it, got him moving and we all went back into the lodge.

"How'd they ever knock you out?" I asked him, when we were back inside. He shook his head.

"This is more serious than I thought," he said, shaking his head. "The only thing that could so affect a Peshniam Memnian like myself—"

"A what?" said the blonde.

"A Peshniam—I am a Memnian from Pesh, Miss," said Dobuk. "I and Mr. Hall are in quest of a Jchoknian Sngrian, or a Sngrian from Jchok. I was pointing out that since I am a Memnian Peshnian, unlike a Zumnian Omnian, that is, an Omnian from Zumn a lighter gravity world to which one branch of our Memnian race has adapted—"

"Get to the point," I interrupted.

"Well," said Dobuk, "the point is that about the only thing on this planet which could render me unconscious would be a jolt of Emirnian nerve gas, one capsule of which Topla Pong was known to have in his possession after his encounter with the cruiser in the Coal Sack. I sadly fear that the Sngrian we are seeking has already joined forces with your Earthly underworld."

"Could be—" I said, frowning. I turned to the blonde.

"What's your name, baby?" I demanded.

"It's Sheila," she answered, shyly. "Sheila Coombes."

"I'll bet it is," I snapped. She colored.

"How did you guess?" she murmured. "The name of my husband in my first unhappy marriage was Swinebender, but after I got my divorce I took back my maiden name— only changing it a little from the original, which was Gumbs."

"I thought so," I said. "I been in the business too long to be fooled by a name like Coombes. Now listen, Sheila, baby. If you want help to get away from Mikey, now's your time to level with us. First, how'd we get here?"

Her lower lip trembled.

"Gorilla and Weasel brought you out," she said. "You were all tied up but, when they went back to town, I took a chance and untied you."

"What were they going to do with us here?"

"Keep you on ice, they said, until Mikey had time to figure out how to dispose of you. I was supposed to keep an eye on you. Mikey said he wanted Gorilla and Weasel back in town for something."

"Yeah?" I said. Things were beginning to make sense to me. "Got a radio anyplace around the dump, Sheila?"

"There's one in the bedroom," she said. We went into the bedroom. Between drapes of flaming pink, a Capehart stood under one window. On top of it was a small table model radio in black leather inlaid with brilliants. Sheila turned it on.

"Get the news," I told her.

She fiddled with the dial. We got music, sports, a lecture by a professor at UCLA, more music—but no news.

"It's no use," said Sheila.

"No, wait," said Dobuk. "I believe I sense—"

The moaner sobbing his tune at us out of the loud-speaker got suddenly cut off in mid-howl. The dry-toast voice of an on-the-spot announcer came crackling out at us.

"—we interrupt this program to bring you a special announcement. It has just been learned that the govern-ments of the world's leading nations have received a com-munication from some organization calling itself the Syndicate and believed in some circles to be the criminal ring behind much of the illegal activities in this country. The communication gives the world's law enforcement agencies twenty-four hours to, quote—get out of business—unquote. In the event that the law enforcement agencies do not comply within the stated time, the Syndicate announces its intention of dropping one atomic bomb each on every major city on the face of the globe. The letter is thought to be a hoax; and if this is so, the hoax will soon be exposed. For it has just been learned that although the news was just now released to the news agencies, the ultimatums were delivered yesterday and the deadline is less than four hours away. We now return to Tommy Mugwu—"

I switched off the set.

"Yesterday!" I said. "How long were we out?"

"Almost twenty hours," said Sheila. Dobuk turned pale.

"Sure it's a hoax," I said. "Where would they get atomic bombs?"

Dobuk turned paler.

"You don't know Sngrians," he said. " 'Snfle beh jkt Sngrian' as the native saying goes. Or, to translate roughly into English, 'Sngrians are all natural-born scientists.' Give Topla Pong a few pinches of middle to heavyweight elements and he can turn out atomic bombs like bjiks—or as you would say—hot rolls."

"But why would he want to blow up all the big cities?" cried Sheila. "That won't help the Syndicate, any."

"The Syndicate itself must be helpless in his grasp," said Dobuk. "Remember, he is not merely an ordinary criminal, but a criminal executive with the very best of up-to-date galactic methods of criminal organization at his antennae-tips. To take over your Syndicate would be pupa's play to the Sngrian who once held undisputed sway over four systems before the IBCA broke his power."

"But the cities—"

"Ah, but there you are," said Dobuk. "He has no scruples. So he destroys the cities today. Slave labor will build them back up again for him tomorrow—and with newer, bigger, better gambling houses and vice dens. No doubt he plans something like criminal conscription where every adult will be forced into some sort of criminal activity, no matter how minor. Ordinary values mean nothing to him. Remember he is a creature of great natural genius and tremendous talent which he gets his greatest happiness from utilizing. To him there is something creative and artistic about building a criminal empire. He does it not for the material, but for the spiritual rewards."

"Dress it up in fancy clothes if you want," I said. "To me, he's still nothing more than a two-bit butterfly with delusions of grandeur. I've met the biggest of them; and when the chips are down they're all punks who think they can make it the easy way."

"No, no," said Dobuk, earnestly, "you don't understand."

"I understand all right," I told him. I reached for my shoulder holster. It was empty. "They took my gun," I said. I turned on Sheila. "Got a gun around the house, baby?"

"Well, let me see—" she frowned and thought. "I have

a twenty-five automatic and a ladies purse model twenty-two. But they're both out being fixed. I know, I've got a little .12 caliber automatic. Will that do?''

"It'll have to," I growled.

"Not a toy," she said. "Built in imitation of one of Germany's most famous firearms. Not an air or a CO2 gun, this is a small-bore gun that actually shoots a clip of six .12 caliber lead bullets." She extracted it from the center drawer of her dressing table and handed it to me. "Excellent for small game, target work, and scaring prowlers."

I picked the twelve up between two fingers and dropped it carefully into my shoulder holster. I felt more natural with a gun on me.

"What are you going to do?" asked Dobuk.

"Time's running short," I grated. "There's only one thing to do. Go to Mikey's town house and get to the bottom of things."

Sheila turned pale.

"The Syndicate West Coast Headquarters?" she cried. "Oh, no, no! I won't let you, Jake. They'll kill you. An army couldn't get into that place."

I shrugged.

"Who's using the army?" I said.

"Then I'll go with you," cried Sheila.

"And I, of course, also," said Dobuk.

We went out and hopped into Sheila's gold and black Cad convertible and lit out for L.A. I was behind the wheel and I kept the needle crowding a hundred and ten all the way in. It was tense driving, especially through the business districts along the way.

We made it in three hours. It had been about five o'clock when we left the lodge; and night had fallen by the time I skidded to a stop at the rear of the estate grounds of Mikey's town residence. I switched off the lights and sat for a minute listening to see if our approach had been noticed. But everything was quiet inside the high stone fence with the broken bottles set in concrete on the top and the electric wire running above them. Through the dark stillness, we could hear the mutters of the hoods on the front gate changing guard, and see the white ghost of the searchlight on top of the mansion sweeping the grounds.

"Perhaps," suggested Dobuk, "perhaps we should inform the local law enforcement agency of our mission?"

"In this suburb of L.A.?" I said. "Don't make me laugh. Mikey's always been careful to play the good, solid home owner in this neighborhood. He gives to the charities and sits on the local committees. They're sold on him. The local law would laugh in our faces."

I got out of the car. Dobuk got out on the other side.

"I'm coming with you!" cried Sheila.

"No," I said.

"Yes!"

"No."

"Yes!"

I hated to have to do it. But I slugged her. Glass jaw—she went out like a light.

"All right," I said to Dobuk. "Now, follow me."

"Where?" inquired Dobuk.

"Over the wall," I said.

"Why not through?" he asked; and walked through the wall. He made a fair-sized hole. I followed.

But the noise of the smashing wall had alarmed the mansion. From the front gate came startled cries; and the searchlight stopped roaming about at random and began a personal hunt in our area of the grounds. I ducked behind some fir trees, dragging Dobuk with me. He was shaking like a leaf.

"What's wrong?" I snapped.

"Oh, these violent emotions!" he groaned. "The place quivers with them. Pesh, why did I ever leave you? I am impaled living on darting shafts of fear and hatred."

"Snap out of it!" I whispered. "If you can't take it from these hoods, how'll you be able to stand up to The Butterfly?"

"He's nowhere near so savage," said Dobuk. "Evil, yes—but as violent, no. You humans!"

I looked at him in the sudden glare of the searchlight that flickered over us without stopping. He was a sad sight. These amateurs are never any good.

"Here, take a jolt of this," I said, handing him the pint I always carry in my hip pocket.

His trembling hand took it and there was a splintering, crunching sound.

"Hey! You nuts?" I yelped in a loud whisper. He had just chewed the neck off the bottle and was about to take a bite out of the rest of it. "You drink it, you don't eat it."

"I'm sorry," he said, humbly, "a little bit of silicon is good for my nerves."

"To hell with your nerves," I said. "I need something to carry my whisky in." I grabbed the bottle back. It was already ruined. "Oh, well," I said; and drank it off. My head was killing me anyway. I handed the bottle back to Dobuk. "Here, finish it off."

"Thank you," he said. There was a little more crunching, a quiet gulp, and we were ready to roll.

We headed for the dim outline of the house, running bent over double. We came up against the back of the building. There was a basement window. Rapidly, I crisscrossed it with scotch tape and broke it open with the butt of the twelve. I reached it, unlatched it, opened it, and we crawled in.

The basement was dark and silent. Suddenly the lights went on.

"Who's there?" snarled a voice; and a rough-looking character came galloping down the stairs. I let him have it between the eyes with the twelve.

"Pick up his body," I said to Dobuk. "Stack it out of sight behind the furnace."

"Whuzzat?" he said. His eyes were glazed. All of a sudden it hit me. He was drunk as a skunk. I should never have let him have the rest of that bottle.

I backhanded him a couple of times across the face, bruising my knuckles.

"Snap out of it," I growled.

He whimpered and cringed away from me.

"If there's anything I hate," I snarled. "It's a lush. Particularly during business hours."

"Don't," he whimpered. "Don't hate me. I'll be all right."

He looked so bad, I relented.

"Okay, come on then," I said. He followed me upstairs.

In the kitchen were five more hoods playing Hollywood gin at five cents a point. I let them all have it between the eyes. The little twelve was empty. I checked the shoulder holsters of the hoods. They were all carrying thirty-twos. I took one.

"Come on," I said to Dobuk. We moved out through the kitchen door. As I stepped through, I had a glimpse of someone swinging at me. I ducked, but not quickly enough. For a moment the room went black; and then I had staggered to my feet and let the man who tried to slug me have it between the eyes. He was dressed in a monkey suit; and for a second I didn't get it. Then I realized he must be the butler.

On the dining table was a tray he had evidently been carrying upstairs when he heard me. It held a bottle, ice, and glasses. I poured myself a stiff shot and downed it. My head was killing me.

I searched the butler. He was carrying a thirty-eight and I traded my thirty-two for it. While I was doing this, someone shot at us from the living room, but missed because I was bent over; and the bullet hit nobody but Dobuk, who, of course, it didn't hurt.

"There's someone in the living room," said Dobuk, looking down at the flattened slug where it lay on the chartreuse carpet before him.

"I know," I said.

I sprayed the living room with bullets and we advanced. Inside, Gorilla and Weasel lay dead with bullet holes between the eyes. Gorilla had my forty-five clutched in his ham-like mitt. Here, at last, was proof positive of the hookup between Topla Pong and the Syndicate. I pointed this out to Dobuk. He agreed.

I led the way on up the stairs toward the second floor, the forty-five clutched in my hand. It felt good to have it back again, though I noticed Gorilla hadn't been taking good care of it. There was dried blood on the front sight at least twenty-four hours old.

At the top of the stairs, we entered a wide hallway. On the plum-colored carpet lay Sheila, her platinum blonde hair tumbled back from her pale face and a spreading stain on the front of her dress. She was dying.

"What are you doing here?" I asked. "I thought I left you in the car."

"You did—" she gasped. "I went to the front gate after I came to and one of the hoods on duty there brought me in to Mikey. I was going to double-cross you, but when I looked at him and thought of you I couldn't do it. He shot me." She choked suddenly on a rush of blood. "Kiss me once more, Jake."

I crushed her in my arms. It was like drowning in a sea of black flame for the last time. Halfway through the clinch, the flame flickered and went out. Gently, I laid her down on the plum-colored carpet. Her eyes were already closed in death, her face peaceful. She looked like a little girl again—a wayward kid, who at the last minute had found a spark of unexpected decency in herself—a spark that had cost her her life.

Now I was really mad. Dobuk yelped and backed off from me.

"What's the matter with you?" I growled.

"You burnt me," he said. Then I got it. I was in a red hot rage after seeing Sheila, and the poor guy had been standing too close.

"Keep behind me," I said. Sheila's outstretched hand on the carpet seemed to be pointing toward a closed door at the end of the hall. I had a hunch that what Dobuk and I were both looking for would be behind the door. I headed for it, gun in hand.

I kicked the door open. It was a library; and behind a desk stood Mikey, faultlessly attired in evening clothes, a highball in one hand and a gun in the other. He gave me a mechanical smile.

"Drop the rod, Mikey," I said. "I got you covered."

"Nuts," he said, oilily, "drop yours, Jake. I got you covered."

Without lowering my forty-five, I glanced at the gun in his hand. It was true. He was holding a forty-eight. I was outgunned.

Helplessly, I dropped the forty-five on the maroon carpet. Moving with piston-like efficiency, he stalked around the desk and scooped it up.

"Come in and shut the door," he said. "You too, Dobuk."

Dobuk! I had forgotten him. Dobuk was immune to bullets.

"Grab the gun from him, Dobuk!" I yelled.

Dobuk stepped around me and advanced on Mikey. Mikey flashed his vicious, mechanical smile at him.

"I've got the solution to you," he said. "To coin a phrase—'bye, bye, Dobuk!' "

His hand flashed out with piston-like efficiency and ripped Dobuk's belt from his pants. There was a splintering crash and Dobuk disappeared. A gaping hole marred the carpet where he had stood a minute before. Suddenly deprived of his gravity nullifier, Dobuk had reverted to his normal weight of two tons and dropped through two floors down into the basement.

"And now," said Mikey, pointing the forty-eight at me. "For you."

"Hold it!" I said, sharply. "I can see I'm not going to get out of this alive, so you better tell me how you did it."

"Very well," said Mikey. I could almost see the gears

grinding in his head as he mulled over various plans for disposing of me. "Sheila was actually a third cousin of my aunt-by-marriage. Although she did not know it herself, she stood to inherit a large share of Syndicate voting stock, following my aunt's recent death. I was planning to maneuver for a position on the Syndicate Executive Board and needed her stock. The killing of Weasel was actually an accident. I was cleaning that forty-five of yours when it went off of its own accord, letting him have it between the eyes. I realized then that it was not safe to have a gun trained by you around the house. I handed it over to Gorilla without even finishing the job of taking the dried blood off the front sight. . . ."

So that was why the dried blood was still on the front sight. Even the little things checked now. If only I'd put two and two together earlier.

". . . and told Gorilla to take it and Weasel out and bury them. You must have run into them as Gorilla was carrying them out of the living room front door."

That explained why there had been only one shot from the living room—and why the bullet had missed me, only bruising Dobuk slightly between the eyes.

"The rest of it," wound up Mikey, "you know. With Sheila's stock and the know-how of The Butterfly, I saw my way clear to take over the Syndicate Executive Board."

"Where's Topla Pong now?" I demanded.

His eyes had a hard, metallic glint in them.

"Where you'll never find him," he said. He lifted his gun and aimed it at me. The hole in the muzzle looked big enough to crawl into. "And now, to coin a phrase—"

"But *I* will find him!" announced Dobuk suddenly, rising up through the hole in the floor beneath us.

"Dobuk!" I yelled. "But how—? Your gravity nullifier—"

"Though only a plagiarism agent," he replied, "I have had the basic IBCA training. I built a new gravity nullifier out of parts from the thermostat on the basement furnace. And now," he said, turning toward Mikey, "to wind up the case."

"Then you know where Topla Pong is?" I asked.

"Exactly!" replied Dobuk. Striding across the carpet, he picked up Mikey and unscrewed his head. Reaching down inside Mikey's body, he hauled out by one wing the struggling green and purple figure of Topla Pong. The headless body of Mikey dropped to the carpet with a thump. Now I saw why his smiles and so many of his actions had been so mechanical.

"A robot!" I said.

"Exactly," repeated Dobuk. "Controlled from inside by Topla Pong, whom I will now return to interstellar justice."

"No, you won't!" shouted The Butterfly, speaking up now for the first time. "I've done nothing on this planet that the real Mikey wouldn't have done. In my proper person I have committed no crimes. I claim sanctuary on this planet in accordance with Interstellar Law; and there are no courts here in which you can bring a case for extraplanetary extradition."

Dobuk looked stunned. He turned to me in consternation.

"Is this true?" he asked. "Has he actually done no more than the real Mikey would have done?"

"I hate to say yes," I said. "But it's a fact."

Topla Pong began to laugh wickedly.

"Then—then I'm helpless," said Dobuk, his shoulders dropping. "I felt sure he would have committed at least one crime here in his proper person."

"But he has!" I shoulted. "What about Mikey, himself? He had to get rid of Mikey before he could pose as Mikey."

"True!" cried Dobuk. He turned to Topla Pong. "Where's Mikey?"

"Dissolved," retorted Topla Pong. " 'Snfle beh jkt Sngrian' as the old saying goes, or in English—'All Sngrians are natural born scientists.' I dissolved him in acid and evaporated the acid. You'll never get me on that. As I need hardly point out—no corpus delicti."

"That does it," groaned Dobuk.

"No, no, wait—" I said. "We're forgetting the one

crime he did that there's a living witness to. Right after he got here, he slugged me and stole my forty-five.''

"My word against yours," smirked Topla Pong.

"I—I'm afraid—" stammered Dobuk.

"What?" I shouted. "You don't mean you aren't going to get him on that?"

"Well—after all—" fumbled Dobuk. "There were no other witnesses—were there?"

"But you came in and found me unconscious, yourself."

"Oh, yes," said Dobuk. "But consider the business you're in. Almost anybody is liable to knock you unconscious. Perhaps it was another would-be client. Inference is not evidence, you know. Short of an out and out confession—"

"Do you mean," I demanded, "that this butterfly is going to be turned loose to build more criminal empires, to conscript more honest citizens into the ranks of the underworld, to start anew his career of blood and dope-soaked organizing?"

"Yes."

"We'll see about that!" I snapped. There was a newspaper lying on the desk. I rolled it up and slammed Topla Pong with it.

"Help!" he shouted. "Dobuk, help!"

"Jake—no!" cried Dobuk.

"Stay out of this," I snarled. "Stand back before I hate you."

"No, no, not that—" said Dobuk. "I—I'll go outside. I can't stand this."

He turned and staggered out of the room. I swatted Topla Pong again.

"Confess!" I snarled.

I gritted my teeth and steeled myself. My stomach was going queasy on me and for a minute I thought I couldn't go through with it. Then I thought of what this insect had done to Sheila and knew I could. Luckily, there was something that made it easier for me. I hate bugs.

I continued. Within a few seconds, Topla Pong broke.

"Stop it!" he yelled. "I'll confess. Get Dobuk back in

here." I went out in the hall and got Dobuk, who was shaking like a leaf.

"He broke," I said, bringing him back into the room.

"So I see," said Dobuk. "Luckily I have my first aid kit here with me. I'll fix you up, Pong. There! That was a bad break."

"It sure was. Thanks," said The Butterfly. "Naturally, I put on a complete nerve block when this human started batting me around; but this is my second best body and I'd hate to have a lot of regrowth scars. I confess."

"In that case I hereby put you under hypnotic compulsion to return to Sngr and go on trial for your interstellar crimes."

"I go," said Topla Pong, and flew out a window.

Dobuk turned to me.

"You will, of course," he said, "submit a full report of this in writing?"

"Count on me," I said. "There's just one thing, though. What was it that tipped you off to the fact that Mikey was really a robot with Topla Pong inside?"

"I'll tell you," said Dobuk. "Like every master criminal, it was the fact that he could not resist the commission of one minor crime that tripped him up. Before depriving me of my nullifier belt he spoke the words—*to coin a phrase—bye, bye, Dobuk.* He forgot that I am essentially a Plagiarism Expert; and as such I immediately recognized his words for the Interstellar Misdemeanor (non-extraditable) that they were. The original of that phrase, which could not conceivably be known to a human like Mikey, is found in A TOUCH OF WELIGIAN POISON by A. Zzanzr Lllg, protected by total Interstellar copyright, covering all known verbal and non-verbal reproductions in all languages, including thought—copyright number 82743906645382—569. It is found on spool thirty, eight hundred and forty-three syllables from the end and goes, correctly—*to coin a phrase—bye, bye, Ugluck!*"

"I get it," I said.

In Iron Years

Slightly after midday, the rain began. Jeebee wiped his glasses and turned the visor of his cap down to keep as much of the falling moisture off them as possible. Wet, they gave him a blurred, untrustworthy image of his surroundings; and although this rolling plains country with its sparse patches of timber and only an occasional devastated farmstead seemed deserted enough, nothing could be certain. In the beginning, in spite of it being March, the rain was not cold; and although it soon soaked through the blanket material of his jacket at the inside of his elbows and upper back, above the packsack, and with each step made damper and more heavy the front of his trousers above the knees, he was not uncomfortable.

But, as the afternoon wore on, the darkness of the heavy cloud cover increased, the temperature dropped, and the rain turned to sleet, whipped against the naked skin of his face as the wind strengthened from the east. Like an animal, he thought of shelter and began to cast around for it, so that when a little later he came to the pile of lumber that had once been a farmhouse, before being dynamited or bulldozed into a scrap heap, he gave up travel for the day and began searching for a gap in the rubble. He found

143

one at last, a hole that seemed to lead far enough in under the loose material to indicate a fairly waterproof overhead. He crawled inside, pushing his pack before him, braced against having stumbled on the den of some wild dog—or worse.

But no human or beast appeared to dispute his entrance, and the opening went back in further than he had guessed. He was pleased to hear the patter of the rain only distantly through what was above him, while feeling everything completely dry and dusty around him. He kept on crawling, as far in as he could until suddenly his right hand, reaching out before him, slid over an edge into emptiness.

He stopped to check, found some space above his head, and risked lighting a stub of candle. Its light shone ahead of him, down into an untouched basement garage, with walls of cinder blocks and a solid roof of collapsed house overhead.

He memorized this scene below as best he could, put the candle out to save as much of it as possible, and let himself down into the thick, dust-smelling darkness, until he felt level floor under his bootsoles. Once down, he relit the candle stub and looked around.

The place was a treasure trove. Plainly no one had set foot here since the moment in which the house had been destroyed, and nothing had been looted from the cellar's original contents.

That night he slept warm and dry with even the luxury of a kerosene lantern to light him; and when he left the place three days later through a separate, carefully tunneled hole much larger than the one by which he had entered, he was rich. He left still more riches behind him. There was more than he could carry, but it was not just a lack of charity to his fellow human beings that made him carefully cover and disguise both openings to the place he had found. It was the hard-learned lesson to cover his trail, so that no one would suspect someone else had been here and would try to track him for what he carried. Otherwise, he would not have cared about the goods he left behind, for his path led still westward to Montana, to his brother Martin's Twin Peaks ranch—eight hundred miles yet distant.

His riches, however, could not help going to his head a little. For one thing, though he realized he was taking a calculated risk, he had ridden off on the motorcycle he had found among other items in the cellar. It was true that it was a light little trail bike and worth a fortune if he could only come across some community civilized enough to trade, rather than simply kill him for it. It was also true that on it, in open country like this, he could probably outrun anyone else, including riders on horseback. But it could be heard coming from a mile away, and gas was scarce. Also, possession of the bike was as open an invitation to attack and robbery as a fat wallet flourished in a den of thieves.

Outside of the motorcycle, however, Jeebee had selected well. He was now wearing some other man's old but still solidly seamed leather jacket; his belt was tight with screwdrivers, pruning knives, and other simple hand tools, and his pockets were newly heavy with boxes of .22-long rifle shells, ammunition for the .22 bolt-action rifle he had been carrying. In addition, he had canned goods, some of which might still be eatable—you could never tell until you opened a can and smelled its contents— and wrapped around his waist above the belt was a good twenty feet of heavy, solid-linked metal chain taken from under the ruins of what had evidently been a doghouse, in the back yard behind the debris of the main building.

He had sense enough by this time not to follow any roads. So he cut off between the hills, on the same compass course westward that he had been holding to for the past two weeks, ever since he had run for his life to get away from Abbotsville. Even to think of Abbotsville now set a cold sickness crawling about in the pit of his stomach. It had taken a miracle to save him. His buck fever had held true to the last; and, at the last, when Bule Mannerly had risen up out of the weeds with the shotgun pointed at his head, he had been unable to shoot, though Bule was only seconds away from shooting him. Only the dumb luck of someone else from the village firing at Jeebee just then and scaring Bule into hitting the dirt had cleared the way to the hills.

It was not just lack of guts on his part that had kept him from firing, Jeebee reminded himself now, strongly, steering the bike along a hillside in the sunlight and the light March breeze. He, more than anyone else, should be able to remember that, like everyone else, he was the product of his own psychobiological pattern; and it was that, more than anything else, which had stopped him from shooting Bule.

Once, in a civilized world, reactions like his had signaled a survival type of pb pattern. Now, they signaled the opposite. He glanced at his reflection in the rearview mirror on the rod projecting from the left handlebar of the bike. The image of his lower face looked back at him, brutal with untrimmed beard and crafty with wrinkles dried into skin tanned by the sun and wind. But above these signs, as he tilted his head to look, the visor of his cap had shaded the skin and his forehead was still pale, the eyes behind the round glasses still blue and innocent. The upper half of his features gave him away. He had no instinctive courage—only a sense of duty—a duty to the fledgling science which had barely managed to be born before the world had fallen apart.

It was that duty that pushed him now. On his own, his spirit would have failed at the thought of the hundreds of unprotected miles between him and the safety of the Twin Peaks ranch, where he could shelter behind a brother more adapted to these times. But what he had learned and worked at drove him—the importance of this knowledge that must be saved for the future. All around the world now there would be forty, perhaps as many as sixty, men and women—psychobiological mathematicians like himself

—who would have come independently to the same conclusion as he had. For a second the symbols of his math danced in order in his mind's eye, spelling out the inarguable truth about the human race in this spring of dissolution and disaster.

Like him, the others would have come to the conclusion that the knowledge of pb patterns must be protected, taken someplace safe and hidden against the time—five hundred years, two thousand years from now—when the majority of the race would begin to change back again toward civilized patterns. Only if all those understanding pb math tried their best would there be even a chance of one of them succeeding in saving this great new tool for the next upswing of mankind. It was a knowledge that could read both the present and the future. Because of it, they who had worked with it knew how vital it was that it must not be lost. Only—the very civilized intellectual nature of their own individual patterns made them nonsurvival types in the world that had now created itself around them. It was bitter to know that they were the weakest, not the strongest, vessels to preserve what they alone knew must be preserved.

But they could try. He could try. Perhaps he could come to some terms with this time of savagery. It was ironic, after all the promises of worldwide nuclear destruction and such, that the world had actually died with a whimper, after all.

No—he corrected himself—not with a whimper. A snarl. It had begun with a universal economic breakdown, complemented by overpopulation, overcrowding, overpollution —of noise and idea as well as of waste and heat. A time of frustration, mounting to frenzy, with unemployment soaring, worldwide. Inflation soaring, worldwide. Strikes, crime, disease . . .

—All the prosaic, predictable things, but reinforcing each other, had come to a head at once. And for a reason which had never been suspected, until the math of psychobiological patterns had been created—independently, but almost simultaneously, by people like Piotr Arazavin, Noshiobi Hideki . . . and Jeeris Belany Walthar, yours truly . . .

First there had come the large breakdowns—of the international economy, then of the national economy, then of local economies. Then, following economic systems into chaos, had gone the systems of world trade, of food production and other necessary supplies. Law and order had struggled for a while and gone down in the maelstrom. Cities became battlefields of the dead left by riot and revolution. Isolated communities developed into small, primitive, self-fortified territories. And the Four Horsemen of the Apocalypse were abroad once more.

It was a time of bloodletting, of a paring down of the population to those with the pb patterns for survival under fang-and-claw conditions. A new medievalism was upon the globe. The iron years had come again; and those who were best fitted to exist were those to whom ethics, conscience, and anything else beyond the pure pragmatism of physical power were excess baggage.

And so it would continue, the pb mathematics calculated, until a new, young order could emerge once more, binding the little village-fortresses into alliances, the alliances into kingdoms, and the kingdoms into sovereign nations which could begin once more to treat with one another in systems. Five hundred years, two thousand years—however long that would take.

. . . And, meanwhile, a small anachronism of the time now dead, a weak individual of the soft centuries, struggled to cross the newly lawless country, carrying a precious child of the mind to where it might sleep in safety for as many centuries as necessary until reason and civilization should be born again—

Jeebee caught himself up at the brink of a bath in self-pity. Not that he was particularly ashamed of self-pity—or, at least, he did not think he was particularly ashamed of it. But emotional navel-contemplating of any kind withdrew his attention from his surroundings; and that could be dangerous. And, in fact, no sooner had he jerked himself out of his mood than his nostrils caught a faint but oily scent on the breeze.

In a moment he had killed the motor of the bike, was off it, and had dragged it with him into the cover of some nearby willow saplings. He lay there, making as little noise as possible and trying to identify what he had just smelled.

The fact that he could not identify it immediately did not make it less alarming. Any unusual phenomena—noise, odor, or other—were potential warnings of the presence of other humans. And if there were other humans around, Jeebee wanted to look them over at leisure before he gave them a chance to look at him.

In this case the scent was unidentifiable, but, he could swear, not totally unfamiliar. Somewhere he had encountered it before. After lying some minutes hidden in the willows with ears and eyes straining for additional information, Jeebee cautiously got to his feet and, pushing the bike without starting the motor, began to try to track down the wind-born odor to its source.

It was some little distance over two rises of land before the smell got noticeably stronger. But the moment came when, with the bike ten feet back, and lying on his stomach, he looked down a long slope at a milling mass of grey and black bodies. It was a large flock of Targhee sheep— the elusive memory of the smell of a sheep barn at a state fair twelve years before snapped back into his mind. With the flock below were three boys, riding bareback on small hairy ponies. No dogs were in view.

The thought of dogs sent a twinge of alarm along the nerves of Jeebee. He was about to crawl back to his bike and start moving away when a ram burst suddenly from the flock, with a sheep dog close behind it, a small brown-and-white collie breed that had been hidden by the milling dark backs and white faces about it. The sheep was headed directly up the slope where Jeebee lay hidden.

He lay holding his breath until the dog, nipping at the heels of the ram, turned it back into the mass of the flock. He breathed out in relief; but at that moment the dog, having seen the ram safely back among the other sheep, spun about and faced up in Jeebee's direction, nose testing the wind.

The wind was from dog to Jeebee. There was no way the animal could smell him, he told himself; and yet the canine nose continued to test the air. After a second the dog began to bark, looking straight in the direction of where Jeebee lay hidden.

"What's it, Snappy?" cried one of the boys on horseback. He wheeled his mount around and cantered toward the dog, up the pitch of the slope.

Jeebee panicked. On hands and knees he scrambled backward, hearing a sudden high-pitched whoop from below as he became visible on the skyline, followed by the abrupt pounding of horses' hooves in a gallop.

"Get him—*get'm!*" sang a voice. A rifle cracked. Knowing he was now fully in view, Jeebee leaped frantically on the trail bike and kicked down on its starter. Mercifully, it started immediately, and he roared off without looking backward, paying no attention to the direction of his going except that it was away from those behind him and along a route as free of bumps and obstacles as he could find.

The rifle cracked again. He heard several voices now, yelping with excitement and the pleasure of the chase. There was a whistling near his head as a bullet passed close. The little trail bike was slow to build up speed, and the sound of its motor washed out the galloping beat of the horses' hooves behind him. But he was headed downslope, and slowly the bounding, oscillating needle of the speedometer was picking up space above the zero miles-per-hour pin.

The rifle sounded again, somewhat further behind him;

and this time he heard no whistle of a passing slug. The shots had been infrequent enough to indicate that only one of the boys was armed; and the rifle used was probably a single shot, needing to be reloaded after firing—not an easy thing to do on the back of a galloping horse with no saddle leather or stirrups to cling to. He risked a glance over his shoulder.

The three had already given up the chase. He saw them on the crest of a rise behind him, sitting their horses, watching. They had given up almost too easily, he thought—and then he remembered the sheep. They would not want to go too far from the flock for which they were responsible.

He continued on, throttling back only a little on his speed. Now that they had seen him, he was anxious to get as far out of their area as possible, before they should pass the word to more adult riders on better horses and armed with better weapons. But he did begin, instinctively, to pay a little more attention to the dangers of rocks and holes in his way.

There was a new, gnawing uneasiness inside him. Dogs meant trouble for him—as one had just demonstrated. Other humans he could watch for and slip by unseen, but dogs had noses and ears to sense him in darkness or behind cover. And sheepherders meant dogs—lots of them. He had never expected to run into sheep this far east. According to his calculations—he had lost his only map some days ago—he should be no further west than barely into Nebraska or the Dakotas, by now.

A sudden, desperate loneliness swept over him. He was an outcast, and there was no one and no hope of anyone to stand by him. If he had even one companion to make this long hazardous journey with him, there might be a real chance of his reaching the Twin Peaks. As it was, what he feared most deeply was that in one of these moments of despair he would simply give up, would stop and turn, to wait to be shot down by the armed riders following him; or he would walk nakedly into some camp or town to be killed and robbed—just to get it all over with.

Now he fought the feeling of loneliness, the despair, forcing himself to think constructively. What was the best thing for him to do under the circumstances? He would be safer apart from the trail bike, but without it he would not cover ground anywhere near so swiftly. With luck, using the bike, he could be out of this sheep area in a day or so. He had two five-gallon containers of gas strapped behind his saddle on the bike; that much fuel gave him a range of nearly four hundred miles, even allowing for the roughest going. Four hundred miles—it was like the thought of gold to a miser. The bike was too valuable to abandon. Yes, it would be better to push through and simply hope to outrun trouble, as he just had, if he encountered any more of it.

He could, of course, hide out somewhere during the days and travel nights only; but travel at night was more dangerous. Even with a good moon he would have trouble spotting all the rocks and potholes in the path of the bike. No, the best plan was to make as much time as he could while the day lasted. When night came, he would decide then whether to ride on . . .

Thinking this, he topped the small rise he had been climbing and looked down at a river, a good two hundred yards across, flowing swiftly from south to north across his direct path west.

Jeebee stared at the river in dismay. Then, carefully, he rode down the slope before him until he halted the bike at the very edge of the swiftly flowing water.

It was a stream clearly swollen by the spring runoff. It was dangerously full of floating debris and swift of current. He got off the bike and squatted to dip a hand in its waters. They numbed his fingers with a temperature like that of freshly melted snow. He got to his feet and remounted the bike, shaking his head. Calm water, warm water, he could have risked swimming, pushing the bike and his other possessions ahead of him on a makeshift raft. But not a river like this.

He would have to go up or downstream until he could find some bridge on which to cross it. Which way? He looked to right and to left. To right was downstream; and downstream, traditionally, led to civilization—which in this case meant habitation and possible enemies. He turned the bike upstream and rode off.

Luckily, the land alongside the river here was flat and open. He made good time, cutting across sections where the river looped back on itself and saving as much time as possible. Almost without warning he came around a bend and upon a bridge, straight and high above the grey, swift waters.

It was a railroad bridge.

For a second time he felt dismay; a purely conditioned reflex out of a civilized time when it was dangerous to try to cross a railway bridge for fear of being caught halfway over by traffic on the rails. Then that outworn feeling passed, and his heart and hopes leaped up together. For his purposes a railway bridge was the best thing he could have encountered.

There would be no traffic on these rails. And for something like the light trail bike he rode, the right-of-way beside the track should be almost as good as a superhighway. He rode the bike up the embankment, stopped to lift it onto the ties between the rails, and remounted. A brief bumpy ride took him safely over the river that moments before had been an uncrossable barrier.

On the far side of the river, as he had expected, there was plenty of room beyond the ends of the ties, on either side, for him to ride the bike. He lifted the machine off the ties to the gravel and took up his journey. The embankment top was pitted at intervals where rain had washed some of the top surfacing down the slope and away, but for the most part it was like traveling a well-kept dirt road, and he made steady time with the throttle nearly wide open.

There was another advantage to traveling along the railroad right-of-way that he had not thought of until he found himself doing it. This was that the embankment lifted him above the surrounding country and he could keep a good watch ahead for possible dangers. He was now past the rolling landscape he had been passing through earlier. Now, on either side of the track, the land was flat to the horizon, except in the far distance ahead, where the track curved out of sight among some low hills. And nowhere in view were there any sheep, or in fact any sign of man or beast.

For a rare moment he relaxed and let himself hope. Anywhere west of the Mississippi, across the prairie country, a railroad could run for miles without intersecting any human habitation. With luck, he could be out of this sheep country before he knew it. Farther west, Martin had written in the last letters Jeebee had gotten from his brother, the isolated ranchers of the cattle country had been less affected than most by the breakdown of the machinery of civilization, and law and order, after a fashion, still existed. He could trade off the loot he had picked up from the cellar in comparative safety for the things he needed.

First of these was a more effective rifle than the .22. The .22 was a good little gun, but it lacked punch. Its slug was too light to have the sort of impact that would stop a charging man, or large beast. And there were still wolf, bear, and even an occasional mountain lion in the territory to which he was headed—to say nothing of wild range cattle, which could be dangerous enough.

Moreover, with a heavier gun he could bring down such cattle, or even deer or mountain sheep—if he was lucky enough to stumble across them—to supplement whatever other food supplies he was carrying. Which brought him to his second greatest need, the proper type of food supplies. Canned goods were very convenient, but they were heavy and impractical to carry by packsack. What he really needed was some freeze-dried meat. Or, failing that, some powdered soups, plain flour, dried beans, or such, and possibly bacon.

He had a packsack full of the best of that sort of supplies when he had finally tried to make his escape alive from Abbotsville. In fact, when he had packed it he had not really believed that the locals would not just let him go, that they really intended to kill him. In spite of the previous three months of near-isolation in the community, he had still felt that after five years of living there, he was one of them.

But of course, he had never been one of them. What had led him to think he knew them was their casual politeness in the supermarket or the post office, plus the real friendship he had had with his housekeeper, Ardyce Prine. Mrs. Prine had lived there all her life and, in her sixties, was in a position of belonging to the local authoritative generation. But when the riots became too dangerous for him to risk traveling into Detroit to the think-tank at the university, the local Abbotsville folks must have begun to consider that they were stuck with him. And there was no real place for him in their lives, particularly as those lives began to shift toward an inward-looking economy, with local produce and meat being traded for locally made shoes and clothing. Jeebee produced nothing they needed. While Ardyce was still his housekeeper, they tolerated him; but the day came when she did not—only a short stiff note was delivered by her grandson, saying that she could no longer work for him.

After that, he had felt the invisible enmity of his neighbors beginning to hem him in. When he did try to leave and head west to Twin Peaks, he found they had been lying in wait with guns for him for some time. At the moment of his leaving he had not been able to understand why. But he knew now. If he had tried to leave naked, they might have let him go. But even the clothes he wore they regarded as Abbotsville property with which he was running off, like a thief in the night. Bule Mannerly, the druggist, had risen like a demon out of the darkness of the hillside, shotgun in hand, to bar his going—and only that lucky misshot from somewhere in the surrounding darkness had let Jeebee get away.

But then, once away, he had foolishly gone through the supplies he carried like a spendthrift, never dreaming that it would be as difficult as it turned out to be to replace them with anything eatable at all, let alone more of their special and expensive kind.

But he had learned his lesson, now, three months later. At least half of him had become bearded and wise and animal-wary—ears pricked, eyes moving all the time, nose sensitive to sound, sight, or smell that might mean danger . . .

He fell to dreaming of the things he would want to trade for as soon as he found someplace where it was safe to do so. In addition to a heavier rifle, he badly needed a spare pair of boots. The ones he wore would not last him all the way to Montana, if the bike broke down or he had to abandon or trade it off for any reason. Also, a revolver and ammunition for it would be invaluable—but of course to dream of a handgun like that was like dreaming of a slice of heaven. Weapons were the last thing anyone was likely to trade off, these days.

He became so involved in his own thoughts that he found himself entering the low line of further hills before he was really aware of it. The railroad track curved off between two heavy, grassy shoulders of land and disappeared in the shadow of a clump of cottonwood trees that lay at the far end of their curve. He followed the tracks around, chugged into the shadow of the cottonwoods and out the other side—to find himself in a small valley, looking down at a railroad station, some sheep-loading pens and a cluster of buildings, all less than half a mile away.

As it had when he had smelled the sheep, reflex led him to kill the motor of the bike and seek the ground beside the track with it and himself alike, all in one unthinking motion. He lay where he was on the rough stones of the track ballast, staring through a screen of tall, dry grass at the buildings.

Even as he lay there, he knew his hitting the ground like this had almost certainly been a futile effort. If there was anyone in the little community ahead, they must have heard the motor of his trail bike even before it came into view from under the trees. He continued to lie there; but there was no sign of movement in or around the small village, or whatever he was observing, although the tin chimneys on several of the buildings were sending up thin banners of grey smoke against the blue sky.

Overall, what he was observing, ahead and below, looked like a sheep-loading station that had grown into a semicommunity. There were two buildings down there that might be stores, but the majority of the structures he saw—frame buildings sided with grey unpainted boards—could be anything from home to warehouse.

He rolled half over on his side and twisted his body about to get at his packsack and take out a pair of binoculars. They were actually toy binoculars, a pair he had brought for Martin's youngest son, a five-year-old. They were all he had been able to get his hands on before leaving Abbotsville, and they were something that in ordinary times he would not have bothered to put in his pack. But they did magnify several times, although the material of their lenses was hardly of a higher grade than window glass.

He put the binoculars to his eyes and squinted at the buildings through the eyepieces. This time, after a long and painful survey, he did discover one dog, apparently asleep beside the three wooden steps leading up to the one long, windowed building he had guessed might be a store. He stared at the dog for a long time, but it did not move.

Jeebee held the glasses to his eyes until they began to water. Then he lowered the glasses, took his weight off his elbows, which had been badly punished, even through the leather jacket, by the gravel and stones beneath him, and tried to conjecture what he had stumbled upon.

It was, of course, possible—the wild wishful supposition came sliding into his head unbidden—that he had stumbled across some community where disease or some other reason had destroyed the population—including the dogs. In which case, all he had to do was step down there and help himself to whatever property might be lying around.

The ridiculousness of such an impossible streak of good fortune coming his way was a proper antidote to the fanciful notion itself. But certainly the buildings seemed, if not deserted, almost too quiet to be true. Of course, it was the middle of the day; and if this was stockmen's country, most of the people in it could be out tending or guarding sheep . . .

Even that was a far-fetched notion. No matter how many might go out, no one in these days would leave this many buildings, with whatever they might contain, unprotected from possible looters. No, there must be people below—they were simply inside the buildings and out of sight.

At once the answer burst on Jeebee's mind, and he glanced at his watch. Of course. It was noon. Anyone around below and ahead of him would be eating a midday meal.

He lay and waited. Within about twenty minutes the door outside which the dog lay opened, and the first of several figures came out. With the first one the dog was on his feet, in what—as far as Jeebee could tell from this distance—was a friendly greeting. The dog stayed alert, and one by one, half a dozen people emerged, to scatter out and disappear within other buildings. All seemed to be male and adult. Shortly after the last one had disappeared, the door opened again and a figure in skirts emerged, threw something to the dog, and went back inside. The dog lay down to chew on whatever it had been given.

Jeebee lay where he was, thinking. He could hold his position until night and then push the bike around the station and continue on down the track beyond at some safe distance. While he was still thinking this, the whanging of a one-cylinder engine burst distantly to life, and a moment later a motorized railcar rolled into sight on the track beyond the buildings. It continued up the track, away from him and the station until it was lost to sound and sight.

Jeebee chilled where he lay, looking after it. A car like that could get its speed up to sixty miles an hour along good railway track. It could run down his motorcycle with no trouble at all. He had just been fortunate that it had not headed toward him, instead of in the other direction. Of course, he could have gotten off the embankment and into the ditch, among the tall weeds before he could have been spotted. But all the same . . .

Suddenly, he had made up his mind. There had to be an end to guessing, sometime. Somewhere he would have to take a chance on trying to trade, and this place looked as good as any. He got back on the trail bike and kicked its motor to life.

Openly and noisily he rode down the track and in among the buildings.

There was a clamor of barking as he entered. A near dozen dogs of diverse breeds, but all of sheep dog type, gathered around him as he rode the bike directly to the steps where he had seen the original dog and where all the people had emerged. The original dog was one of those now following him clamorously. Like the others, it crowded close but made no serious attempt to bite, which was—he thought—a good sign as far as the attitudes toward strangers of those owning the dogs were concerned.

He stopped the bike, got off, and with the .22 in hand,

packsack on back, he climbed the three steps to the door. He knocked. There was no answer.

After a second he knocked again; and when there was still no answer, put his hand on the knob. It turned easily and the door opened. He went in, leaving the yelping of the station dog pack behind him. Their noise did not stop once he had disappeared from their view, but it was muted by the walls and windows of the building.

Jeebee looked around himself at the room into which he had stepped. It was fair-sized, with six round tables and four chairs apiece that all dated back to before the breakdown. Along one wall was a short, high bar, but with nothing but some glasses upside down on the shelves behind it. Beyond the bar was a further door, closed, which Jeebee assumed to lead deeper into the building. Stacked on one end of the bar were some dishes, cups, and silverware looking as if they had just been left behind by diners, the figures Jeebee had seen coming out of this building a small while since as he lay and watched from the embankment.

The clamor of the dogs outside suddenly increased in volume, then unaccountably faded away into whimpers and silence. Jeebee moved swiftly to the window and looked out.

Coming toward the steps leading to the building's entrance was a strange female figure. A woman who must have been as large as Jeebee himself, but dressed in a muffling nineteenth-century dress of rusty black cloth that fell to the tops of her heavy boots below and ended in a literal poke bonnet at the top. She walked with long and heavy strides, one hand holding a short chain leash. But the leash seemed unnecessary. It dropped slackly from its connection with the leather collar of the large dog pacing beside her, as if it was trained to heel.

It was this dog which had caused the rest of the pack to fall silent. It was no sheep dog, but a German shepherd half again as large as any of the other canines around it, its coat rough with the thick hair of a dog which had spent most of its winter out in the weather. Its collar was heavy and studded with bright metallic points, which, as it came closer, Jeebee made out to be sharp-pointed spikes.

It paid no attention to the other dogs at all. It ignored them as if they did not exist, walking by the side of the big woman with no signal of body or tail to show anything other than that it was on some purposeful errand. The other dogs had drawn back from it, had sat down or lain down, and were now silent, licking their jaws with wet uneasy tongues. Woman and dog came up the steps, opened the door and stepped into the room where Jeebee waited. As the woman closed the door behind her, the barking outside made a halfhearted attempt to start again, then dwindled into silence.

"Heard you on your way in here," said the woman to Jeebee in a hoarse deep voice like the voice of a very old person. "I just stepped out to get my watchdog, here."

Jeebee felt the metal of the trigger guard of the .22 slippery in his right hand. The woman, he saw now that she was close, was wearing a black leather belt tight around her waist, with a small holster and the butt of what looked like a short-barreled revolver sticking out of the holster. He did not doubt that she could use it. He did not doubt that the dog would attack if she gave it the order. And, flooding all through him, was the old doubt that he could lift the .22 and fire, even to defend his own life.

"Sit," said the woman to the huge dog. "Guard."

The German shepherd sat down before the outer door. His black nose pointed and twitched in Jeebee's direction for a second, but that was all the reaction he showed. The woman lifted her head, looking directly at Jeebee. Her face was tanned, masculine-looking, with heavy bones and thin lips. Deep parentheses of lines cut their curves from nose to chin on each side of her mouth. She must be, Jeebee thought, at least fifty.

"All right," said the woman. "What brings you to town?"

"I came in to trade some things," said Jeebee.

His own voice sounded strange in his ears, like the creaky tones of an old-fashioned phonograph record where most of the low range had been lost in recording.

"What you got?"

"Different things," said Jeebee. "How about you? Have you or somebody else here got shoes, food, and maybe some other things you can trade me?"

His voice was sounding more normal now. He had pulled his cap low over his eyes before he had come into town; and hopefully, in this interior dimness, lit only by the windows to his right, she could not see the pale innocence of his eyes and forehead.

"I can trade you what you want—prob'ly," the woman said. "Come on. —You, too."

The last words were addressed to the dog. It rose silently to four feet and padded after them. She led Jeebee to the further door and through it into another room that looked as if it might once have been a poor excuse for a hotel lobby. A corridor led off from a far wall, and doors could be glimpsed on either side along it.

The lobby room was equipped with what had probably been a clerk's counter. This, plus half a dozen more of the round tables, were piled with what at first glimpse appeared to be every kind of junk imaginable, from old tire casings to metal coffeepots that showed the dints and marks of long use. A second look showed Jeebee a rough order to things in the room. Clothing filled two of the tables, and all of the cooking utensils were heaped with the coffeepots on another.

"Guard," said the woman to the dog again, and once more it took a seated position before the closed door by which they had all just entered.

"Let's see what you got," said the woman. She motioned to an end of the clerk's counter that was clear.

Jeebee unbuckled his recently acquired leather jacket—the dog's nose tested the air again—and began unloading his belt of the screwdrivers, chisels, files, and other small hand tools he had brought. When he was done, he unwrapped the metal chain from his waist and laid it on the wooden surface of the counter where it chinked heavily.

"Maybe you can use this," said Jeebee, nodding at the dog as casually as possible.

"Maybe," said the woman, with a perfect flatness of voice. "But he don't need much holding. He works to orders."

"Sheep dog?" asked Jeebee, as she began to examine the tools.

She looked up squarely into his face.

"You know better than that," she said. "He's no stock dog. He's a killer." She stared at him for a second. "Or, do you know? What are you—cattleman?"

"Not me," said Jeebee. "My brother is. I'm on my way to his place, now."

"Where?" she asked, bluntly.

"West," he said. "You probably wouldn't know him." He met her eyes. It was a time to claim as much as he could. "But he's got a good-sized ranch, he's out there—and he's waiting for me to show up."

The last, lying part came out with what Jeebee felt sounded like conviction. Perhaps a little of the truth preceding it had carried over. The woman, however, looked at him without any change of expression whatsoever, then bent to her examination of the hand tools again.

"What made you think I was a cattleman?" Jeebee asked. Her silence was unnerving. Something in him wanted to keep her talking, as if, so long as she continued to speak, nothing much could go wrong.

"Cattleman's jacket," she said, not looking up.

"Ja—" he stopped himself. Of course, she was talking about the leather jacket he was wearing. He had not realized that there would be any perceptible difference in

clothing between sheep and cattlemen. Didn't sheepmen
wear leather jackets, too? Evidently not—or at least, not in
the same style.

"This is sheep country," the woman said, still not
looking up. Jeebee felt the statement like a gun hanging in
the air, aimed at him and ready to go off at any minute.

"That so?" he said.

"Yes, that's so," she answered. "No cattlemen left here,
now. *That* was a cattle dog." She jerked her thumb at the
guard dog, swept the tools and the chain together into a
pile before her as if she already owned them. "All right,
what you want?"

"A pair of good boots," he said. "Some bacon, beans,
or flour. A handgun—a revolver."

She looked up at him on the last words.

"Revolver," she said with contempt. She shoved the
pile of tools and chain toward him. "You better move
on."

"All right," he said. "Didn't hurt to ask, did it?"

"Revolver!" she said again, deep in her throat, as if she
was getting ready to spit. "I'll give you ten pounds of
parched corn and five pounds of mutton fat. And you can
look for a pair of boots on the table over there. That's it."

"Now, wait . . ." he said. The miles he had come since
Abbotsville had not left him completely uneducated to the
times he now lived in. "Don't talk like that. You know—I
know—those tools there are worth a lot more than that.
You can't get metal stuff like that any more. You want to
cheat me some, that's all right. But let's talk a little more
sense."

"No talk," she said. She came around the counter and
faced him. Jeebee could feel her gaze searching in under
the shadow of his cap's visor to see his weakness and his
vulnerability. "Who else you going to trade with?"

She stared at him. Suddenly the great wave of loneliness, of weariness, washed through Jeebee again. The
thinking front of his mind recognized that her words were

only the first step in a bargaining. Now it was time for him to counteroffer, to sneer at what she had, to rave and protest—but he could not. Emotionally he was too isolated, too empty inside. Silently he began to sweep the chain and the hand tools into a pile and return them to his belt.

"What you doing?" yelled the woman, suddenly.

He stopped and looked at her.

"It's all right," he said. "I'll take them someplace else."

Even as he said the words, he wondered if she would call the dog and whether he would, indeed, make it out of this station alive.

"Someplace else?" she snarled. "Didn't I just say there isn't anyplace else anywhere near? What's wrong with you?—You never traded before?"

He stopped putting the tools back in his belt and looked at her.

"Look!" she said, reaching under the counter. "You wanted to trade for a revolver. Look at it!"

He reached out and picked up the nickel-plated short-muzzled weapon she had dumped before him. It was speckled with rust, and when he pulled the hammer back, there was a thick accumulation of dirt to be seen on its lower part. Even at its best, it had been somebody's cheap Saturday night special, worth fifteen or twenty dollars. Jeebee did not really know guns, but it was plain what he was being offered.

His head cleared, suddenly. If she really wanted to trade, there was hope after all.

"No," he said, shoving the cheap and dirty revolver back at her. "Let's skip the nonsense. I'll give you all of this for a rifle. A deer rifle—something about .30 caliber, and ammunition. Skip the food, the boots and the rest."

"Throw in that motorcycle," she said.

He laughed. And he was as shocked to hear himself as if he had heard a corpse laugh.

"You know better than that," he said. He waved his hand at the pile on the counter. "All right, you can make new hand tools out of a leaf from old auto springs—if you want to sweat like hell. But there's one thing you can't make, and that's chain like that. That chain's worth a lot. Particularly to somebody like you with stuff to protect. And if this is sheep country, you're not short of guns. Show me a .30-06 and half a dozen boxes of shells for it."

"Two boxes!" she spat.

"Two boxes and five sticks of dynamite." Jeebee's head was whirling with the success of his bargaining.

"I got no dynamite. Only damn fools keep that stuff around."

"Six boxes, then."

"Three."

"Five," he said.

"Three." She straightened up behind the counter. "That's it. Shall I get the rifle?"

"Get it," he said.

She turned and went down the corridor to the second door on the left. There was the grating sound of a key in a lock, and she went inside. A moment later she reemerged, relocked the door, and brought him a rifle with two boxes of shells, all of which she laid on the counter.

Jeebee picked up the gun eagerly and went through the motions of examining it. The truth of the matter was that he was not even sure if what he was holding was a .30-06. But he had lived with the .22 long enough to know where to look for signs of wear and dirt in a rifle. What he had seemed clean, recently oiled and in good shape.

"You look that over, mister," said the woman. "I got another one you might like better, but it's not here. I'll go get it."

She turned and went toward the door.

"Guard!" she said to the dog, and it came to all four feet, its eyes fixed on Jeebee. She passed through the door, closing it behind her.

Jeebee stood motionless, listening until he heard the distant sound of the outside door slamming re-echo through the building. Then, moving slowly so as not to trigger off any reflex in the dog, he slid his hand to one of the boxes of cartridges the woman had brought, opened it with the fingers of one hand and extracted two of the shells. He laid one on the counter and slowly fed the other into the clip slot of the rifle. He hesitated, but the dog had not moved. With one swift move, he jacked the round into firing position . . .

—Or tried to. The firing chamber would not close. Manually, he pulled back its cover and swore silently. The woman had outthought him, even in this. The shells she had brought him were of the wrong caliber for this particular rifle. The shell he had just put in was too big to more than barely nose itself into firing position.

Slowly, he took the shell out and laid the gun down on the counter. The proper size ammunition, of course, would be in that room down the corridor, but his chances of getting there . . .

On the other hand, he might as well try. He took a step away from the counter toward the corridor.

Immediately the dog moved. It took one step forward toward him. He stared at it. It stood like a statue, its tail unmoving, no sound or sign of anger showing in it, but neither any sign of a relaxation of its watchfulness. It was the picture of a professional on duty. Of course, he thought, of course it would never let him reach the door of the room with the guns, let alone smash the door lock and break in. He stared at the dog. It must weigh close to a hundred and fifty pounds, and it was a flesh-and-blood engine of destruction. Some years back he had seen video film of such dogs being trained—

The distant sound of voices, barely above the range of audibility, attracted his attention. They were coming from outside the building.

He took a step toward the windows. This moved him

also toward the dog, and at this first step the animal did not move. But when he stepped again, the dog moved toward him. It did not growl or threaten, but in its furry skull its eyes shone like bits of china, opaque and without feeling.

But his movement had brought him far enough out in the room so that he could look at an angle through the windows and glimpse the area in front of the building where the three steps stood to the entrance door. The woman stood there, now surrounded by five men, all with rifles or shotguns. As he stood, straining his ears in the hot, silent room, the sense of their words came faintly to him through the intervening glass and distance.

". . . Where y'been?" The woman was raging. "He was ready to walk out on me. I want two of you to go around back—"

"Now, you wait," one of the men interrupted her. "He's got that little rifle. No one's getting no .22 through him just because you want his bike."

"Did I say I wanted it for myself?" demanded the woman. "The whole station can use it. Isn't it worth that?"

"Not getting shot for, it ain't," said the man who had spoken. "Sic your dog on him."

"And get the dog shot!" shouted the woman, hoarsely, deeply.

"Why not?" said one of the other men. "It's no damn good, that dog. Killed four good sheep dogs already, and nobody dare go close to it. For that matter, it don't do what you want, so easy. You should have shot it yourself, back when we pulled down Callahan's place."

"That's a valuable dog! Like this's a valuable machine!" The woman waved at the motorcycle. "You got to take some risks to make a profit."

"You go in and send him out here!" said one of the men, stubbornly. "You send him out not suspecting anything and give us a chance to shoot him with some safe."

"If'n he comes out," said the woman. "He's going to want to come out traded, with a loaded carbine instead of that .22. You want to face that, damn you? You going to argy with me? I done my share of facing him. Now it's up to you all—"

The argument went on. The loneliness and emptiness crested inside Jeebee. He sank down into a sitting position on the boards of the floor, dropping the .22 across his knees and covering his face with his hands. Let them come. Let it be over . . .

But he sat there as the seconds ticked away, and he found that he was not quite ready to die yet. He lifted his head and saw the muzzle of the dog staring eye-to-eye with him—not six inches between their faces.

For a moment the dog stood there, then it extended its neck, and sniffed at him. Its black nose began to move over his upper body, sniff by sniff exploring the jacket; and a sudden wild hope stirred in Jeebee. Casually, he closed his hands on the rifle still in his lap and with his left hand tilted its muzzle toward the head of the dog above it as his left hand felt for the trigger. At this close range, even a small slug like this right through the brain of the dog . . .

His finger found the trigger and trembled there. The dog paid no attention. His nose was pushed in the unbuttoned opening at the top of the jacket, sniffing. Abruptly he withdrew his head and looked squarely into Jeebee's eyes.

In that moment Jeebee knew that he could not do it. Not like this. He could not even kill this dog. His buck fever was back on him . . . and what did it matter? Even if he killed the animal, the men outside would kill him eventually. And what kind of a fool guard dog was it, that would let him put a gun directly to its head and pull the trigger?

"Get away!" he snarled at it, slamming it with his fist on the side of the head.

The head rocked away from him with the blow. But it turned back; the china eyes looked undecipherably into his;

and the head dropped, dropped . . . until a rough red tongue rasped on the back of the hand with which he had struck.

He stared at the door. Then, almost before he had time to think, habit and instinct—his whole out-of-date pattern —moved him unthinkingly. He reached out and gently soothed the thick fur of the bowed neck.

"Sorry, boy. Sorry . . ." he whispered.

The big dog leaned its weight against him, almost tumbling him over backward. But even now it did not wag its tail in ordinary canine fashion. The tail moved horizontally, tentatively and slightly, and then went back to being still. The great jaws caught Jeebee's stroking hand by the wrist and chewed gently and lovingly upon it. The eyes looked directly into Jeebee's again; and now they were no longer opaque china, but glass windows opening on long twin tunnels down to where a savage single-purpose fire burned.

Like the waters from a bursting dam, the offering of affection from the animal exploded into Jeebee's arid soul. Like water to a parched throat, it was almost painful in its first touch—and then Jeebee found himself with both arms around the neck of the big dog, hugging the beast to him.

But, even as he blossomed interiorly, Jeebee's mind began its working. It was the jacket, of course, his mind told him. The jacket, and the dog alike, must have come from the ruined house where he had found the chain and taken shelter that night. The jacket must still smell of the cattleman who had owned the dog originally, and several days of wearing the leather garment had mingled its original owner's scent with Jeebee's until they were one scent only. Also, above all, the jacket and Jeebee both would not smell of sheep and sheep handling, of which all this station, its people and buildings, must reek to the dog's sensitive nose.

Nonetheless, what had happened was a miracle. He could not get over that. He almost cried and laughed at once, sitting on the floor with his arms around the dog, dodging the wet tongue searching for his face. He should have remembered, he told himself, that back when the years had been of iron there had been miracles as well. And both had come to life again.

That thought reminded him of the danger in which he still stood. He scrambled to his feet and ran to the locked door of the room the woman had entered, the dog close at his heels. A blow of the rifle butt of the .22 broke the cheap lock of the door handle, and the door itself swung open to show him a rack of rifles and shotguns—a hanging row of handguns.

He grabbed a revolver and the one rifle he recognized, a Weatherby Magnum 300, and found boxes of ammunition for both weapons among the many other such boxes filling a shelf along the far side of the small room. He loaded the Weatherby and the revolver and shoved the revolver into his belt, boxes of the two kinds of shells into his pockets. Then, with the big dog following, he ran out again into the corridor, toward its far end.

A little farther on, the corridor turned left at a ninety-degree angle and cut across the width of the building to a dead end, pierced by a window shielded by a glass curtain. Jeebee looked out the window and saw two men, with three of the station dogs, standing and waiting, watching.

Hidden behind the curtain, Jeebee smashed the glass of the window with the muzzle of the .22 and fired it steadily out of the broken window into the air until it was empty. Then he threw up the window and jumped out.

The two men outside, unhurt, were running away. They disappeared from sight around the far end of the building, the three dogs at their heels. Jeebee looked about, saw the loom of the hills over the roofs to his right, and ran that way between two buildings.

He loped between the buildings, suddenly remembering that half of his possessions were back on the bike and the bike was lost forever. A tingle of fear tried to be born in him, but was drowned in the adrenalin of the moment. This was no time to think of anything but getting away. He dodged from one alley between a pair of buildings to another and broke out at last beyond a final pair of the structures to see his way clear to the hills, with only a long slope of waist-high stunted-looking corn before him. Just emerging from the cornfield and headed toward the station, only fifty feet from him, was a man with a shotgun and a pair of dogs trotting ahead of him.

The man halted at the sight of Jeebee and lifted his shotgun uncertainly. The guard dog went past Jeebee in a silent rush toward the two smaller dogs. One of the two spun and bolted. The second stood its ground a second too long and went down with a howl that turned into a choked-off death yelp as the guard dog's jaws closed on its neck.

The man's shotgun, which had been lifting to aim at Jeebee, swung instead to point at the guard dog.

Jeebee dropped the .22 and jerked up the Weatherby. This time, without thinking, he fired to kill.

A few minutes later, hidden among the corn, he turned to look down through the stalks at the station. A number of figures milled around down there between the buildings and the edge of the planted field, but none of them were trying to follow.

He turned and headed away between two of the hills, keeping the corn as cover between himself and the station. He had lost the .22 in that last moment when he had shot the man coming out of the cornfield; half of his goods and bike were abandoned behind him. But the big dog pressed close against his leg as they both moved on, and Montana was a certain destination now. He was no longer alone. The world as it was, and he as he had become, had moved toward each other finally.

A strengthened vessel carried knowledge westward.

The Monster and the Maiden

That summer more activity took place upon the shores of the loch and more boats appeared on its waters than at any time in memory. Among them was even one of the sort of boats that went underwater. It moved around in the loch slowly, diving quite deep at times. From the boats, swimmers with various gear about them descended on lines—but not so deep—swam around blindly for a while, and then returned to the surface.

Brought word of all this in her cave, First Mother worried and speculated on disaster. First Uncle, though equally concerned, was less fearful. He pointed out that the Family had survived here for thousands of years; and that it could not all end in a single year—or a single day.

Indeed, the warm months of summer passed one by one with no real disturbance to their way of life.

Suddenly fall came. One night, the first snow filled the air briefly above the loch. The Youngest danced on the surface in the darkness, sticking out her tongue to taste the cold flakes. Then the snow ceased, the sky cleared for an hour, and the banks could be seen gleaming white under a high and watery moon. But the clouds covered the moon again; and because of the relative warmth of the loch water

173

nearby, in the morning, when the sun rose, the shores were once more green.

With dawn, boats began coming and going on the loch again and the Family went deep, out of sight. In spite of this precaution, trouble struck from one of these craft shortly before noon. First Uncle was warming the eggs on the loch bottom in the hatchhole, a neatly cleaned shallow depression scooped out by Second Mother, near Glen Urquhart, when something heavy and round descended on a long line, landing just outside the hole and raising an almost-invisible puff of silt in the blackness of the deep, icy water. The line tightened and began to drag the heavy thing about.

First Uncle had his huge length coiled about the clutch of eggs, making a dome of his body and enclosing them between the smooth skin of his underside and the cleaned lakebed. Fresh, hot blood pulsed to the undersurface of his smooth skin, keeping the water warm in the enclosed area. He dared not leave the clutch to chill in the cold loch, so he sent a furious signal for Second Mother, who, hearing that her eggs were in danger, came swiftly from her feeding. The Youngest heard also and swam up as fast as she could in mingled alarm and excitement.

She reached the hatchhole just in time to find Second Mother coiling herself around the eggs, her belly skin already beginning to radiate heat from the warm blood that was being shunted to its surface. Released from his duties, First Uncle shot up through the dark, peaty water like a sixty-foot missile, up along the hanging line, with the Youngest close behind him.

They could see nothing for more than a few feet because of the murkiness. But neither First Uncle nor the Youngest relied much on the sense of sight, which was used primarily for protection on the surface of the loch, in any case. Besides, First Uncle was already beginning to lose his vision with age, so he seldom went to the surface nowadays, preferring to do his breathing in the caves, where it was safer. The Youngest had asked him once if he did not miss the sunlight, even the misty and often cloud-dulled sunlight of the open sky over the loch, with its instinctive pull at ancestral memories of the ocean, retold in the legends. No, he had told her, he had grown beyond such things. But she found it hard to believe him; for in her, the yearning for the mysterious and fascinating world above the waters was still strong. The Family had no word for it. If they did, they might have called her a romantic.

Now, through the pressure-sensitive cells in the cheek areas of her narrow head, she picked up the movements of a creature no more than six feet in length. Carrying some long, narrow made thing, the intruder was above them, though descending rapidly, parallel to the line.

"Stay back," First Uncle signaled her sharply; and, suddenly fearful, she lagged behind. From the vibrations she felt, their visitor could only be one of the upright animals from the world above that walked about on its hind legs and used "made" things. There was an ancient taboo about touching one of these creatures.

The Youngest hung back, then, continuing to rise through the water at a more normal pace.

Above her, through her cheek cells, she felt and interpreted the turbulence that came from First Uncle's movements. He flashed up, level with the descending animal, and with one swirl of his massive body snapped the taut descending line. The animal was sent tumbling—untouched by First Uncle's bulk (according to the taboo), but stunned and buffeted and thrust aside by the water-blow like a leaf in a sudden gust of wind when autumn sends the dry tears of the trees drifting down upon the shore waters of the loch.

The thing the animal had carried, as well as the lower half of the broken line, began to sink to the bottom. The top of the line trailed aimlessly. Soon the upright animal, hanging limp in the water, was drifting rapidly away from it. First Uncle, satisfied that he had protected the location of the hatchhole for the moment, at least—though later in the day they would move the eggs to a new location, anyway, as a safety precaution—turned and headed back down to release Second Mother once more to her feeding.

Still fearful, but fascinated by the drifting figure, the Youngest rose timidly through the water on an angle that gradually brought her close to it. She extended her small head on its long, graceful neck to feel about it from close range with her pressure-sensitive cheek cells. Here, within inches of the floating form, she could read minute differences, even in its surface textures. It seemed to be encased in an unnatural outer skin—one of those skins the creatures wore which were not actually theirs—made of some material that soaked up the loch water. This soaked-up water was evidently heated by the interior temperature of the creature, much as members of the Family could warm their belly skins with shunted blood, which protected the animal's body inside by cutting down the otherwise too-rapid radiation of its heat into the cold liquid of the loch.

The Youngest noticed something bulky and hard on the creature's head, in front, where the eyes and mouth were. Attached to the back was a larger, doubled something, also hard and almost a third as long as the creature itself. The Youngest had never before seen a diver's wetsuit, swim mask, and air tanks with pressure regulator, but she had heard them described by her elders. First Mother had once watched from a safe distance while a creature so equipped had maneuvered below the surface of the loch, and she had concluded that the things he wore were devices to enable him to swim underwater without breathing as often as his kind seemed to need to, ordinarily.

Only this one was not swimming. He was drifting away with an underwater current of the loch, rising slowly as he traveled toward its south end. If he continued like this, he would come to the surface near the center of the loch. By that time the afternoon would be over. It would be dark.

Clearly, he had been damaged. The blow of the water

that had been slammed at him by the body of First Uncle had hurt him in some way. But he was still alive. The Youngest knew this, because she could feel through her cheek cells the slowed beating of his heart and the movement of gases and fluids in his body. Occasionally, a small thread of bubbles came from his head to drift surfaceward.

It was a puzzle to her where he carried such a reservoir of air. She herself could contain enough oxygen for six hours without breathing, but only a portion of that was in gaseous form in her lungs. Most was held in pure form, saturating special tissues throughout her body.

Nonetheless, for the moment the creature seemed to have more than enough air stored about him; and he still lived. However, it could not be good for him to be drifting like this into the open loch with night coming on. Particularly if he was hurt, he would be needing some place safe out in the air, just as members of the Family did when they were old or sick. These upright creatures, the Youngest knew, were slow and feeble swimmers. Not one of them could have fed himself, as she did, by chasing and catching the fish of the loch; and very often when one fell into the water at any distance from the shore, he would struggle only a little while and then die.

This one would die also, in spite of the things fastened to him, if he stayed in the water. The thought raised a sadness in her. There was so much death. In any century, out of perhaps five clutches of a dozen eggs to a clutch, only one embryo might live to hatch. The legends claimed that once, when the Family had lived in the sea, matters had been different. But now, one survivor out of several clutches was the most to be hoped for. A hatchling who survived would be just about the size of this creature, the Youngest thought, though of course not with his funny shape. Nevertheless, watching him was a little like watching a new hatchling, knowing it would die.

It was an unhappy thought. But there was nothing to be

done. Even if the diver were on the surface now, the chances were small that his own People could locate him.

Struck by a thought, the Youngest went up to look around. The situation was as she had guessed. No boats were close by. The nearest was the one from which the diver had descended; but it was still anchored close to the location of the hatchhole, nearly half a mile from where she and the creature now were.

Clearly, those still aboard thought to find him near where they had lost him. The Youngest went back down, and found him still drifting, now not more than thirty feet below the surface, but rising only gradually.

Her emotions stirred as she looked at him. He was not a cold life-form like the salmons, eels, and other fishes on which the Family fed. He was warm—as she was—and if the legends were all true, there had been a time and a place on the wide oceans where one of his ancestors and one of her ancestors might have looked at each other, equal and unafraid, in the open air and the sunlight.

So, it seemed wrong to let him just drift and die like this. He had shown the courage to go down into the depths of the loch, this small, frail thing. And such courage required some recognition from one of the Family, like herself. After all, it was loyalty and courage that had kept the Family going all these centuries: their loyalty to each other and the courage to conserve their strength and go on, hoping that someday the ice would come once more, the land would sink, and they would be set free into the seas again. Then surviving hatchlings would once more be numerous, and the Family would begin to grow again into what the legends had once called them, a "True People." Anyone who believed in loyalty and courage, the Youngest told herself, ought to respect those qualities wherever she found them—even in one of the upright creatures.

He should not simply be left to die. It was a daring thought that she might interfere.

She felt her own heart beating more rapidly as she

followed him through the water, her cheek cells only inches from his dangling shape. After all, there was the taboo. But perhaps, if she could somehow help him without actually touching him . . . ?

"Him," of course, should not include the "made" things about him. But even if she could move him by these made parts alone, where could she take him?

Back to where the others of his kind still searched for him?

No, that was not only a deliberate flouting of the taboo but was very dangerous. Behind the taboo was the command to avoid letting any of his kind know about the Family. To take him back was to deliberately risk that kind of exposure for her People. She would die before doing that. The Family had existed all these centuries only because each member of it was faithful to the legends, to the duties, and to the taboos.

But, after all, she thought, it wasn't that she was actually going to break the taboo. She was only going to do something that went around the edge of it, because the diver had shown courage and because it was not his fault that he had happened to drop his heavy thing right beside the hatchhole. If he had dropped it anyplace else in the loch, he could have gone up and down its cable all summer and the Family members would merely have avoided that area.

What he needed, she decided, was a place out of the water where he could recover. She could take him to one of the banks of the loch. She rose to the surface again and looked around.

What she saw made her hesitate. In the darkening afternoon, the headlights of the cars moving up and down the roadways on each side of the loch were still visible in unusual numbers. From Fort Augustus at the south end of the loch to Castle Ness at the north, she saw more headlights about than ever before at this time of year, especially congregating by St. Ninian's, where the diver's boat was docked, nights.

No, it was too risky, trying to take him ashore. But she knew of a cave, too small by Family standards for any of the older adults, south of Urquhart Castle. The diver had gone down over the hatchhole, which had been constructed by Second Mother in the mouth of Urquhart Glen, close by St. Ninian's; and he had been drifting south ever since. Now he was below Castle Urquhart and almost level with the cave. It was a good, small cave for an animal his size, with ledge of rock that was dry above the water at this time of year; and during the day even a little light would filter through cracks where tree roots from above had penetrated its rocky roof.

The Youngest could bring him there quite easily. She hesitated again, but then extended her head toward the air tanks on his back, took the tanks in her jaws, and began to carry him in the direction of the cave.

As she had expected, it was empty. This late in the day there was no light inside; but since, underwater, her cheek cells reported accurately on conditions about her and, above water, she had her memory, which was ultimately reliable, she brought him—still unconscious—to the ledge at the back of the cave and reared her head a good eight feet out of the water to lift him up on it. As she set him down softly on the bare rock, one of his legs brushed her neck, and a thrill of icy horror ran through the warm interior of her body.

Now she had done it! She had broken the taboo. Panic seized her.

She turned and plunged back into the water, out through the entrance to the cave and into the open loch. The taboo had never been broken before, as far as she knew—never. Suddenly she was terribly frightened. She headed at top speed for the hatchhole. All she wanted was to find Second Mother, or the Uncle, or anyone, and confess what she had done, so that they could tell her that the situation was not irreparable, not a signal marking an end of every-thing for them all.

Halfway to the hatchhole, however, she woke to the fact that it had already been abandoned. She turned immedi-ately and began to range the loch bottom southward, her instinct and training counseling her that First Uncle and Second Mother would have gone in that direction, south toward Inverfarigaig, to set up a new hatchhole.

As she swam, however, her panic began to lessen and guilt moved in to take its place. How could she tell them? She almost wept inside herself. Here it was not many months ago that they had talked about how she was begin-ning to look and think like an adult; and she had behaved as thoughtlessly as if she was still the near-hatchling she had been thirty years ago.

Level with Castle Kitchie, she sensed the new location and homed in on it, finding it already set up off the mouth of the stream which flowed past that castle into the loch. The bed of the loch about the new hatchhole had been neatly swept and the saucer-shaped depression dug, in which Second Mother now lay warming the eggs. First Uncle was close by enough to feel the Youngest arrive, and he swept in to speak to her as she halted above Second Mother.

"Where did you go after I broke the line?" he de-manded before she herself could signal.

"I wanted to see what would happen to the diver," she signaled back. "Did you need me? I would have come back, but you and Second Mother were both there."

"We had to move right away," Second Mother sig-naled. She was agitated. "It was frightening!"

"They dropped another line," First Uncle said, "with a thing on it that they pulled back and forth as if to find the first one they dropped. I thought it not wise to break a second one. One break could be a chance happening. Two, and even small animals might wonder."

"But we couldn't keep the hole there with that thing

dragging back and forth near the eggs," explained Second Mother. "So we took them and moved without waiting to make the new hole here, first. The Uncle and I carried them, searching as we went. If you'd been here, you could have held half of them while I made the hole by myself, the way I wanted it. But you weren't. We would have sent for First Mother to come from her cave and help us, but neither one of us wanted to risk carrying the eggs about so much. So we had to work together here while still holding the eggs."

"Forgive me," said the Youngest. She wished she were dead.

"You're young," said Second Mother. "Next time you'll be wiser. But you do know that one of the earliest legends says the eggs should be moved only with the utmost care until hatching time; and you know we think that may be one reason so few hatch."

"If none hatch now," said First Uncle to the Youngest, less forgiving than Second Mother, even though they were not his eggs, "you'll remember this and consider that maybe you're to blame."

"Yes," mourned the Youngest.

She had a sudden, frightening vision of this one and all Second Mother's future clutches failing to hatch and she herself proving unable to lay when her time came. It was almost unheard of that a female of the Family should be barren, but a legend said that such a thing did occasionally happen. In her mind's eye she held a terrible picture of First Mother long dead, First Uncle and Second Mother grown old and feeble, unable to stir out of their caves, and she herself—the last of her line—dying alone, with no one to curl about her to warm or comfort her.

She had intended, when she caught up with the other two members of the Family, to tell them everything about what she had done with the diver. But she could not bring herself to it now. Her confession stuck in her mind. If it turned out that the clutch had been harmed by her inattention while she had actually been breaking the taboo with one of the very animals who had threatened the clutch in the first place . . .

She should have considered more carefully. But, of course, she was still too ignorant and irresponsible. First Uncle and Second Mother were the wise ones. First Mother, also, of course; but she was now too old to see a clutch of eggs through to hatching stage by herself alone, or with just the help of someone presently as callow and untrustworthy as the Youngest.

"Can I— It's dark now," she signaled. "Can I go feed, now? Is it all right to go?"

"Of course," said Second Mother, who switched her signaling to First Uncle. "You're too hard sometimes. She's still only half grown."

The Youngest felt even worse, intercepting that. She slunk off through the underwater, wishing something terrible could happen to her so that when the older ones did find out what she had done they would feel pity for her, instead of hating her. For a while she played with mental images of what this might involve. One of the boats on the surface could get her tangled in their lines in such a way that she could not get free. Then they would tow her to shore, and since she was so tangled in the line she could not get up to the surface, and since she had not breathed for many hours, she would drown on the way. Or perhaps the boat that could go underwater would find her and start chasing her and turn out to be much faster than any of them had ever suspected. It might even catch her and ram her and kill her.

By the time she had run through a number of these dark scenarios, she had begun almost automatically to hunt, for the time was in fact well past her usual second feeding period and she was hungry. As she realized this, her hunt became serious. Gradually she filled herself with salmon; and as she did so, she began to feel better. For all her bulk, she was swifter than any fish in the loch. The wide swim paddle at the end of each of her four limbs could turn her instantly; and with her long neck and relatively small head outstretched, the streamlining of even her twenty-eight-foot body parted the waters she displaced with an absolute minimum of resistance. Last, and most important of all, was the great engine of her enormously powerful, lashing tail: that was the real drive behind her ability to flash above the loch bottom at speeds of up to fifty knots.

She was, in fact, beautifully designed to lead the life she led, designed by evolution over the generations from that early land-dwelling, omnivorous early mammal that was her ancestor. Actually, she was herself a member of the mammalian sub-class prototheria, a large and distant cousin of monotremes like the platypus and the echidna. Her cretaceous forebears had drifted over and become practicing carnivores in the process of readapting to life in the sea.

She did not know this herself, of course. The legends of the Family were incredibly ancient, passed down by the letter-perfect memories of the individual generations; but they actually were not true memories of what had been, but merely deductions about the past gradually evolved as her People had acquired communication and intelligence. In many ways, the Youngest was very like a human savage: a member of a Stone Age tribe where elaborate ritual and custom directed every action of her life except for a small area of individual freedom. And in that area of individual freedom she was as prone to ignorance and misjudgments about the world beyond the waters of her loch as any Stone Age human primitive was in dealing with the technological world beyond his familiar few square miles of jungle.

Because of this—and because she was young and healthy—by the time she had filled herself with salmon, the exercise of hunting her dinner had burned off a good deal of her feelings of shame and guilt. She saw, or thought she saw, more clearly that her real fault was in not staying close to the hatchhole after the first incident. The diver's leg touching her neck had been entirely accidental; and besides, the diver had been unconscious and unaware of her presence at that time. So no harm could have been done. Essentially, the taboo was still unbroken. But she must learn to stay on guard as the adults did, to anticipate additional trouble, once some had put in an appearance, and to hold herself ready at all times.

She resolved to do so. She made a solemn promise to herself not to forget the hatchhole again—ever.

Her stomach was full. Emboldened by the freedom of the night-empty waters above, for the loch was always clear of boats after sundown, she swam to the surface, emerging only a couple of hundred yards from shore. Lying there, she watched the unusual number of lights from cars still driving on the roads that skirted the loch.

But suddenly her attention was distracted from them. The clouds overhead had evidently cleared some time since. Now it was a clear, frosty night and more than half the sky was glowing and melting with the northern lights. She floated, watching them. So beautiful, she thought, so beautiful. Her mind evoked pictures of all the Family who must have lain and watched the lights like this since time began, drifting in the arctic seas or resting on some skerry or ocean rock where only birds walked. The desire to see all the wide skies and seas of all the world swept over her like a physical hunger.

It was no use, however. The mountains had risen and they held the Family here, now. Blocked off from its primary dream, her hunger for adventure turned to a more possible goal. The temptation came to go and investigate the loch-going "made" things from which her diver had descended.

She found herself up near Dores, but she turned and went back down opposite St. Ninian's. The dock to which this particular boat was customarily moored was actually a mile below the village and had no illumination. But the boat had a cabin on its deck, amidships, and through the square windows lights now glowed. Their glow was different from that of the lights shown by the cars. The Youngest noted this difference without being able to account for it, not understanding that the headlights she had been watching were electric, but the illumination she now saw shining out of the cabin windows of the large, flat-hulled boat before her came from gas lanterns. She heard sounds coming from inside the cabin.

Curious, the Youngest approached the boat from the darkness of the lake, her head now lifted a good six feet out of the water so that she could look over the side railing. Two large, awkward-looking shapes rested on the broad deck in front of the cabin—one just in front, the other right up in the bow with its far end overhanging the water. Four more shapes, like the one in the bow but smaller, were spaced along the sides of the foredeck, two to a side. The Youngest slid through the little waves until she was barely a couple of dozen feet from the side of the boat. At that moment, two men came out of the cabin, strode onto the deck, and stopped by the shape just in front of the cabin.

The Youngest, though she knew she could not be seen against the dark expanse of the loch, instinctively sank down until only her head was above water. The two men stood, almost overhead, and spoke to each other.

Their voices had a strangely slow, sonorous ring to the ears of Youngest, who was used to hearing sound waves traveling through the water at four times the speed they moved in air. She did understand, of course, that they were engaged in meaningful communication, much as she and the others of the Family were when they signaled to each other. This much her People had learned about the upright animals; they communicated by making sounds. A few of these sounds—the *"Ness"* sound, which, like the other sound, *"loch,"* seemed to refer to the water in which the Family lived—were by now familiar. But she recognized no such noises among those made by the two above her; in fact, it would have been surprising if she had, for while the language was the one she was used to hearing, the accent of one of the two was a different English, different enough from that of those living in the vicinity of the loch to make what she heard completely unintelligible.

". . . poor bastard," the other voice said.

"Mon, you forget that 'poor bastard' talk, I tell you! He knew what he doing when he go down that line. He know what a temperature like that mean. A reading like that big enough for a blue whale. He just want the glory—he all alone swimming down with a speargun to drug that great beast. It the newspaper headlines, man; that's what he after!"

"Gives me the creeps, anyway. Think we'll ever fish up the sensor head?"

"You kidding. Lucky we find *him*. No, we use the spare, like I say, starting early tomorrow. And I mean it, early!"

"I don't like it. I tell you, he's got to have relatives who'll want to know why we didn't stop after we lost him. It's his boat. It's his equipment. They'll ask who gave us permission to go on spending money they got coming, with him dead."

"You pay me some heed. We've got to try to find him, that's only right. We use the equipment we got—what else we got to use? Never mind his rich relatives. They just like him. He don't never give no damn for you or me or what it cost him, this expedition. He was born with money and all he want to do is write the book about how he an adventurer. We know what we hunt be down there, now. We capture it, then everybody happy. And you and me, we get what's in the contract, the five thousand extra apiece for taking it. Otherwise we don't get nothing—you back to that machine shop, me to the whaling, with the pockets empty. We out in the cold then, you recall that!"

"All right."

"You damn right, it all right. Starting tomorrow sunup."

"I said *all right!*" The voice paused for a second before going on. "But I'm telling you one thing. If we run into it, you better get it fast with a drug spear because I'm not waiting. If I see it, I'm getting on the harpoon gun."

The other voice laughed.

"That's why he never let you near the gun when we out before. But I don't care. Contract, it say alive or dead we get what he promise us. Come on now, up the inn and have us food and drink."

"I want a drink! Christ, this water's empty after dark, with that law about no fishing after sundown. Anything could be out there!"

"Anything is. Come on, mon."

The Youngest heard the sound of their footsteps backing off the boat and moving away down the dock until they became inaudible within the night of the land.

Left alone, she lifted her head gradually out of the water once more and cautiously examined everything before her: big boat and small ones nearby, dock and shore. There was no sound or other indication of anything living. Slowly, she once more approached the craft the two had just left and craned her neck over its side.

The large shape in front of the cabin was box-like like the boat, but smaller and without any apertures in it. Its top sloped from the side facing the bow of the craft to the opposite side. On that sloping face she saw circles of some material that, although as hard as the rest of the object, still had a subtly different texture when she pressed her cheek cells directly against them. Farther down from these, which were in fact the glass faces of meters, was a raised plate with grooves in it. The Youngest would not have understood what the grooves meant, even if she had had enough light to see them plainly; and even if their sense could have been translated to her, the words "caloric sensor" would have meant nothing to her.

A few seconds later, she was, however, puzzled to discover on the deck beside this object another shape which her memory insisted was an exact duplicate of the heavy round thing that had been dropped to the loch bed beside the old hatchhole. She felt all over it carefully with her cheek cells, but discovered nothing beyond the dimensions of its almost plumb-bob shape and the fact that a line was attached to it in the same way a line had been attached to the other. In this case, the line was one end of a heavy coil that had a farther end connected to the box-like shape with the sloping top.

Baffled by this discovery, the Youngest moved forward to examine the strange object in the bow of the boat with its end overhanging the water. This one had a shape that was hard to understand. It was more complex, made up of a number of smaller shapes both round and boxy. Essentially, however, it looked like a mound with something long and narrow set on top of it, such as a piece of waterlogged tree from which the limbs had long since dropped off. The four smaller things like it, spaced two on each side of the foredeck, were not quite like the big one, but they were enough alike so that she ignored them in favor of examining the large one. Feeling around the end of the object that extended over the bow of the boat and hovered above the water, the Youngest discovered the log shape rotated at a touch and even tilted up and down with the mound beneath it as a balance point. On further investigation, she found that the log shape was hollow at the water end and was projecting beyond the hooks the animals often let down into the water with little dead fish or other things attached, to try to catch the larger fish of the loch. This end, however, was attached not to a curved length of metal, but to a straight metal rod lying loosely in the hollow log space. To the rod part, behind the barbed head, was joined the end of another heavy coil of line wound about a round thing on the deck. This line was much thicker than the one attached to the box with the sloping top. Experimentally, she tested it with her teeth. It gave—but did not cut when she closed her jaws on it—then sprang back, apparently unharmed, when she let it go.

All very interesting, but puzzling—as well it might be. A harpoon gun and spearguns with heads designed to inject a powerful tranquilizing drug on impact were completely outside the reasonable dimensions of the world as the Youngest knew it. The heat-sensing equipment that had been used to locate First Uncle's huge body as it lay on the loch bed warming the eggs was closer to being something she could understand. She and the rest of the Family used heat sensing themselves to locate and identify one another, though their natural abilities were nowhere near as sensitive as those of the instrument she had examined on the foredeck. At any rate, for now, she merely dismissed from her mind the question of what these things were. Perhaps, she thought, the upright animals simply liked to have odd shapes of "made" things around them. That notion reminded her of her diver; and she felt a sudden, deep curiosity about him, a desire to see if he had yet recovered and found his way out of the cave to shore.

She backed off from the dock and turned toward the south end of the loch, not specifically heading for the cave where she had left him but traveling in that general direction and turning over in her head the idea that perhaps she might take one more look at the cave. But she would not be drawn into the same sort of irresponsibility she had fallen prey to earlier in the day, when she had taken him to the cave! Not twice would she concern herself with one of the animals when she was needed by others of the Family. She decided, instead, to go check on Second Mother and the new hatchhole.

When she got to the hole, however, she found that Second Mother had no present need of her. The older female, tired from the exacting events of the day and heavy from feeding later than her usual time—for she had been too nervous, at first, to leave the eggs in First Uncle's care and so had not finished her feeding period until well after dark—was half asleep. She only untucked her head from the coil she had made of her body around and above the eggs long enough to make sure that the Youngest had not brought warning of some new threat. Reassured, she coiled up tightly again about the clutch and closed her eyes.

The Youngest gazed at her with a touch of envy. It must be a nice feeling, she thought, to shut out everything but yourself and your eggs. There was plainly nothing that Youngest was wanted for, here—and she had never felt less like sleeping herself. The night was full of mysteries and excitements. She headed once more north, up the lake.

She had not deliberately picked a direction, but suddenly she realized that unconsciously she was once more heading toward the cave where she had left the diver. She felt a strange sense of freedom. Second Mother was sleeping with her eggs. First Uncle by this time would have his heavy bulk curled up in his favorite cave and his head on its long neck resting on a ledge at the water's edge, so that he had the best of both the worlds of air and loch at the same time. The Youngest had the loch to herself, with neither Family nor animals to worry about. It was all hers, from Fort Augustus clear to Castle Ness.

The thought gave her a sense of power. Abruptly, she decided that there was no reason at all why she should not go see what had happened to the diver. She turned directly toward the cave, putting on speed.

At the last moment, however, she decided to enter the cave quietly. If he was really recovered and alert, she might want to leave again without being noticed. Like a cloud shadow moving silently across the surface of the waves, she slid through the underwater entrance of the cave, invisible in the blackness, her cheek cells reassuring her that there was no moving body in the water inside.

Once within, she paused again to check for heat radia-

tion that would betray a living body in the water even if it
was being held perfectly still. But she felt no heat. Satisfied, she lifted her head silently from the water inside the
cave and approached the rock ledge where she had left
him.

Her hearing told that he was still here, though her eyes
were as useless in this total darkness as his must be.
Gradually, that same, sensitive hearing filled in the image
of his presence for her.

He still lay on the ledge, apparently on his side. She
could hear the almost rhythmic scraping of a sort of metal
clip he wore on the right side of his belt. It was scratching
against the rock as he made steady, small movements. He
must have come to enough to take off his head-things and
back-things, however, for she heard no scraping from
these. His breathing was rapid and hoarse, almost a pant-
ing. Slowly, sound by sound, she built up a picture of
him, there in the dark. He was curled up in a tight ball,
shivering.

The understanding that he was lying, trembling from the
cold, struck the Youngest in her most vulnerable area.
Like all the Family, she had vivid memories of what it had
been like to be a hatchling. As eggs, the clutch was kept in
open water with as high an oxygen content as possible
until the moment for hatching came close. Then they were
swiftly transported to one of the caves so that they would
emerge from their shell into the land and air environment
that their warm-blooded, air-breathing ancestry required.
And a hatchling could not drown on a cave ledge. But,
although he or she was protected there from the water, a
hatchling was still vulnerable to the cold; and the caves
were no warmer than the water—which was snow-fed
from the mountains most of the year. Furthermore, the
hatchling would not develop the layers of blubber-like fat
that insulated an adult of the Family for several years. The
life of someone like the Youngest began with the sharp
sensations of cold as a newborn, and ended the same way,

when aged body processes were no longer able to generate enough interior heat to keep the great hulk going. The first instinct of the hatchling was to huddle close to the warm belly skin of the adult on guard. And the first instinct of the adult was to warm the small, new life.

She stood in the shallow water of the cave, irresolute. The taboo, and everything that she had ever known, argued fiercely in her against any contact with the upright animal. But this one had already made a breach in her cosmos, had already been promoted from an "it" to a "he" in her thoughts; and her instincts cried out as strongly as her teachings, against letting him chill there on the cold stone ledge when she had within her the heat to warm him.

It was a short, hard, internal struggle; but her instincts won. After all, she rationalized, it was she who had brought him here to tremble in the cold. The fact that by doing so she had saved his life was beside the point.

Completely hidden in the psychological machinery that moved her toward him now was the lack in her life that was the result of being the last, solitary child of her kind. From the moment of hatching on, she had never had a playmate, never known anyone with whom she could share the adventures of growing up. An unconscious part of her was desperately hungry for a friend, a toy, anything that could be completely and exclusively hers, apart from the adult world that encompassed everything around her.

Slowly, silently, she slipped out of the water and up onto the ledge and flowed around his shaking form. She did not quite dare to touch him; but she built walls about him and a roof over him out of her body, the inward-facing skin of which was already beginning to pulse with hot blood pumped from deep within her.

Either dulled by his semi-consciousness or else too wrapped up in his own misery to notice, the creature showed no awareness that she was there. Not until the warmth began to be felt did he instinctively relax the tight ball of his body and, opening out, touch her—not merely with his wetsuit-encased body, but with his unprotected hands and forehead.

The Youngest shuddered all through her length at that first contact. But before she could withdraw, his own reflexes operated. His chilling body felt warmth and did not stop to ask its source. Automatically, he huddled close against the surfaces he touched.

The Youngest bowed her head. It was too late. It was done.

This was no momentary, unconscious contact. She could feel his shivering directly now through her own skin surface. Nothing remained but to accept what had happened. She folded herself close about him, covering as much of his small, cold, trembling body as possible with her own warm surface, just as she would have if he had been a new hatchling who suffered from the chill. He gave a quavering sigh of relief and pressed close against her.

Gradually he warmed and his trembling stopped. Long before that, he had fallen into a deep, torporlike slumber. She could hear the near-snores of his heavy breathing.

Grown bolder by contact with him and abandoning herself to an affection for him, she explored his slumbering shape with her sensitive cheek cells. He had no true swim paddles, of course—she already knew this about the upright animals. But she had never guessed how delicate and intricate were the several-times split appendages that he possessed on his upper limbs where swim paddles might have been. His body was very narrow, its skeleton hardly clothed in flesh. Now that she knew that his kind were as vulnerable to cold as new hatchlings, she did not wonder that it should be so with them: they had hardly anything over their bones to protect them from the temperature of the water and air. No wonder they covered themselves with non-living skins.

His head was not long at all, but quite round. His mouth was small and his jaws flat, so that he would be able to take only very small bites of things. There was a sort of protuberance above the mouth and a pair of eyes, side by side. Around the mouth and below the eyes his skin was full of tiny, sharp points; and on the top of his head was a strange, springy mat of very fine filaments. The Youngest rested the cells of her right cheek for a moment on the filaments, finding a strange inner warmth and pleasure in the touch of them. It was a completely inexplicable pleasure, for the legends had forgotten what old, primitive parts of her brain remembered: a time when her ancestors on land had worn fur and known the feel of it in their close body contacts.

Wrapped up in the subconscious evocation of ancient companionship, she lay in the darkness spinning impossible fantasies in which she would be able to keep him. He could live in this cave, she thought, and she would catch salmon—since that was what his kind, with their hooks and filaments, seemed most to search for—to bring to him for food. If he wanted "made" things about him, she could probably visit docks and suchlike about the loch and find some to bring here to him. When he got to know her better, since he had the things that let him hold his breath underwater, they could venture out into the loch together. Of course, once that time was reached, she would have to tell Second Mother and First Uncle about him. No doubt it would disturb them greatly, the fact that the taboo had been broken; but once they had met him underwater, and seen how sensible and friendly he was—how wise, even, for a small animal like himself . . .

Even as she lay dreaming these dreams, however, a sane part of her mind was still on duty. Realistically, she knew that what she was thinking was nonsense. Centuries of legend, duty, and taboo were not to be upset in a few days by any combination of accidents. Nor, even if no problem arose from the Family side, could she really expect him to live in a cave, forsaking his own species. His kind needed light as well as air. They needed the freedom to come and go on shore. Even if she could manage to keep him with her in the cave for a while, eventually the time would come when he would yearn for the land under his feet and the open sky overhead, at one and the same time. No, her imaginings could never be; and, because she knew this, when her internal time sense warned her that the night was nearly over, she silently uncoiled from around him and slipped back into the water, leaving the cave before the first light, which filtered in past the tree roots in the cave roof, could let him see who it was that had kept him alive through the hours of darkness.

Left uncovered on the ledge but warm again, he slept heavily on, unaware.

Out in the waters of the loch, in the pre-dawn gloom, the Youngest felt fatigue for the first time. She could easily go twenty-four hours without sleep; but this twenty-four hours just past had been emotionally charged ones. She had an irresistible urge to find one of the caves she favored herself and to lose herself in slumber. She shook it off. Before anything else, she must check with Second Mother.

Going swiftly to the new hatchhole, she found Second Mother fully awake, alert, and eager to talk to her. Evidently Second Mother had awakened early and spent some time thinking.

"You're young," she signaled the Youngest, "far too young to share the duty of guarding a clutch of eggs, even with someone as wise as your First Uncle. Happily, there's no problem physically. You're mature enough so that milk would come, if a hatchling should try to nurse from you. But, sensibly, you're still far too young to take on this sort of responsibility. Nonetheless, if something should happen to me, there would only be you and the Uncle to see this clutch to the hatching point. Therefore, we have to think of the possibility that you might have to take over for me."

"No. No, I couldn't," said the Youngest.

"You may have to. It's still only a remote possibility; but I should have taken it into consideration before. Since there're only the four of us, if anything happened to one of us, the remaining would have to see the eggs through to hatching. You and I could do it, I'm not worried about that situation. But with a clutch there must be a mother. Your uncle can be everything but that, and First Mother is really too old. Somehow, we must make you ready before your time to take on that duty."

"If you say so . . ." said the Youngest, unhappily.

"Our situation says so. Now, all you need to know, really, is told in the legends. But knowing them and understanding them are two different things . . ."

Then Second Mother launched into a retelling of the long chain of stories associated with the subject of eggs and hatchlings. The Youngest, of course, had heard them all before. More than that, she had them stored, signal by signal, in her memory as perfectly as had Second Mother herself. But she understood that Second Mother wanted her not only to recall each of these packages of stored wisdom, but to think about what was stated in them. Also—so much wiser had she already become in twenty-four hours—she realized that the events of yesterday had suddenly shocked Second Mother, giving her a feeling of helplessness should the upright animals ever really chance to stumble upon the hatchhole. For she could never abandon her eggs, and if she stayed with them the best she could hope for would be to give herself up to the land-dwellers in hope that this would satisfy them and they would look no further.

It was hard to try and ponder the legends, sleepy as the Youngest was, but she tried her best; and when at last Second Mother turned her loose, she swam groggily off to the nearest cave and curled up. It was now broad-enough daylight for her early feeding period, but she was too tired to think of food. In seconds, she was sleeping almost as deeply as the diver had been when she left him.

She came awake suddenly and was in motion almost before her eyes were open. First Uncle's signal of alarm was ringing all through the loch. She plunged from her cave into the outer waters. Vibrations told her that he and Second Mother were headed north, down the deep center of the loch as fast as they could travel, carrying the clutch of eggs. She drove on to join them, sending ahead her own signal that she was coming.

"Quick! Oh, quick!" signaled Second Mother.

Unencumbered, she began to converge on them at double their speed. Even in this moment her training paid off. She shot through the water, barely fifty feet above the bed of the loch, like a dolphin in the salt sea; and her perfect shape and smooth skin caused no turbulence at all to drag at her passage and slow her down.

She caught up with them halfway between Inverfarigaig and Dores and took her half of the eggs from Second Mother, leaving the older female free to find a new hatchhole. Unburdened, Second Mother leaped ahead and began to range the loch bed in search of a safe place.

"What happened?" signaled Youngest.

"Again!" First Uncle answered. "They dropped another 'made' thing, just like the first, almost in the hatchhole this time!" he told her.

Second Mother had been warming the eggs. Luckily he had been close. He had swept in; but not daring to break the line a second time for fear of giving clear evidence of the Family, he had simply scooped a hole in the loch bed, pushed the thing in, buried it and pressed down hard on the loch bed material with which he had covered it. He had buried it deeply enough so that the animals above were pulling up on their line with caution, for fear that they themselves might break it. Eventually, they would get it loose. Until then, the Family had a little time in which to find another location for the eggs.

A massive shape loomed suddenly out of the peaty

darkness, facing them. It was First Mother, roused from her cave by the emergency.

"I can still carry eggs. Give them here, and you go back," she ordered First Uncle. "Find out what's being done with that 'made' thing you buried and what's going on with those creatures. Two hatchholes stumbled on in two days is too much for chance."

First Uncle swirled about and headed back.

The Youngest slowed down. First Mother was still tremendously powerful, of course, more so than any of them; but she no longer had the energy reserves to move at the speed at which First Uncle and the Youngest had been traveling. Youngest felt a surge of admiration for First Mother, battling the chill of the open loch water and the infirmities of her age to give help now, when the Family needed it.

"Here! This way!" Second Mother called.

They turned sharply toward the east bank of the loch and homed in on Second Mother's signal. She had found a good place for a new hatchhole. True, it was not near the mouth of a stream; but the loch bed was clean and this was one of the few spots where the rocky slope underwater from the shore angled backward when it reached a depth below four hundred feet, so that the loch at this point was actually in under the rock and had a roof overhead. Here, there was no way that a "made" thing could be dropped down on a line to come anywhere close to the hatchhole.

When First Mother and the Youngest got there, Second Mother was already at work making and cleaning the hole. The hole had barely been finished and Second Mother settled down with the clutch under her, when First Uncle arrived.

"They have their 'made' thing back," he reported. "They pulled on its line with little, repeated jerkings until they loosened it from its bed, and then they lifted it back up."

He told how he had followed it up through the water

until he was just under the ''made'' thing and rode on the loch surface. Holding himself there, hidden by the thing itself, he had listened, trying to make sense out of what the animals were doing from what he could hear.

They had made a great deal of noise after they hoisted the thing back on board. They had moved it around a good deal and done things with it, before finally leaving it alone and starting back toward the dock near St. Ninian's. First Uncle had followed them until he was sure that was where they were headed; then he had come to find the new hatchhole and the rest of the Family.

After he was done signaling, they all waited for First Mother to respond, since she was the oldest and wisest. She lay thinking for some moments.

''They didn't drop the 'made' thing down into the water again, you say?'' she asked at last.

''No,'' signaled First Uncle.

''And none of them went down into the water themselves?''

''No.''

''It's very strange,'' said First Mother. ''All we know is that they've twice almost found the hatchhole. All I can guess is that this isn't a chance thing, but that they're acting with some purpose. They may not be searching for our eggs, but they seem to be searching for *something*.''

The Youngest felt a sudden chilling inside her. But First Mother was already signalling directly to First Uncle.

''From now on you should watch them whenever the thing in which they move about the loch surface isn't touching shore. If you need help, the Youngest can help you. If they show any signs of coming close to here, we must move the eggs immediately. I'll come out twice a day to relieve Second Mother for her feeding, so that you can be free to do that watching. No''—she signaled sharply before they could object—''I *will* do this. I can go for some days warming the eggs for two short periods a day, before I'll be out of strength; and this effort of mine is needed. The eggs *should* be safe here, but if it proves that the creatures have some means of finding them, wherever the hatchhole is placed in the open loch, we'll have to move the clutch into the caves.''

Second Mother cried out in protest.

"I know," First Mother said, "the legends counsel against ever taking the eggs into the caves until time for hatching. But we may have no choice."

"My eggs will die!" wept Second Mother.

"They're your eggs, and the decision to take them inside has to be yours," said First Mother. "But they won't live if the animals find them. In the caves there may be a chance of life for them. Besides, our duty as a Family is to survive. It's the Family we have to think of, not a single clutch of eggs or a single individual. If worse comes to worst and it turns out we're not safe from the animals even in the caves, we'll try the journey of the Lost Father from Loch Morar before we'll let ourselves all be killed off.''

"What Lost Father?" the Youngest demanded. "No one ever told me a legend about a Lost Father from Loch Morar. What's Loch Morar?"

"It's not a legend usually told to those too young to have full wisdom," said First Mother. "But these are new and dangerous times. Loch Morar is a loch a long way from here, and some of our People were also left there when the ice went and the land rose. They were of our People, but a different Family."

"But what about a Lost Father?" the Youngest persisted, because First Mother had stopped talking as if she would say no more about it. "How could a Father be lost?"

"He was lost to Loch Morar," First Mother explained, "because he grew old and died here in Loch Ness."

"But how did he get here?"

"He couldn't, that's the point," said First Uncle, grumpily. "There are legends *and* legends. That's why some are not told to young ones until they've matured enough to understand. The journey the Lost Father's supposed to have made is impossible. Tell it to some youngster and he or she's just as likely to try and duplicate it.''

"But you said we might try it!" The Youngest appealed to First Mother.

"Only if there were no other alternative," First Mother answered. "I'd try flying out over the mountains if that was the only alternative left, because it's our duty to keep trying to survive as a Family as long as we're alive. So, as a last resort, we'd try the journey of the Lost Father, even though as the Uncle says, it's impossible.''

"Why? Tell me what it was. You've already begun to tell me. Shouldn't I know all of it?"

"I suppose . . ." said First Mother, wearily. "Very well. Loch Morar isn't surrounded by mountains as we are here. It's even fairly close to the sea, so that if a good way could be found for such as us to travel over dry land, members of the People living there might be able to go home to the sea we all recall by the legends. Well, this legend says that there once was a Father in Loch Morar who dreamed all his life of leading his Family home to the sea. But we've grown too heavy nowadays to travel any distance overland, normally. One winter day, when a new snow had just fallen, the legend says this Father discovered a way of traveling on land that worked.''

In sparse sentences, First Mother rehearsed the legend to a fascinated Youngest. It told that the snow provided a slippery surface over which the great bodies of the People could slide under the impetus of the same powerful tail muscles that drove them through the water, their swim paddles acting as rudders—or brakes—on downslopes. Actually, what the legend described was a way of swimming on land. Loch Ness never froze and First Mother therefore had no knowledge of ice-skating, so she could not explain that what the legend spoke of was the same principle that makes a steel ice blade glide over ice—the weight upon it causing the ice to melt under the sharp edge of the blade so that, effectively, it slides on a cushion of water. With the People, their ability to shunt a controlled amount of warmth to the skin in contact with the ice and snow did the same thing.

In the legend, the Father who discovered this tried to take his Family from Loch Morar back to the sea, but they were all afraid to try going, except for him. So he went alone and found his way to the ocean more easily than he had thought possible. He spent some years in the sea, but found it lonely and came back to land to return to Loch Morar. However, though it was winter, he could not find enough snow along the route he had taken to the sea in order to get back to Loch Morar. He hunted northward for a snow-covered route inland, north past the isle of Sleat, past Glenelg; and finally, under Benn Attow, he found a snow route that led him ultimately to Glen Moriston and into Loch Ness.

He went as far back south through Loch Ness as he could go, even trying some distance down what is now the southern part of the Caledonian Canal before he became convinced that the route back to Loch Morar by that way would be too long and hazardous to be practical. He decided to return to the sea and wait for snow to make him a way over his original route to Morar.

But, meanwhile, he had become needed in Loch Ness and grown fond of the Family there. He wished to take them with him to the sea. The others, however, were afraid to try the long overland journey; and while they hesitated and put off going, he grew too old to lead them; and so they never did go. Nevertheless, the legend told of his route and, memories being what they were among the People, no member of the Family in Loch Ness, after First Mother had finished telling the legend to the Youngest, could not have retraced the Lost Father's steps exactly.

"I don't think we should wait," the Youngest said, eagerly, when First Mother was through. "I think we should go now—I mean, as soon as we get a snow on the banks of the loch so that we can travel. Once we're away from the loch, there'll be snow all the time, because it's only the warmth of the loch that keeps the snow off around here. Then we could all go home to the sea, where we belong, away from the animals and their 'made' things. Most of the eggs laid there would hatch—''

"I told you so," First Uncle interrupted, speaking to First Mother. "Didn't I tell you so?"

"And what about my eggs now?" said Second Mother.

"We'll try something like that only if the animals start to destroy us," First Mother said to the Youngest with finality. "Not before. If it comes to that, Second Mother's present clutch of eggs will be lost, anyway. Otherwise, we'd never leave them, you should know that. Now, I'll go back to the cave and rest until late feeding period for Second Mother."

She went off. First Uncle also went off, to make sure that the animals had really gone to the dock and were still there. The Youngest, after asking Second Mother if there was any way she could be useful and being told there was none, went off to her delayed first feeding period.

She was indeed hungry, with the ravenous hunger of youth. But once she had taken the edge off her appetite, an uneasy feeling began to grow inside her, and not even stuffing herself with rich-fleshed salmon made it go away.

What was bothering her, she finally admitted to herself, was the sudden, cold thought that had intruded on her when First Mother had said that the creatures seemed to be searching for something. The Youngest was very much afraid she knew what they were searching for. It was their fellow, the diver she had taken to the cave. If she had not done anything, they would have found his body before this; but because she had saved him, they were still looking; and because he was in a cave, they could not find him. So they would keep on searching, and sooner or later they would come close to the new hatchhole; and then Second Mother would take the clutch into one of the caves, and the eggs would die, and it would be her own fault, the Youngest's fault alone.

She was crying inside. She did not dare cry out loud because the others would hear and want to know what was troubling her. She was ashamed to tell them what she had done. Somehow, she must put things right herself, without telling them—at least until some later time, when it would be all over and unimportant.

The diver must go back to his own people—if he had not already.

She turned and swam toward the cave, making sure to approach it from deep in the loch. Through the entrance of the cave, she stood up in the shallow interior pool and lifted her head out of water; and he was still there.

Enough light was filtering in through the ceiling cracks of the cave to make a sort of dim twilight inside. She saw him plainly—and he saw her.

She had forgotten that he would have no idea of what she looked like. He had been sitting up on the rock ledge; but when her head and its long neck rose out of the water, he stared and then scrambled back—as far back from her as he could get, to the rock wall of the cave behind the ledge. He stood pressed against it, still staring at her, his mouth open in a soundless circle.

She paused, irresolute. She had never intended to frighten him. She had forgotten that he might consider her at all frightening. All her foolish imaginings of keeping him here in the cave and of swimming with him in the loch crumbled before the bitter reality of his terror at the sight of her. Of course, he had had no idea of who had been coiled about him in the dark. He had only known that something large had been bringing the warmth of life back into him. But surely he would make the connection, now that he saw her?

She waited.

He did not seem to be making it. He simply stayed where he was, as if paralyzed by her presence. She felt an exasperation with him rising inside her. According to the legends, his kind had at least a share of intelligence, possibly even some aspect of wisdom, although that was doubtful. But now, crouched against the back of the cave, he looked like nothing more than another wild animal— like one of the otters, strayed from nearby streams, she had occasionally encountered in these caves. And as with such an otter, for all its small size ready to scratch or bite, she felt a caution about approaching him.

Nevertheless, something had to be done. At any moment now, the others like him would be out on the loch in their "made" thing, once more hunting for him and threatening to rediscover the hatchhole.

Cautiously, slowly, so as not to send him into a fighting reflex, she approached the ledge and crept up on it sideways, making an arc of her body and moving in until she half surrounded him, an arm's length from him. She was ready to pull back at the first sign of a hostile move, but no action was triggered in him. He merely stayed where he was, pressing against the rock wall as if he would like to step through it, his eyes fixed on her and his jaws still in the half-open position. Settled about him, however, she shunted blood into her skin area and began to radiate heat.

It took a little while for him to feel the warmth coming from her and some little while more to understand what she was trying to tell him. But then, gradually, his tense body relaxed. He slipped down the rock against which he was pressed and ended up sitting, gazing at her with a different shape to his eyes and mouth.

He made some noises with his mouth. These conveyed no sense to the Youngest, of course, but she thought that at least they did not sound like unfriendly noises.

"So now you know who I am," she signaled, although she knew perfectly well he could not understand her. "Now, you've got to swim out of here and go back on the land. Go back to your People."

She had corrected herself instinctively on the last term.

She had been about to say "go back to the other animals"; but something inside her dictated the change—which was foolish, because he would not know the difference anyway.

He straightened against the wall and stood up. Suddenly, he reached out an upper limb toward her.

She flinched from his touch instinctively, then braced herself to stay put. If she wanted him not to be afraid of her, she would have to show him the same fearlessness. Even the otters, if left alone, would calm down somewhat, though they would take the first opportunity to slip past and escape from the cave where they had been found.

She held still, accordingly. The divided ends of his limb touched her and rubbed lightly over her skin. It was not an unpleasant feeling, but she did not like it. It had been different when he was helpless and had touched her unconsciously.

She now swung her head down close to watch him and had the satisfaction of seeing him start when her own eyes and jaws came within a foot or so of his. He pulled his limbs back quickly, and made more noises. They were still not angry noises, though, and this fact, together with his quick withdrawal, gave her an impression that he was trying to be conciliatory, even friendly.

Well, at least she had his attention. She turned, backed off the ledge into the water, then reached up with her nose and pushed toward him the "made" things he originally had had attached to his back and head. Then, turning, she ducked under the water, swam out of the cave into the loch, and waited just under the surface for him to follow.

He did not.

She waited for more than enough time for him to reattach his things and make up his mind to follow, then she swam back inside. To her disgust, he was now sitting down again and his "made" things were still unattached to him.

She came sharply up to the edge of the rock and tumbled the two things literally on top of him.

"Put them on!" she signaled. "Put them on, you stupid animal!"

He stared at her and made noises with his mouth. He stood up and moved his upper limbs about in the air. But he made no move to pick up the "made" things at his feet. Angrily, she shoved them against his lower limb ends once more.

He stopped making noises and merely looked at her. Slowly, although she could not define all of the changes that signaled it to her, an alteration of manner seemed to take place in him. The position of his upright body changed subtly. The noises he was making changed; they became slower and more separate, one from another. He bent down and picked up the larger of the things, the one that he had had attached to his back; but he did not put it on.

Instead, he held it up in the air before him as if drawing her attention to it. He turned it over in the air and shook it slightly, then held it in that position some more. He rapped it with the curled-over sections of one of his limb-ends, so that it rang with a hollow sound from both its doubled parts. Then he put it down on the ledge again and pushed it from him with one of his lower limb ends.

The Youngest stared at him, puzzled, but nonetheless hopeful for the first time. At last he seemed to be trying to communicate something to her, even though what he was doing right now seemed to make no sense. Could it be that this was some sort of game the upright animals played with their "made" things; and he either wanted to play it, or wanted her to play it with him, before he would put the things on and get in the water? When she was much younger, she had played with things herself—interesting pieces of rock or waterlogged material she found on the loch bed, or flotsam she had encountered on the surface at night, when it was safe to spend time in the open.

No, on second thought that explanation hardly seemed likely. If it was a game he wanted to play with her, it was more reasonable for him to push the things at her instead of just pushing the bigger one away and ignoring it. She watched him, baffled. Now he had picked up the larger thing again and was repeating his actions exactly.

The creature went through the same motions several more times, eventually picking up and putting the smaller "made" thing about his head and muzzle, but still shaking and pushing away the larger thing. Eventually he made a louder noise which, for the first time, sounded really angry; threw the larger thing to one end of the ledge; and went off to sit down at the far end of the ledge, his back to her.

Still puzzled, the Youngest stretched her neck up over the ledge to feel the rejected "made" thing again with her cheek cells. It was still an enigmatic, cold, hard, double-shaped object that made no sense to her. What he's doing can't be playing, she thought. Not that he was playing at the last, there. And besides, he doesn't act as if he liked it and liked to play with it, he's acting as if he hated it—

Illumination came to her, abruptly.

"Of course!" she signaled at him.

But of course the signal did not even register on him. He still sat with his back to her.

What he had been trying to tell her, she suddenly realized, was that for some reason the "made" thing was no good for him any longer. Whether he had used it to play with, to comfort himself, or, as she had originally guessed, it had something to do with making it possible for him to stay underwater, for some reason it was now no good for that purpose.

The thought that it might indeed be something to help him stay underwater suddenly fitted in her mind with the fact that he no longer considered it any good. She sat back on her tail, mentally berating herself for being so foolish. Of course, that was what he had been trying to tell her. It would not help him stay underwater anymore; and to get out of the cave he had to go underwater—not very far, of course, but still a small distance.

On the other hand, how was he to know it was only a small distance? He had been unconscious when she had brought him here.

Now that she had worked out what she thought he had been trying to tell her, she was up against a new puzzle. By what means was she to get across to him that she had understood?

She thought about this for a time, then picked up the thing in her teeth and threw it herself against the rock wall at the back.

He turned around, evidently alerted by the sounds it made. She stretched out her neck, picked up the thing, brought it back to the water edge of the ledge, and then threw it at the wall again.

Then she looked at him.

He made sounds with his mouth and turned all the way around. Was it possible he had understood, she wondered? But he made no further moves, just sat there. She picked up and threw the "made" thing a couple of more times; then she paused once again to see what he might do.

He stood, hesitating, then inched forward to where the thing had fallen, picked up and threw it himself. But he threw it, as she had thrown it—at the rock wall behind the ledge.

The Youngest felt triumph. They were finally signalling each other—after a fashion.

But now where did they go from here? She wanted to ask him if there was anything they could do about the "made" thing being useless, but she could not think how to act that question out.

He, however, evidently had something in mind. He went to the edge of the rock shelf, knelt down and placed one of his multi-divided limb ends flat on the water surface, but with its inward-grasping surface upward. Then he moved it across the surface of the water so that the outer surface, or back, of it was in the water but the inner surface was still dry.

She stared at him. Once more he was doing something incomprehensible. He repeated the gesture several more times, but still it conveyed no meaning to her. He gave up, finally, and sat for a few minutes looking at her; then he got up, went back to the rock wall, turned around, walked once more to the edge of the ledge, and sat down.

Then he held up one of his upper limb ends with all but two of the divisions curled up. The two that were not curled up he pointed downward, and lowered them until their ends rested on the rock ledge. Then, pivoting first on the end of one of the divisions, then on the other, he moved the limb end back toward the wall as far as he could stretch, then turned it around and moved it forward again to the water's edge, where he folded up the two extended divisions, and held the limb end still.

He did this again. And again.

The Youngest concentrated. There was some meaning here; but with all the attention she could bring to bear on it, she still failed to see what it was. This was even harder than extracting wisdom from the legends. As she watched, he got up once more, walked back to the rock wall, came forward again and sat down. He did this twice.

Then he did the limb-end, two-division-movement thing twice.

Then he walked again, three times.

Then he did the limb-end thing three more times—

Understanding suddenly burst upon the Youngest. He was trying to make some comparison between his walking to the back of the ledge and forward again, and moving his limb ends in that odd fashion, first backward and then forward. The two divisions, with their little joints, moved much like his two lower limbs when he walked on them. It was extremely interesting to take part of your body and make it act like your whole body doing something. Youngest wished that her swim paddles had divisions on the ends, like his, so she could try it.

She was becoming fascinated with the diver all over

again. She had almost forgotten the threat to the eggs that others like him posed as long as he stayed hidden in this cave. Her conscience caught her up sharply. She should check right now and see if things were all right with the Family. She turned to leave, and then checked herself. She wanted to reassure him that she was coming back.

For a second only she was baffled for a means to do this; then she remembered that she had already left the cave once, thinking he would follow her, and then come back when she had given up on his doing so. If he saw her go and come several times, he should expect that she would go on returning, even though the interval might vary.

She turned and dived out through the hole into the loch, paused for a minute or two, then went back in. She did this two more times before leaving the cave finally. He had given her no real sign that he understood what she was trying to convey, but he had already showed signs of that intelligence the legends credited his species with. Hopefully, he would figure it out. If he did not—well, since she was going back anyway, the only harm would be that he might worry a bit about being abandoned there.

She surfaced briefly, in the center of the loch, to see if many of the "made" things were abroad on it today. But none were in sight and there was little or no sign of activity on the banks. The sky was heavy with dark, low-lying clouds; and the hint of snow, heavy snow, was in the sharp air. She thought again of the journey of the Lost Father of Loch Morar, and of the sea it could take them to—their safe home, the sea. They should go. They should go without waiting. If only she could convince them to go . . .

She dropped by the hatchhole, found First Mother warming the eggs while Second Mother was off feeding, and heard from First Mother that the craft had not left its place on shore all day. Discussing this problem almost as equals with First Mother—of whom she had always been very much in awe—emboldened the Youngest to the point where she shyly suggested she might try warming the clutch herself, occasionally, so as to relieve First Mother from these twice-daily stints, which must end by draining her strength and killing her.

"It would be up to Second Mother, in any case," First Mother answered, "but you're still really too small to be sure of giving adequate warmth to a full clutch. In an emergency, of course, you shouldn't hesitate to do your best with the eggs, but I don't think we're quite that desperate, yet."

Having signaled this, however, First Mother apparently softened.

"Besides," she said, "the time to be young and free of responsibilities is short enough. Enjoy it while you can. With the Family reduced to the four of us and this clutch, you'll have a hard enough adulthood, even if Second Mother manages to produce as many as two hatchlings out of the five or six clutches she can still have before her laying days are over. The odds of hatching females over males are four to one; but still, it could be that she might produce only a couple of males—and then everything would be up to you. So, use your time in your own way while it's still yours to use. But keep alert. If you're called, come immediately!"

The Youngest promised that she would. She left First Mother and went to find First Uncle, who was keeping watch in the neighborhood of the dock to which the craft was moored. When she found him, he was hanging in the loch about thirty feet deep and about a hundred feet off-shore from the craft, using his sensitive hearing to keep track of what was happening in the craft and on the dock.

"I'm glad you're here," he signaled to the Youngest when she arrived. "It's time for my second feeding; and I think there're none of the animals on the 'made' thing, right now. But it wouldn't hurt to keep a watch, anyway. Do you want to stay here and listen while I go and feed?"

Actually, Youngest was not to anxious to do so. Her plan had been to check with the Uncle, then do some feeding herself and get back to her diver while daylight was still coming into his cave. But she could hardly explain that to First Uncle.

"Of course," she said. "I'll stay here until you get back."

"Good," said the Uncle; and went off.

Left with nothing to do but listen and think, the Youngest hung in the water. Her imagination, which really required very little to start it working, had recaptured the notion of making friends with the diver. It was not so important, really, that he had gotten a look at her. Over the centuries a number of incidents had occurred in which members of the Family were seen briefly by one or more of the animals, and no bad results had come from those sightings. But it was important that the land-dwellers not realize there was a true Family. If she could just convince the diver that she was the last and only one of her People, it might be quite safe to see him from time to time—of course, only when he was alone and when they were in a safe place of her choosing, since though he might be trustworthy, his fellows who had twice threatened the hatchhold clearly were not.

The new excitement about getting to know him had come from starting to be able to "talk" with him. If she and he kept at it, they could probably work out ways to tell all sort of things to each other eventually.

That thought reminded her that she had not yet figured out why it was important to him that she understand that moving his divided limb ends in a certain way could stand for his walking. He must have had some reason for showing her that. Maybe it was connected with his earlier moving of his limb ends over the surface of the water?

Before she had a chance to ponder the possible connection, a sound from above, reaching down through the water, alerted her to the fact that some of the creatures were once more coming out onto the dock. She drifted in closer, and heard the sounds move to the end of the dock and onto the craft.

Apparently they were bringing something heavy aboard, because along with the noise of their lower limb ends on the structure came the thumping and rumbling of something which ended at last—to judge from the sounds—somewhere up on the forward deck where she had examined the box with the sloping top and the other "made" thing in the bow.

Following this, she heard some more sounds moving from the foredeck area into the cabin.

A little recklessly, the Youngest drifted in until she was almost under the craft and only about fifteen feet below the surface, and so verified that it was, indeed, in that part of the boat where the box with the sloping box stood that most of the activity was going on. Then the noise in that area slowed down and stopped, and she heard the sound of the animals walking back off the craft, down the dock and ashore. Things became once more silent.

First Uncle had not yet returned. The Youngest wrestled with her conscience. She had not been specifically told not to risk coming up to the surface near the dock; but she knew that was simply because it had not occurred to any of the older members of the Family that she would be daring enough to do such a thing. Of course, she had never told any of them how she had examined the foredeck of the craft once before. But now, having already done so, she had a hard time convincing herself it was too risky to do again. After all, hadn't she heard the animals leave the area? No matter how quiet one of them might try to be, her hearing was good enough to pick up little sounds of his presence, if he was still aboard.

In the end, she gave in to temptation—which is not to say she moved without taking every precaution. She drifted in, underwater, so slowly and quietly that a little crowd of curious minnows formed around her. Approaching the foredeck from the loch side of the craft, she stayed well underwater until she was right up against the hull. Touching it, she hung in the water, listening. When she still heard nothing, she lifted her head quickly, just enough for a glimpse over the side; then she ducked back under again and shot away and down to a safe distance.

Eighty feet deep and a hundred feet offshore, she paused to consider what she had seen.

Her memory, like that of everyone in the Family, was essentially photographic when she concentrated on remembering, as she had during her brief look over the side of the craft. But being able to recall exactly what she had looked at was not the same thing as realizing its import. In this case, what she had been looking for was what had just been brought aboard. By comparing what she had just seen with what she had observed on her night visit earlier, she had hoped to pick out any addition to the "made" things she had noted then.

At first glance, no difference had seemed visible. She noticed the box with the sloping top and the thing in the bow with the barbed rod inside. A number of other, smaller things were about the deck, too, some of which she had examined briefly the time before and some that she had barely noticed. Familiar were several of the doubled things like the one the diver had thrown from him in order to open up communications between them at first. Largely unfamiliar were a number of smaller boxes, some round things, other things that were combinations of round and angular shapes, and a sort of tall open frame, upright and holding several rods with barbed ends like the ones which the thing in the bow contained.

She puzzled over the assortment of things—and then without warning an answer came. But provokingly, as often happened with her, it was not the answer to the question she now had, but to an earlier one.

It had suddenly struck her that the diver's actions in rejecting the "made" thing he had worn on his back, and all his original signals to her, might mean that for some reason it was not the one he wanted, or needed, in order to leave the cave. Why there should be that kind of difference between it and these things left her baffled. The one with him now in the cave had been the right one; but maybe it was not the right one, today. Perhaps—she had a sudden inspiration—"made" things could die like animals or fish, or even like People, and the one he now had was dead. In any case, maybe what he needed was another of that particular kind of thing.

Perhaps this insight had come from the fact that several of these same "made" things were on the deck; and also, there was obviously only one diver, since First Uncle had not reported any of the other animals going down into the water. She was immediately tempted to go and get another one of the things, so that she could take it back to the diver. If he put it on, that meant she was right. Even if he did not, she might learn something by the way he handled it.

If it had been daring to take one look at the deck, it was inconceivably so to return now and actually try to take something from it. Her sense of duty struggled with her inclinations but slowly was overwhelmed. After all, she knew now—knew positively—that none of the animals were aboard the boat and none could have come aboard in the last few minutes because she was still close enough to hear them. But if she went, she would have to hurry if she was going to do it before the Uncle got back and forbade any such action.

She swam back to the craft in a rush, came to the surface beside it, rose in the water, craned her neck far enough inboard to snatch up one of the things in her teeth and escape with it.

A few seconds later, she had it two hundred feet down on the bed of the loch and was burying it in silt. Three minutes later she was back on station watching the craft, calmly enough but with her heart beating fast. Happily, there was still no sign of First Uncle's return.

Her heartbeat slowed. She went back to puzzling over what it was on the foredeck that could be the thing she had heard the creatures bring aboard. Of course, she now had three memory images of the area to compare . . .

Recognition came.

There *was* a discrepancy between the last two mental images and the first one, a discrepancy about one of the "made" things to which she had devoted close attention, that first time.

The difference was the line attached to the box with the sloping top. It was not the same line at all. It was a drum of other line at least twice as thick as the one which had connected the heavy thing and the box previously—almost as thick as the thick line connecting the barbed rod to the thing in the bow that contained it. Clearly, the animals of the craft had tried to make sure that they would run no danger of losing their dropweight if it became buried again. Possibly they had foolishly hoped that it was so strong that not even First Uncle could break it as he had the first.

That meant they were not going to give up. Here was clear evidence they were going to go on searching for their diver. She *must* get him back to them as soon as possible.

She began to swim restlessly, to and fro in the underwater, anxious to see the Uncle return so that she could tell him what had been done.

He came not long afterward, although it seemed to her that she had waited and worried for a considerable time before he appeared. When she told him about the new line, he was concerned enough by the information so that he barely reprimanded her for taking the risk of going in close to the craft.

"I must tell First Mother, right away—" He checked himself and looked up through the twenty or so feet of water that covered them. "No, there're only a few more hours of daylight left. I need to think, anyway. I'll stay on guard here until dark, then I'll go see First Mother in her

cave. Youngest, for right now don't say anything to Second Mother, or even to First Mother if you happen to talk
to her. I'll tell both of them myself after I've had time to
think about it."

"Then I can go now?" asked the Youngest, almost
standing on her tail in the underwater in her eagerness to
be off.

"Yes, yes," signaled the Uncle.

The Youngest turned and dove toward the spot where
she had buried the "made" thing she had taken and about
which she had been careful to say nothing to First Uncle.
She had no time to explain about the diver now, and any
mention of the thing would bring demands for a full
explanation from her elders. Five minutes later, the thing
in her teeth, she was splitting the water in the direction of
the cave where she had left the diver.

She had never meant to leave him alone this long. An
irrational fear grew in her that something had happened to
him in the time she had been gone. Perhaps he had started
chilling again and had lost too much warmth, like one of
the old ones, and was now dead. If he was dead, would
the other animals be satisfied just to have his body back?
But she did not want to think of him dead: He was not a
bad little animal, in spite of his acting in such an ugly
fashion when he had seen her for the first time. She should
have realized that in the daylight, seeing her as he had
without warning for the first time—

The thought of daylight reminded her that First Uncle
had talked about there being only a few hours of it left.
Surely there must be more than that. The day could not
have gone quickly.

She took a quick slant up to the surface to check. No,
she was right. There must be at least four hours yet before
the sun would sink below the mountains. However, in his
own way the Uncle had been right, also, because the
clouds were very heavy now. It would be too dark to see
much, even long before actual nightfall. Snow was certain

by dark, possibly even before. As she floated for a moment with her head and neck out of water, a few of the first wandering flakes came down the wind and touched her right cheek cells with tiny, cold fingers.

She dived again. It would indeed be a heavy snowfall; the Family could start out tonight on their way to the sea, if only they wanted to. It might even be possible to carry the eggs, distributed among the four of them, just two or three carried pressed between a swim paddle and warm body skin. First Mother might tire easily; but after the first night, when they had gotten well away from the loch, and with new snow falling to cover their footsteps, they could go by short stages. There would be no danger that the others would run out of heat or strength. Even the Youngest, small as she was, had fat reserves for a couple of months without eating and with ordinary activity. The Lost Father had made it to Loch Ness from the sea in a week or so.

If only they would go now. If only she were old enough and wise enough to convince them to go. For just a moment she gave herself over to a dream of their great sea home, of the People grown strong again, patrolling in their great squadrons past the white-gleaming berg ice or under the tropic stars. Most of the eggs of every clutch would hatch, then. The hatchlings would have the beaches of all the empty islands of the world to hatch on. Later, in the sea, they would grow up strong and safe, with their mighty elders around to guard them from anything that moved in the salt waters. In their last years, the old ones would bask under the hot sun in warm, hidden places and never need to chill again. The sea. That was where they belonged. Where they must go home to, someday. And that day should be soon . . .

The Youngest was almost to the cave now. She brought her thoughts, with a wrench, back to the diver. Alive or dead, he too must go back—to his own kind. Fervently, she hoped that she was right about another "made" thing being what he needed before he would swim out of the cave. If not, if he just threw this one away as he had the other one, then she had no choice. She would simply have to pick him up in her teeth and carry him out of the cave without it. Of course, she must be careful to hold him so that he could not reach her to scratch or bite; and she must get his head back above water as soon as they got out of the cave into the open loch, so that he would not drown.

By the time she had gotten this far in her thinking, she was at the cave. Ducking inside, she exploded up through the surface of the water within. The diver was seated with his back against the cave wall, looking haggard and savage. He was getting quite dark-colored around the jaws, now. The little points he had there seemed to be growing. She dumped the new "made" thing at his feet.

For a moment he merely stared down at it, stupidly. Then he fumbled the object up into his arms and did something to it with those active little divided sections of his two upper limb ends. A hissing sound came from the thing that made her start back, warily. So, the "made" things were alive, after all!

The diver was busy attaching to himself the various things he had worn when she had first found him—with the exception that the new thing she had brought him, rather than its old counterpart, was going on his back. Abruptly, though, he stopped, his head-thing still not on and still in the process of putting on the paddle-like things that attached to his lower limb ends. He got up and came forward to the edge of the water, looking at her.

He had changed again. From the moment he had gotten the new thing to make the hissing noise, he had gone into yet a different way of standing and acting. Now he came within limb reach of her and stared at her so self-assuredly that she almost felt she was the animal trapped in a cave and he was free. Then he crouched down by the water and once more began to make motions with his upper limbs and limb ends.

First, he made the on-top-of-the-water sliding motion
with the back of one limb end that she now began to
understand must mean the craft he had gone overboard
from. Once she made the connection it was obvious: the
craft, like his hand, was in the water only with its underside. Its top side was dry and in the air. As she watched,
he circled his "craft" limb end around in the water and
brought it back to touch the ledge. Then, with his other
limb end, he "walked" two of its divisions up to the
"craft" and continued to "walk" them onto it.

She stared. He was apparently signaling something about
his getting on the craft. But why?

However, now he was doing something else. He lifted
his walking-self limb end off the "craft" and put it standing on its two stiff divisions, back on the ledge. Then he
moved the "craft" out over the water, away from the
ledge, and held it there. Next, to her surprise, he "walked"
his other limb end right off the ledge into the water. Still
"walking" so that he churned the still surface of the cave
water to a slight roughness, he moved that limb end slowly
to the unmoving "craft." When the "walking" limb end
reached the "craft," it once more stepped up onto it.

The diver now pulled his upper limbs back, sat crouched
on the ledge, and looked at the Youngest for a long
moment. Then he made the same signals again. He did it a
third time, and she began to understand. He was showing
himself swimming to his craft. Of course, he had no idea
how far he actually was from it, here in the cave—an
unreasonable distance for as weak a swimmer as one of his
kind was.

But now he was signaling yet something else. His "walking" limb end stood at the water's edge. His other limb
end was not merely on the water, but in it, below the
surface. As she watched, a single one of that other limb
end's divisions rose through the surface and stood, slightly
crooked, so that its upper joint was almost at right angles
to the part sticking through the surface. Seeing her gaze on

this part of him, the diver began to move that solitary joint through the water in the direction its crooked top was pointing. He brought it in this fashion all the way to the rock ledge and halted it opposite the "walking" limb end standing there.

He held both limb ends still in position and looked at her, as if waiting for a sign of understanding.

She gazed back, once more at a loss. The joint sticking up out of the water was like nothing in her memory but the limb of a waterlogged tree, its top more or less looking at the "walking" limb end that stood for the diver. But if the "walking" limb end was *he*—? Suddenly she understood. The division protruding from the water signalized *her!*

To show she understood, she backed off from the ledge, crouched down in the shallow water of the cave until nothing but her upper neck and head protruded from the water, and then—trying to look as much like his crooked division as possible—approached him on the ledge.

He made noises. There was no way of being sure, of course, but she felt she was beginning to read the tone of some of the sounds he made; and these latest sounds, she was convinced, sounded pleased and satisfied.

He tried something else.

He made the "walking" shape on the ledge, then added something. In addition to the two limb-end divisions standing on the rock, he unfolded another—a short, thick division, one at the edge of that particular limb end, and moved it in circular fashion, horizontally. Then he stood up on the ledge himself and swung one of his upper limbs at full length, in similar, circular fashion. He did this several times.

In no way could she imitate that kind of gesture, though she comprehended immediately that the movement of the extra, short division above the "walking" form was supposed to indicate him standing and swinging his upper limb like now. She merely stayed as she was and waited to see what he would do next.

He got down by the water, made the "craft" shape, "swam" his "walking" shape to it, climbed the "walking" shape up on the "craft," then had the "walking" shape turn and make the upper-limb swinging motion.

The Youngest watched, puzzled, but caught up in this strange game of communication she and the diver had found to play together. Evidently he wanted to go back to his craft, get on it, and then wave his upper limb like that, for some reason. It made no sense so far—but he was already doing something more.

He now had the "walking" shape standing on the ledge, making the upper-limb swinging motion, and he was showing the crooked division that was she approaching through the water.

That was easy: he wanted her to come to the ledge when he swung his upper limb.

Sure enough, after a couple of demonstrations of the last shape signals, he stood up on the ledge and swung his arm. Agreeably, she went out in the water, crouched down, and approached the ledge. He made pleased noises. This was all rather ridiculous, she thought, but enjoyable nonetheless. She was standing half her length out from the edge, where she had stopped, and was trying to think of a body signal she could give that would make him swim to her, when she noticed that he was going on to further signals.

He had his "walking" shape standing on the "craft" shape, in the water out from the ledge, and signaling "Come." But then he took his "walking" shape away from the "craft" shape, put it under the water a little distance off, and came up with it as the "her" shape. He showed the "her" shape approaching the "craft" shape with her neck and head out of water.

She was to come to his craft? In response to this "Come" signal?

No!

She was so furious with him for suggesting such a thing

that she had no trouble at all thinking of a way to convey her reaction. Turning around, she plunged underwater, down through the cave entrance and out into the loch. Her first impulse was to flash off and leave him there to do whatever he wanted—stay forever, go back to his kind, or engage in any other nonsensical activity his small head could dream up. Did he think she had no wisdom at all? To suggest that she come right up to his craft with her head and neck out of water when he signaled—as if there had never been a taboo against her People having anything to do with his! He must not understand her in the slightest degree.

Common sense caught up with her, halted her, and turned her about not far from the cave mouth. Going off like this would do her no good—more, it would do the Family no good. On the other hand, she could not bring herself to go back into the cave, now. She hung in the water, undecided, unable to conquer the conscience that would not let her swim off, but also unable to make herself re-enter.

Vibrations from the water in the cave solved her problem. He had evidently put on the "made" thing she had brought him and was coming out. She stayed where she was, reading the vibrations.

He came to the mouth of the cave and swam slowly, straight up, to the surface. Level with him, but far enough away to be out of sight in the murky water, the Youngest rose, too. He lifted his head at last into the open air and looked around him.

He's looking for me, thought the Youngest, with a sense of satisfaction that he would see no sign of her and would assume she had left him for good. Now, go ashore and go back to your own kind, she commanded in her thoughts.

But he did not go ashore, though shore was only a matter of feet from him. Instead, he pulled his head underwater once more and began to swim back down.

She almost exploded with exasperation. He was headed toward the cave mouth! He was going back inside!

"You stupid animal!" she signaled to him. *"Go ashore!"*

But of course he did not even perceive the signal, let alone understand it. Losing all patience, the Youngest swooped down upon him, hauled him to the surface once more, and let him go.

For a second he merely floated there, motionless, and she felt a sudden fear that she had brought him up through the water too swiftly. She knew of some small fish that spent all their time down in the deepest parts of the loch, and if you brought one of them too quickly up the nine hundred feet or so to the surface, it twitched and died, even though it had been carried gently. Sometimes part of the insides of these fish bulged out through their mouths and gill slits after they were brought up quickly.

After a second, the diver moved and looked at her.

Concerned for him, she had stayed on the surface with him, her head just barely out of the water. Now he saw her. He kicked with the "made" paddles on his lower limbs to raise himself partly out of the water and, a little awkwardly, with his upper limb ends made the signal of him swimming to his craft.

She did not respond. He did it several more times, but she stayed stubbornly non-communicative. It was bad enough that she had let him see her again after his unthinkable suggestion.

He gave up making signals. Ignoring the shore close at hand, he turned from her and began to swim slowly south and out into the center of the loch.

He was going in the wrong direction if he was thinking of swimming all the way to his craft. And after his signaling it was pretty clear that this was what he had in mind. Let him find out his mistake for himself, the Youngest thought, coldly.

But she found that she could not go through with that. Angrily, she shot after him, caught the thing on his back with her teeth, and, lifting him by it enough so that his head was just above the surface, began to swim wth him in the right direction.

She went slowly—according to her own ideas of speed—but even so a noticeable bow wave built up before him. She lifted him a little higher out of the water to be on the safe side; but she did not go any faster: perhaps he could not endure too much speed. As it was, the clumsy shape of his small body hung about with "made" things was creating surprising turbulence for its size. It was a good thing the present hatchhole (and, therefore, First Mother's current resting cave and the area in which First Uncle and Second Mother would do their feeding) was as distant as they were; otherwise First Uncle, at least, would certainly have been alarmed by the vibrations and have come to investigate.

It was also a good thing that the day was as dark as it was, with its late hour and the snow that was now beginning to fall with some seriousness; otherwise she would not have wanted to travel this distance on the surface in daylight. But the snow was now so general that both shores were lost to sight in its white, whirling multitude of flakes, and certainly no animal on shore would be able to see her and the diver out here.

There was privacy and freedom, being hidden by the snow like this—like the freedom she felt on dark nights when the whole loch was free of the animals and all hers. If only it could be this way all the time. To live free and happy was so good. Under conditions like these, she could not even fear or dislike the animals, other than her diver, who were a threat to the Family.

At the same time, she remained firm in her belief that the Family should go, now. None of the others had ever before told her that any of the legends were untrustworthy, and she did not believe that the one about the Lost Father was so. It was not that that legend was untrustworthy, but that they had grown conservative with age and feared to leave the loch; while she, who was still young, still dared to try great things for possibly great rewards.

She had never admitted it to the older ones, but one midwinter day when she had been very young and quite small—barely old enough to be allowed to swim around in the loch by herself—she had ventured up one of the streams flowing into the loch. It was a stream far too shallow for an adult of the Family; and some distance up it, she found several otters playing on an ice slide they had made. She had joined them, sliding along with them for half a day without ever being seen by any upright animal. She remembered this all very well, particularly her scrambling around on the snow to get to the head of the slide; and that she had used her tail muscles to skid herself along on her warm belly surface, just as the Lost Father had described.

If she could get the others to slip ashore long enough to try the snowy loch banks before day-warmth combined with loch-warmth to clear them of the white stuff . . . But even as she thought this, she knew they would never agree to try. They would not even consider the journey home to the sea until, as First Mother said, it became clear that that was the only alternative to extinction at the hands of the upright animals.

It was a fact, and she must face it. But maybe she could think of some way to make plain to them that the animals had, indeed, become that dangerous. For the first time, it occurred to her that her association with the diver could turn out to be something that would help them all. Perhaps, through him, she could gain evidence about his kind that would convince the rest of the Family that they should leave the loch.

It was an exciting thought. It would do no disservice to him to use him in that fashion, because clearly he was different from others of his kind: he had realized that not only was she warm as he was, but as intelligent or more so than he. He would have no interest in being a danger to her People, and might even cooperate—if she could make him understand what she wanted—in convincing the Family of the dangers his own race posed to them. Testimony from one of the animals directly would be an argument to convince even First Uncle.

For no particular reason, she suddenly remembered how he had instinctively huddled against her when he had discovered her warming him. The memory roused a feeling of tenderness in her. She found herself wishing there were some way she could signal that feeling to him. But they were almost to his craft, now. It and the dock were beginning to be visible—dark shapes lost in the dancing white—with the dimmer dark shapes of trees and other things ashore behind them.

Now that they were close enough to see a shore, the falling snow did not seem so thick, nor so all-enclosing as it had out in the middle of the loch. But there was still a privacy to the world it created, a feeling of security. Even sounds seemed to be hushed.

Through the water, Youngest could feel vibrations from the craft. At least one, possibly two, of the other animals were aboard it. As soon as she was close enough to be sure her diver could see the craft, she let go of the thing on his back and sank abruptly to about twenty feet below the surface, where she hung and waited, checking the vibrations of his movements to make sure he made it safely to his destination.

At first, when she let him go, he trod water where he was and turned around and around as if searching for her. He pushed himself up in the water and made the "Come" signal several times; but she refused to respond. Finally, he turned and swam to the edge of the craft.

He climbed on board very slowly, making so little noise that the two in the cabin evidently did not hear him. Surprisingly, he did not seem in any hurry to join them or to let them know he was back.

The Youngest rose to just under the surface and lifted her head above to see what he was doing. He was still standing on the foredeck, where he had climbed aboard, not moving. Now, as she watched, he walked heavily forward to the bow and stood beside the ''made'' thing there, gazing out in her direction.

He lifted his arm as if to make the ''Come'' signal, then dropped it to his side.

The Youngest knew that in absolutely no way could he make out the small portion of her head above the waves, with the snow coming down the way it was and day drawing swiftly to its dark close. She stared at him. She noticed something weary and sad about the way he stood. I should leave now, she thought. But she did not move. With the other two animals still unaware in the cabin, and the snow continuing to fall, there seemed no reason to hurry off. She would miss him, she told herself, feeling a sudden pang of loss. Looking at him, it came to her suddenly that from the way he was acting he might well miss her, too.

Watching, she remembered how he had half lifted his limb as if to signal and then dropped it again. Maybe his limb is tired, she thought.

A sudden impulse took her. I'll go in close, underwater, and lift my head high for just a moment, she thought, so he can see me. He'll know then that I haven't left him for good. He already understands I wouldn't come on board that thing of his under any circumstance. Maybe if he sees me again for a second, now, he'll understand that if he gets back in the water and swims to me, we can go on learning signals from each other. Then, maybe, someday, we'll know enough signals together so that he can convince the older ones to leave.

Even as she thought this, she was drifting in, underwater, until she was only twenty feet from the craft. She rose suddenly and lifted her head and neck clear of the water.

For a long second, she saw he was staring right at her but not responding. Then she realized that he might not be seeing her after all, just staring blindly out at the loch and the snow. She moved a little sideways to attract his attention, and saw his head move. Then he *was* seeing her? Then why didn't he do something?

She wondered if something was wrong with him. After all, he had been gone for nearly two days from his own People and must have missed at least a couple of his feeding periods in that time. Concern impelled her to a closer look at him. She began to drift in toward the boat.

He jerked upright suddenly and swung an upper limb at her.

But he was swinging it all wrong. It was not the "Come" signal he was making, at all. It was more like the "Come" signal in reverse—as if he was pushing her back and away from him. Puzzled, and even a little hurt, because the way he was acting reminded her of how he had acted when he first saw her in the cave and did not know she had been with him earlier, the Youngest moved in even closer.

He flung both his upper limbs furiously at her in that new, "rejecting" motion and shouted at her—a loud, angry noise. Behind him, came an explosion of different noise from inside the cabin, and the other two animals burst out onto the deck. Her diver turned, making noises, waving both his limbs at them the way he had just waved them at her. The Youngest, who had been about to duck down below the safety of the loch surface, stopped. Maybe this was some new signal he wanted her to learn, one that had some reference to his two companions?

But the others were making noises back at him. The taller one ran to one of the "made" things that were like, but smaller than, the one in the bow of the boat. The diver shouted again, but the tall one ignored him, only seizing one end of the thing he had run to and pulling that end around toward him. The Youngest watched, fascinated, as the other end of the "made" thing swung to point at her.

Then the diver made a very large angry noise, turned, and seized the end of the largest "made" thing before him in the bow of the boat.

Frightened suddenly, for it had finally sunk in that for some reason he had been signaling her to get away, she turned and dived. Then, as she did so, she realized that she had turned, not away from, but into line with the outer end of the thing in the bow of the craft.

She caught a flicker of movement, almost too fast to see, from the thing's hollow outer end. Immediately, the loudest sound she had ever heard exploded around her, and a tremendous blow struck her behind her left shoulder as she entered the underwater.

She signaled for help instinctively, in shock and fear, plunging for the deep bottom of the loch. From far off, a moment later, came the answer of First Uncle. Blindly, she turned to flee to him.

As she did, she thought to look and see what had happened to her. Swinging her head around, she saw a long, but shallow, gash across her shoulder and down her side. Relief surged in her. It was not even painful yet, though it might be later; but it was nothing to cripple her, or even to slow her down.

How could her diver have done such a thing to her? The thought was checked almost as soon as it was born—by the basic honesty of her training. *He* had not done this. *She* had done it by diving into the path of the barbed rod cast from the thing in the bow. If she had not done that, it would have missed her entirely.

But why should he make the thing throw the barbed rod at all? She had thought he had come to like her, as she liked him.

Abruptly, comprehension came; and it felt as if her heart leaped in her. For all at once it was perfectly clear what he had been trying to do. She should have had more faith in him. She halted her flight toward the Uncle and turned back toward the boat.

Just below it, she found what she wanted. The barbed rod, still leaving a taste of her blood in the water, was hanging point down from its line, in about two hundred feet of water. It was being drawn back up, slowly but steadily.

She surged in close to it, and her jaws clamped on the line she had tried to bite before and found resistant. But now she was serious in her intent to sever it. Her jaws scissored and her teeth ripped at it, though she was careful to rise with the line and put no strain upon it that would warn the animals above about what she was doing. The tough strands began to part under her assault.

Just above her, the sound of animal noises now came clearly through the water: her diver and the others making sounds at each other.

". . . I tell you we're through!" It was her diver speaking. "It's over. I don't care what you saw. It's my boat. I paid for it; and I'm quitting."

"It not *your* boat, man. It a boat belong to the company, the company that belong all three of us. We got contracts."

"I'll pay off your damned contracts."

"There's more to this than money, now. We know that great beast in there, now. We get our contract money, and maybe a lot more, going on the TV and telling how we catch it and bring it in. No, man, you don't stop us now."

"I say, it's my boat. I'll get a lawyer and court order—"

"You do that. You get a lawyer and a judge and a pretty court order, and we'll give you the boat. You do that. Until then, it belong to the company and it keep after that beast."

She heard the sound of footsteps—her diver's footsteps, she could tell, after all this time of seeing him walk his lower limbs—leaving the boat deck, stepping onto the dock, going away.

The line was almost parted. She and the barbed rod were only about forty feet below the boat.

"What'd you have to do that for?" That was the voice of the third creature. "He'll do that! He'll get a lawyer and take the boat and we won't even get our minimum pay. Whyn't you let him pay us off, the way he said?''

"Hush, you fooking fool. How long you think it take him get a lawyer, a judge, and a writ? Four days, maybe five—''

The line parted. She caught the barbed rod in her jaws as it started to sink. The ragged end of the line lifted and vanished above her.

"—and meanwhile, you and me, we go hunting with this boat. We know the beast there, now. We know what to look for. We find it in four, five day, easy.''

"But even if we get it, he'll just take it away from us again with his lawyer—''

"I tell you, no. We'll get ourselves a lawyer, also. This company formed to take the beast; and he got to admit he tried to call off the hunt. And we both seen what he do. He've fired that harpoon gun to scare it off, so I can't get it with the drug lance and capture it. We testify to that, we got him—Ah!''

"What is it?''

"What is it? You got no eyes, man? The harpoon gone. It in that beast after all, being carried around. We don't need no four, five days, I tell you now. That be a good, long piece of steel, and we got the locators to find metal like that. We hunt that beast and bring it in tomorrow. Tomorrow, man, I promise you! It not going to go too fast, too far, with that harpoon.''

But he could not see below the snow and the black surface of the water. The Youngest was already moving very fast indeed through the deep loch to meet the approaching First Uncle. In her jaws she carried the harpoon, and on her back she bore the wound it had made. The elders could have no doubt, now, about the intentions of the upright animals (other than her diver) and their ability to destroy the Family.

They must call First Mother, and this time there would be no hesitation. She would see the harpoon and the wound and decide for them all. Tonight they would leave by the route of the Lost Father, while the snow was still thick on the banks of the loch. They might have to leave the eggs behind, after all; but if so, Second Mother could have more clutches, and maybe later they would even find a way ashore again to Loch Morar and meet others of their own People at last.

But, in any case, they would go now to live free in the sea; and in the sea most of Second Mother's future eggs would hatch and the Family would grow numerous and strong again.

She could see them in her mind's eye, now. They would leave the loch by the mouth of Glen Moriston—First Mother, Second Mother, First Uncle, herself—and take to the snow-covered banks when the water became too shallow . . .

They would travel steadily into the mountains, and the new snow falling behind them would hide the marks of their going from the eyes of the animals. They would pass by deserted ways through the silent rocks to the ocean. They would come at last to its endless waters, to the shining bergs of the north and the endless warmth of the Equator sun. The ocean, their home, was welcoming them back, at last. There would be no more doubt, no more fear or waiting. They were going home to the sea . . . they were going home to the sea . . .

A Matter of Perspective

The day of the launch of Apollo 14, buses for the working writers got us to the press site, three and a half miles from the bird, four hours before launch time. With at least two hours yet to go before lift-off, I was sitting in an upper part of the press stand, still talking to artist Kelly Freas about the VAB, or Vehicle Assembly Building, which lifted out of the flat Cape Kennedy landscape to our left.

"I don't understand," I was saying to Kelly. "From here it still looks like a big building. But it doesn't begin to look half as big as I know it is, after being inside it. Can you figure out why?"

"I'm not sure," said Kelly. "It could be a matter of perspective. If you're close enough to compare the building to anything beside it, you're too close to see it all at once. If you're far enough back to see it all, anything else beside it is too small to measure it by. So your eye gives it dimensions you can believe in."

He was right, of course, this gigantic building sits on the horizon like a department store in the middle of a parking lot—in this case a parking lot five miles wide—and is unbelievable. Its magical proportions and ingenious use of

236

space have already earned it an architectural award for functional design. Every change of viewpoint, atmosphere and time of day presents unexpected realignments of plane and texture. It looks delicate and airy from a distance; but by the time you are close enough to be aware of the reality of steel and concrete, you have lost awareness of it as a total structure. The fact that it covers eight acres doesn't mean much until you notice that the place is uncommon quiet; it's so damn big it doesn't even echo!

The discussion Kelly and I were having about it was not exactly an idle one. We were both down in Florida to cover the launch for *Analog*. It had been decided that an artist like Kelly was needed to capture in sketches what defied the best of camera work—the sheer, unbelievably outsize dimensions of some of the hardware involved in the space program.

I was concerned with matters of size—and with something else. A question that had kept coming at me in the last two years, particularly from radio and TV interviewers and non-science-fiction readers among the audiences to whom I sometimes spoke.

"What can you science-fiction people think up to write about," the question ran, "now that man has landed on the Moon? Isn't all the science fiction told by this time?"

The same question had been put to me in somewhat more practical terms by a news editor I had talked with before coming down.

"It's a problem," he said. "Naturally, we have to cover the Apollo shot. On the other hand, the public has pretty well had this Moon flight business. It was all right for space-age poets, like yourself, before the actual thing got going. Now the engineers have taken over. There's not much poetry in engineering."

I had come down to Kennedy feeling instinctively that editor was wrong; but unable to say why. However, when I got to the Cape, what I found there first seemed to support his attitude, rather than mine. The first exhibit we stopped at was the launch site from which Alan Shepard had lifted for his first suborbital flight on May 5, 1961. Looking at the site right now, I realized that it jarred me to see the blockhouse so close to the launch pad, and that on the edge of the pad itself, less than a dozen steps from the center of it, was a fire hose behind a thin, metal shield. But the largest jolt came from the sight of the rocket itself standing upright on display there, a Redstone launch vehicle, duplicate of the one with which Shepard had actually reached an altitude of 116.5 miles and a speed of 5,100 m.p.h. for five minutes of weightless flight.

Reaching back ten years, I went up to the launch vehicle and put my hand on its painted metal side, already hot from the morning hours of Florida winter sun. The Redstone rocket, standing on its tail and exclusive of the spacecraft it carried, was 69 feet tall and 70 inches in diameter—and those figures had always seemed impressive enough. But, as I stood there in the sunlight touching it, it struck me what a flimsy vehicle it was in which to fire a man a hundred miles up and three hundred miles downrange. For the first time, I began to realize how the engineering developments of the space effort had changed my own point of view, even as they had affected my radio and TV interviewers, and the editor I had spoken with before coming here. Once, such a rocket had seemed more than large enough to carry a man that distance.

I left the Redstone and walked over to the fire extinguisher behind its shield. It was a cannon-type nozzle mounted on a post with a wheel crank driving a gear to raise and lower the angle of the nozzle. The whole mechanism had been painted a fire-engine red, but the rod connecting the crank wheel to the gear had been eaten away by salt air until it looked chewed and blackened and in one spot was no thicker than heavy wire. Ten years of history moved between me and the fire hose like an invisible, but heavy, curtain. Suddenly, the pad and rocket seemed ancient and primitive, almost quaint, like a Model T Ford on display at a present-day auto show.

The feeling of looking at things from a simpler, cruder time, stuck with me as we went on through the Space Museum. We passed a number of exhibits from World War II and later, guided missiles and rockets which had been frankly constructed as weapons. With two exceptions these were smaller than the Redstone. One exception was a 90-foot Thor-Delta. The other was an Atlas launch vehicle, like the one first fired from Cape Kennedy in November, 1958. The Atlas on display lay on its side; but it was a younger and larger launch vehicle than the Redstone, a 1½ stage rocket, with a 120-inch diameter. As a single first-stage only, in conjunction with the 22-foot Agena B stage, an Atlas had helped launch the 447-pound Mariner 2 Venus probe on August 27, 1962. That had been a reaching out to a sister planet—space flight in the real sense of the word. And yet, even the Atlas I saw lying there was touched and seemed shrunken by the same cloak of past history that seemed to diminish my view of the Redstone.

The reason was not hard to dig out. I *knew*, even as I looked at these creatures of the Space Museum, that the Saturn vehicle I was about to see was so much larger than these exhibits that it would make them seem like toys . . . scaled-down playthings for the children of the present-day giant, whose actual massive tools were alive and fuming, only a few miles away.

We got back in the press bus and were driven over blacktop roads from the Patrick Air Force Base sections of the Kennedy area toward the NASA—National Aeronautics and Space Administration—section. On the way we passed an Atlas-Centaur in upright, ready-to-lift position on a launch pad; and the cloak of history began to dissolve a little. Above the 75-foot Atlas first-stage, the Centaur second-stage was 32 feet long, as opposed to the shorter

Agena B. Also, between Centaur and Atlas, there was a 13-foot interstage adapter and separation system. This most powerful of the Atlas-combination carriers can put 2,300 pounds of probe into escape trajectory, or soft-land a payload of 700 pounds on the Moon. It is out of the class of playthings, even for giant children, and watching the Atlas-Centaur from a distance, as our bus rolled past it, I began to think I had bridged the gap in time and perception; and that I was ready now for the Apollo 14, with its Saturn stages.

We passed from Patrick Air Force Base on to NASA ground and at the entry point to the latter a uniformed guard with a side arm came on board the bus, looked up and down the aisle, then got off again without saying a word. The bus went on once more and turned in toward the wall of a big building—I had not been watching, for some reason, and the wall took me by surprise. We turned parallel to the wall, went on for a short distance and came to a high wire fence, a compound enclosing the crawler-carrier that carries the completed launch vehicle and spacecraft from the VAB to the launch pad.

I had thought I was prepared for the Saturn. It had not occurred to me to wonder if I was prepared for the size of the crawler—and I found I was not. We got out of the bus and walked around it; and it was impossible to see, for the same reason you cannot really see a block-square office building or department store. You could get different angles of view upon it; but there was no way to back off far enough to see it as a whole and still distinguish any details.

A baseball diamond on wheels would be a bit smaller. The platform is supported at each corner by what looked like an oversized army tank ten feet high and forty feet long. Its four great double tracks, each wearing 57 tons of tread shoe, are driven by 16 traction motors powered by four 1,000 kilowatt generators driven by two 2,750 h.p.

diesel engines. Together, these moved the crawler's six million pounds, plus its enormous cargo, once it was loaded.

To baby that cargo over the 18,000 feet from VAB to pad, it has a power system for the gigantic hydraulic jacks which keep the bird and its mobile launcher level. These are two 750 kw generators, driven by two 1,065 h.p. diesel engines, which also supply power for lighting and ventilating as well as steering—not that there is much steering except in actually positioning the load. You will notice in pictures that the crawler has an identical control cab at each identical end. All opening and control functions are coordinated in these cabs: one guides it going, the other returning. The machine never needs to turn around, although if it did I do not suppose anyone would ever know.

This is the largest tracked vehicle in the world, as far as is known. As such, it has generated a couple of tales.

Naturally, such a ponderous machine has to have a rather special road to carry the weight. The first tale is that the roadbed was put down originally with a layer of hydraulic fill, a thicker layer of graded lime rock and a final layer of special fill and surface sealer, all nicely compacted into a good, solid road twelve feet thick.

The crawler, the tale goes, roared out of its pen at top speed—one mile per hour—and sank five feet into the surface . . . Now it has a seven-foot thick roadbed.

Another tale has to do with the problem of wheel bearings tough enough to carry the weight of the Crawler/ Transporter, let alone its cargo. It seems that when the original model was tried out the wheel bearings simply collapsed at the first revolution. One version has it that the bearings simply oozed out like toothpaste; the other version says the bearings were crushed and trickled out as a fine powder.

Whether the bearings crunched or squished, they *were*

made of the toughest material available so there was no question of replacement, or substitution. The whole truck mechanism had to be redesigned and rebuilt.

The crawler carries a crew of eleven with three ground crewmen, and almost as an afterthought, it also provides power for the Mobile Launcher through two 1,250 kw generators. Two glass-windowed structures at corners diagonally opposite each other house controls that can drive it from either end. The control structures alone looked large enough to set up family housekeeping in.

After the cameras had stopped snapping, the bus drove on around the building and came on an entrance through which it looked as if several furniture vans could have been driven, side by side. We got out and walked through the entrance, from the eye-dazzling brilliance of the sunshine into a shadowy vastness beyond adequate description. This was the Vehicle Assembly Building; and we were inside it.

To come in on the ground floor of the VAB as we were doing was to realize literally the meaning in the old simile about feeling like an ant. Seen from the ceiling level of that 525-foot high building, a six-foot man could be no more visible than an ant in an ordinary room, if he could be distinguished at all. Standing on the floor and gazing ceilingward the eye went up, and up, and still up—until it did not seem possible to see farther. And yet still it went up, to a darkness that must be the ceiling, but seemed no less untouchable and remote than the sky itself.

Above us, a tenth of a mile of soaring emptiness. About us, eight acres of floor. Four of the Saturn vehicles with spacecraft atop each of them could be constructed and contained in this building at once; and each 363-foot high Saturn craft was the equivalent of a 36-story office building in height and over 33 feet in diameter at the base. The VAB was a structure large enough to make its own weather out of the differences in temperature and humidity between ground level and ceiling.

Above, the eye lost its way in the maze of girders, platforms and catwalks. Looking up, it is not hard to believe that there are 100,000 tons of steel hanging overhead; but the sheer mass of it does not really strike home until your guide mentions that the building rests on pilings— 16-inch steel pipes driven 160 feet into the ground—over 4,000 of them.

The great doors of the High Bay through which the launch vehicle is moved out to the pad allow about ten feet of clearance for bird and its umbilical tower, which stands 446 feet high. Their design allows them to open by sliding vertically, one section behind another, to the top of the building, 525 feet above the floor. Four doors—each 52 feet high—make up the launch vehicle's exitway.

It is through these massive doors that the huge, individual stages, brought in by barge, are placed into position, one on top of the other, as the rocket is assembled. The subsections that make up the completed bird must be aligned with perfect accuracy to produce the longitudinal rigidity necessary to carry the thrust of the engines. The result resembles a tower built of children's blocks—in this case, round tubes—which carry their 400 feet of height on a 30-foot base and have no horizontal strength at all, relatively speaking. The least deviation from perfect alignment, and the bird would snap like a fresh breadstick.

The incredible care with which the rockets must be handled is pointed up by the maneuverability of the great 250-ton bridge cranes used to stack the elements of the vehicle. One of the tests for accurate manipulation of these cranes consists of placing a drop of oil on the floor below the test load. The latter is a water tank which weighs about 70 tons filled. The tank is lowered until it touches the oil—but not the floor. Or it may be lowered to touch an egg without breaking the shell.

The confidence VAB personnel have in both the precision of their cranes and the skill of their operators is indicated by the carefree abandon with which a mechanic will plunge an irreplaceable arm into the space between a dangling load and a steel girder to fasten a clamp or remove a nut. This is part of the feeling of a different place with different rules that permeates the VAB. Appearance and reality confound each other here.

Moving through the VAB, I was continually surprised by the contrast between the appearance of lightness and delicacy which each area presented from a distance, and the no-nonsense solidity of steel and concrete close up. Gradually I began to realize that the designers had literally used full-sized rooms like Belgian Blocks, building walls and partitions of them to enclose the great bays in which the vehicles are assembled. Inside these walls are offices, shops, ready rooms, storerooms and even snack bars. Looking from above down on the nose of the Apollo 15 itself from the upper levels, the eye is stretched, baffled and finally lost in the descending dimensions of girth and distance. What stood there as I looked down was something too big to be imagined in any other way than as a fixed structure. The thought that it could some day lift by itself from the Earth was unbelievable.

Far below, on the floor itself, the wide door by which we had entered now looked no larger than a mousehole. But, later when we went back down and out of it again, it was as wide as ever. Only the world beyond it was not now so much a larger as a merely different place, where the sky seemed hardly any farther away than the ceiling of the VAB had looked to be, inside.

We got back in the bus and drove on toward the launch pad where the Apollo 14 was already standing. I was still numb from the VAB, and did not notice anything outside the bus until I saw heads craning out the windows to our left. I turned then and saw the crawlerway along which the crawler transports the vehicle and its mobile launcher to the launch pad. It was as it had been described to me, looking very much like a superhighway 130 feet wide; two roadway-broad strips with a wide green space of turf in-between them, paralleling the blacktop road we were on. It was along this that the Apollo vehicles moved, exerting surface pressures of 8 to 12 thousand pounds per square foot, as the 17 million pounds of combined load of crawler and vehicle moved ponderously over them toward the launch pad.

At the end of its trip, not only would the crawler carry its load along the level crawlerway, but it would need to mount the 5 percent angle of the ramp sloping upward to the launch pad, carefully tilting its own bearing surface so that the 36-story vehicle it carried would remain upright at all times, like a bottle on a tray in the hands of a skilled waiter. It must keep the top of the bird vertical within 10 minutes of arc, plus or minus. That gives it a margin of error roughly the diameter of a basketball . . .

The Launch Pad and Mobile Service Structure almost deserve an article to themselves; for now with the bird in place, it is at this point that the whole effort comes to-gether; and both pad and structure are of a piece with the rest of this Brobdingnagian wonderland.

For some reason it had not occurred to me how important it would be to exercise some control over the blast of flame from the rocket engines. This control is provided by a miniature Grand Canyon 450 feet long, 58 feet wide, and 42 feet deep, called the Flame Trench. A 700-ton flame deflector at its middle sends the exhaust gases roaring out to each side, producing the familiar sunrise effect, lighting the whole horizon. Most of the billowing clouds visible in pictures of the launch are steam, for the cooling system which washes the pad down after a shot is capable of pumping 45,000 gallons of water per minute.

The pad has a number of interesting safety features in

case of trouble. One is a blast resistant room, 40 feet underground, with seats, safety harnesses and survival gear for 20 men over a period of 24 hours. It is designed to cut a 75 gravity blast force to 4 G's, and is reached by a 200-foot escape tube from the launch platform.

The bus returned us to the Press Headquarters in Cocoa Beach; and the science-fiction people gathered at the home of Joe Green, NASA engineering writer and one of our sf writers. That night, after dark, Joe drove a number of us out on the causeway to look across 17 and ½ miles of open water at the Apollo 14, now free of its scaffolding and spotlighted. Amazingly, even at that distance, the Saturn and its spacecraft were large enough to stand clearly visible.

We were not alone in the watching. All that day the cars had been flooding into the Cape Kennedy area, and now the causeway was parked thickly with them on both sides—people who had come to spend the night to watch the lift-off tomorrow, even from twenty miles or so, at an expected launch time of mid-afternoon on the next day.

"... *The public*," my news editor had said, "*has had this Moonlight business* . . ."

But it did not look so, there, at 10 p.m. on the dark causeway with the cars crammed together along its length and the Apollo 14 shining under its spotlights, seventeen and a half miles away.

The next day, with four hours yet to lift-off, I was in the press stands, talking to Kelly Freas about the deceptive size of the VAB, seen from where we sat.

The press stands are the closest viewing area of any to the bird—theoretically just within the danger area at three and a half miles of distance from the launch pad. Free of everything now but the upright tower of the Mobile Launcher, the waiting Saturn vehicle breathed light plumes of excess vapors into the sunlight. Its size made it seem closer than it was, like a tower on the landscape.

Ahead of the stands was a large digital clock on a little

apron of ground, reaching out perhaps a hundred and fifty yards to the edge of a patch of water, beyond which was flat Florida scrub brush for the rest of the three and a half miles to the rocket. To right and left of the bird, but some distance from it, gleamed the white-painted globular tanks that were pumping fuels into the rocket engines.

In and about the stand itself, the atmosphere was one of busy boredom. The movie and television cameras were set up in a line before the stand and occasionally a loud-speaker would advise us of some small detail. Otherwise we merely sat around talking and waiting. There was a burst of Spanish in a female voice, two rows down and behind me. I turned and saw a small, pretty, dark-haired girl standing talking to two men, as if she were at a cocktail party rather than a space-flight launch.

But I could not blame my fellow reporters and photographers. The buses had brought us all here early, and for four hours we had had nothing to do but to sit and wait. Still, the digital clock out in front of the stands, halfway to the water's edge, was continuing to click off the minutes and seconds. Then there was a hold—a slight delay. It seemed that rain clouds had moved in. In fact, we could see them. We waited, and after a while a couple of light planes could be seen circling the edge of the darkness over us. A few drops of moisture fell.

Then the hold was lifted. The countdown went on. It was close now, less than three minutes to liftoff; and a little stir went through the stands. I found I had stood up, and around me others were standing up, also. Gradually we began to leave the stands for the ground in front of it, walking forward toward the water's edge and the rocket, which stood towering there in its more than 6 million pounds of immobility.

The countdown had less than a minute to go. A sudden squall of rain swept down on us; and there was no shelter.

We, who were in the front, ran ahead to the digital clock facing the stand and tried to find some protection there, but there was none. Around me shirts were turning dark with the wet. My own shirt was sticking to me. I looked back toward the stands, expecting to see most of those who had come out streaming back to the shelter of its roof—but practically no one was turning back and the stands were almost empty.

There was no point in pretending to hide from rain against an upright wall. I gave up, and walked around the clock, on to the water's edge. Already, there was a line of people all along it. I found a spot, wiped the lenses of the binoculars hung around my neck and looked.

The umbilicals had fallen away from the bird. The rain was lightening a little, but still it fell on us. The cloud was still dark overhead. Without warning, orange flame spurted to right and left from beneath the rocket. The length of the flames was incredible. They looked as long as the rocket was tall and there was not a sound to be heard. The Apollo stood there, a huge, immovable structure conducting a fireworks display at its base.

Then the sound came—the first, sharp cracking explosions, building to an impossible volume. And the whole thing began to move. It lifted—it actually lifted those hundreds of feet of length, those millions of pounds, upward and upward, the flames growing shorter and showing brilliantly white at its base. The sound rolled over us, buffeting our minds.

It rose. The clouds were still close overhead. The nose went into the clouds while the tail seemed still to hover only a short distance above the landscape—and everybody was talking. I was talking.

"My God!" I was saying. "My God . . ." It was not just an immovable tower after all. It was alive. It was going—heading out beyond everything. And it was taking three men with it, three men who were already hidden in the clouds.

Roaring, it slipped upward, the whole bird, as if with brute strength it was pushing Earth away from beneath it. It went away from us up into the clouds; and there was no one there who was not saying something.

"Mira! Mira!" The sound of the small, high voice made me turn to look; and I saw her again, the little, dark-haired girl, pointing and exclaiming in Spanish. "Look! Look—"

It was gone then, all but the sound. For a few seconds more, everybody continued to stand there, talking, and then we turned; and the return to the stands became a scramble for the shelter of the buses parked beyond.

But, running with my head down for the bus through what rain that still fell, I had my answer to the puzzle of the size of the VAB, seen from the outside, and the attitude of the news editor, all at once. Kelly was right; it was a matter of perspective. The VAB was too big. If you were close enough to measure it against anything else, you were too close to see it as a whole. If you were far enough back to see it whole, it was too big for any of the things standing about it to serve as measures for comparison. Faced with these choices, the eye gave up and refused to believe it was as big as it was.

So, with the space effort as a whole, and the Moon flights in particular, the press was close enough to make all the measurements and report them—but because of that fact, often too close to see exploration of space . . . as a whole. And the public to whom the press reported was too far from that exploration to make measurements of its true value. The public only saw the mass of the effort as a whole from a distance, and its remote gaze refused to believe that anything could be so big, so mind- and soul-shaking.

But there was no split between the engineers and the poets, after all, no matter what else might appear. Because there was a point at which the work of both came together; and that point was the moment of lift-off in which we in the press stands, who knew all about it and were here as part of our working day, ran forward instinctively to stand in the rain and watch something man had built with his hands leave Earth for space. In that particular moment we betrayed the fact that we were all together part of that vehicle, and one with the three men riding it spaceward. We gave it away by our actions and our voices.

". . . *Mira! Mira!* . . . Look! Look!"

—And indeed, look! To the stars.